**We're laughing and stuffing our packs with riches, with
life itself, and then bullets are snapping all around us.**

Melanie is closest, and I pull her to the ground. We get right
down on the broken glass and try to push ourselves into the
cracks between the tiles. All of us but Scotty. He's standing
with his new, proud posture and shooting his rifle at the
ambushers. Jerry runs and tackles him and pulls him back
from the front of the store. Bullets take pieces of things with
them as they pass. Melanie is screaming. I wrap myself around
her. Bottles of wine are breaking red and white, and the floor is
slick with wine and glass.

I check Melanie but she hasn't been shot. Her screams aren't
screams of pain, but anger. People aren't supposed to be like
this. People *are* like this. I push the shotgun out around a rack
of greeting cards and fire a blast into the parking lot.

THE UNIT

Terry DeHart

www.orbitbooks.net

Orbit
Hachette Book Group
237 Park Avenue, New York, NY 10017
www.HachetteBookGroup.com

First Edition: July 2010

Orbit is an imprint of Hachette Book Group. The Orbit name and logo are trademarks of Little, Brown Book Group Limited.

The characters and events in this book are fictitious. Any similarity to real persons, living or dead, is coincidental and not intended by the author.

Library of Congress Cataloging-in-Publication Data
DeHart, Terry.
    The unit / Terry DeHart. — 1st ed.
        p. cm.
    ISBN 978-0-316-07740-8
    1. Nuclear terrorism—Fiction.   2. Survival skills—Fiction.   I. Title.
    PS3604.E3475U65 2010
    813'.6—dc22
                                    2009041366

10   9   8   7   6   5   4   3   2   1

Printed in the United States of America

For Sabra

THE UNIT

Jerry

It's been two weeks since the cars died, and we're walking out. The bombs have shorted out every electrical circuit in North America, as far as we know. Yellow-brown clouds blot out the sun, and I've never been so cold. My family is here with me in the Sierra Nevada, Susan and our newly adult children, and I don't know if it's a blessing or a curse.

It goes without saying that I'm not expecting anything good to happen, so it doesn't make me happy when I hear a light airplane approaching. We're walking a deer trail that parallels the interstate. The plane is on us very quickly, and I motion for Susan and the kids to get under cover. We run into the pines. We press ourselves against the trees and look up. It's been two weeks since we've heard anything in the sky except the occasional bomber, but this little bird is hanging from its prop and flaps, just above stall speed at tree-scraping altitude. It doesn't fly directly overhead, but I catch a glimpse of painted aluminum above the pines. The plane makes a shallow turn and flies parallel to the interstate. I feel the pressure of searching eyes. When the pilot adds power to hold a sharper turn, we run uphill for better cover.

We get into a thicker stand of trees and form our four-person perimeter. It's a sloppy diamond formation but it allows us to cover the highway with three guns. Susan gives me a flat look. Her lips are moving, and at first I think she's trying to tell me something, but then I see that she's praying, and I wonder if she knows it.

Our son, Scotty, is prone with his scoped .22. God help him, the boy looks like he can't wait to shoot somebody. Our eldest, Melanie, is farthest from the interstate. She refuses to carry a weapon but I'm grateful that she still more or less follows my orders, no matter how it must gall her.

The Cessna drags itself over the freeway. The hum of its engine grows more businesslike, more attentive, and it rises and circles like a carrion bird. The pilot drops something. I watch the lumpy gleam of a bubble-wrapped package falling from the sky. There can't be anything half-assed about it. It's either something very good or something very bad. I watch its flawed shape pass through the trees and into God's nature like a gift or a curse. I'm a naturally pessimistic bastard, and my pessimism has stood me well as of late, so I motion for Susan and the kids to put their heads down. The ground is matted with moldy pine needles. I listen to the buffeting sound of my breath pushing against the offal of trees. Time passes and there isn't an explosion. It isn't an improvised bomb at all and I hear people cheering, the voices of men, women, and children.

Another group is traveling the interstate. They're on foot, and we've been trailing them for most of the day. It's a group of a dozen armed adults and seven children. I've been watching them through my binoculars, choosing safe vantage points and trying to figure them out. The kids in the group are elementary school–aged, and the adults are well beyond their middle years. I think they're grandparents walking with their grandchildren because it's the way of the world, in hostile places, to thin out the connecting population of young adults.

They're herding a handful of cattle and a half dozen sheep. The adults dote on the children, giving them rides on their stiff shoulders and carting them in the wheelbarrows they use to carry their supplies, but I can't trust them yet. No matter how badly I want to place my family into the relative safety of a larger group, we've only been following and watching to see what they're all about.

I don't admit it to Susan, but I'm also using the group to clear the road ahead of us. If there's any heat to be taken, it will fall on them. They're down below us now. I can't see them, but I imagine they're waving and dancing at the prospect of salvation, or at least a meal. For a few seconds I think maybe I've gotten it wrong. Maybe they're really not in somebody's crosshairs. Maybe the bad feeling I have now is the result of my weakness for melodrama, or something I ate, or a lifetime spent looking through a half-empty glass. Maybe the airplane is actually a Civil Air Patrol bird, out trying to help people. Maybe Good Samaritans are still active in the world and maybe they're doing their good works in this very time and place, and soon they'll be dropping fresh steaks and cold beer and apple pie and linen napkins to everyone they see.

Yeah. And when the shooting starts, it's the loud popcorn sound of rapid fire from multiple weapons. I flinch and try to sink into the earth, then I turn to check Susan and the kids. They're okay; the rounds aren't being directed at us, and I let my breath out. I'm relieved that we aren't targets. I'm almost happy, but it has to be a slaughter down there, and my relief dissolves into the chamber of guilt that's been burning in my guts since this fun-time began.

The ambushers are armed with 5.56 rifles. I know the sound well, from my Marine Corps days. Most of the rifles are firing three-round bursts, and that means they're probably modern M-16s or M-4s. And the fighting seems far too one-sided. The people on the road are slow to respond. It's an impossibly long five seconds before they open up with their shotguns, and they only get off a few rounds before their return fire falls silent.

We wriggle and burrow into matted pine needles. Echoes of gunfire roll past us and into the fingers and stubs of mountain canyons. My bladder feels impossibly full, though I haven't had anything to drink since first light. I can't see any movement, but my thumb reaches out to unsafe my rifle. My breath condenses around my head, and the ground steals my body heat. Exposed patches of earth are red with iron oxide, and wailing voices rise behind the gunshots, and my family is here with me, all of us on the brink of a mass murder, and I want to scream.

The firing winds down as the ambushers reload. A child calls twice for its mother, the last call a question, and a fusillade of fresh shots is the reply. Our peacenik daughter, Melanie, has to be eating her guts out. She keeps her head down and lets it happen, but she curses into the musty earth, and it's as good a thing to do as any.

High misses and ricochets snap and crack into the pines on the opposite ridgeline. Twigs and cones and showers of needles fall in their wakes. We hug the ground and wait. I keep my head turned, cheek to dirt, so I can watch the children. I force myself to look into their eyes. I watch to see what the sounds of slaughter are doing to them. I hate myself for it, but I watch to see if the message is getting through: *Don't walk the road. Trust no one. Be ready, always, to dive into cover. Be ready to put rounds on target, RIGHT AWAY, and for the love of Christ listen to your old man.*

Susan has always been a good mother, and she pushes her riot gun in the general direction of the killing. She watches the world over a brass sighting bead. I have no idea what this is doing to her.

Not ten feet away, Scotty holds himself tightly. He moves like a hunting reptile, every movement deliberate and barely perceptible, scanning in the direction of the killing zone through his 4-power scope. I don't think he can see anything through the trees. His Ruger .22 is a short-range weapon, at best, but he's locked onto the sounds of killing. His hands are rock steady, and I'm proud and sad, both. His sister, Melanie, is still cursing without sound. She curls into a ball and grinds the back of her head against the bark of a pine, and if I thought it would do any good, I'd join her.

The firing slows but it doesn't stop. I can't keep my hands under control. I squeeze the forearm of my AR-15 hard enough to make the fiberglass creak beneath my fingers. I have to force myself to relax. I quit smoking twenty years ago, but I get a craving for a Marlboro red. I want to pull smoke into my lungs to calm myself and to occupy my hands, if not my mind, but there's more to it than that. I want to somehow show my solidarity for the people not a quarter-mile away who walked into an ambush. I want to wish them well but I also want to let them know that, nothing personal, we're sitting this one out.

It's a stupid thing to be thinking. I've had no shortage of stupid thoughts since this started. I hold tightly to the ground as the cries turn to moans behind the gunfire. Then a woman's scream rises above the others. Her scream contains grief and outrage and hatred and I know she's fighting back. Every person in the history of the world who ever made a sound like that was fighting back. A shotgun speaks up, and I can't tell the good cries from the bad, but I wish the woman well. I wish her wild success in her wild pain, but I'm selfish, too, because my family is here, and I hope she takes a dozen of the goons with her.

The firing becomes sporadic, high-velocity bullets smacking into soft targets, passing through and whacking the road. There isn't any more outgoing fire from the victims, nor so much as a hope for it. And then the firing goes on for far too long, and there's no doubt in my mind that it's unnecessary shooting. It's target practice now, a ballistic maiming of the dead.

I want to signal my family, tell them to hold very still, but I'd have to move to do it. The ambushers are hot to kill, and they'll be looking to shoot anything that moves. I try to tune out the shooting and pay attention to our close-in perimeter. I hear footsteps. Someone creeps out of the woods and moves downhill toward the fight. I get a glimpse of a man working his way through the trees. I put my rifle on him, but he passes out of my field of fire. I'm guessing it's one of the killers. Their top cover. Their sniper or ground spotter.

I take a breath and lift my head. I don't think he saw us. My heartbeat seems to be bouncing me off the ground. I try to get my breathing under control. I hear a floundering sound behind me. I turn to face it, the front sight of my rifle coming around slowly, too slowly, and it takes me a full second to realize there isn't an immediate threat. I take another breath and let it dribble back out of my new, old-man lungs. The shooting tapers off. A few random finishing shots and then it's over, but for the whooping and looting.

I stifle a cough. I'd sell my soul for a drink, but we don't have any booze. The pine needles beneath us are damp and rotted. We're stretched out on our bellies in perfect insect habitat. I hear whispered curses from Scott and Melanie, and a muted smacking as they slap at their clothes. They roll and writhe on the forest floor. Back before the world went mean, I might've found words to distract them from the revulsion of feeling vermin on skin.

The airplane straightens from its orbit and climbs and flies due south until I can hear only an occasional throb from its engine. I stand and lead us farther uphill. I find a place where half-buried boulders line the forest floor. It's not a bad place to set up for a defensive fight, if it comes to it.

Susan's face is set and pale, but her eyes are green fire. She's very angry. I want to touch her hand. I want to hold her, but she moves away and tells the kids to strip off their packs and clothes. Her voice is as tight as her expression. I want to whisper something private and married into her ear. I want to push her untended hair from her face and kiss her, but I watch while she uses her ragged fingernails to flick and pull insects from the skin of our daughter and son. Fat, red-brown ticks are gorging themselves on the blood of our children.

Melanie turned nineteen this year. Scott is eighteen. I trace the new streaks of gray in my wife's hair, then I turn to face the road. I tell myself that someone has to stand watch, but then I go to them because I'd rather be a good father than anything else.

Scotty has ticks on his back. They stand out like fattening tumors on his pale skin. I turn him around so he's facing downhill. I hand him my rifle.

"Keep an eye out."

"Yeah, huh?"

"The safety's off."

"Good."

I lean close and pull the biting jaws and burrowing mouth-parts away from my son's skin. Thin lines of blood run down his back. He shivers in the mountain air, but he holds himself steady while I tend to him. These days, even the smallest injury or infection is a serious threat. These days there isn't any place for hesitation or embarrassment.

Susan checks and clears Melanie's skin. It takes time. I use the back of my hand to knock the last of the ants from Scotty's legs. He's thin, too thin, but my knuckles are bouncing against solid muscle, too, and it makes me proud. It gives me hope.

We shake out their shirts and pants and coats and they get dressed. Susan asks me to strip and I know I should say something to break the stress, but I can't think of anything that might do the trick. She waits for me to say something. When I don't, she helps me out of my clothes. She delouses me and I delouse her and we dress in the mountain air, old lovers cooled by time and fear.

I'm anxious to get us moving again, but I grind through a long stack of minutes to make sure we're not the next course on the menu. A single gunshot takes me by surprise. The boom of a pistol. We slip behind our chosen boulders and listen and wait, but there aren't any more shots. I hear raised voices but I can't make out the words, then a vehicle approaches on the road. It sounds like a diesel, and then we hear more. I think they have three trucks, in all.

The ambushers load up their plunder and the vehicles head south. I expect them to move quickly away, but they travel at a slow walking speed. At first I think they might be road hunting. Hunting for targets of opportunity. Hunting for us. But then I remember that the dead people had cattle and sheep, and some of the animals must've survived. The ambushers must be taking the beasts with them, probably haltered to the bumpers of their vehicles, fresh meat for the barbecue.

They move onto a plain and I watch them through my binoculars. I guess their number at two dozen. They stop and manage to drag the animals aboard their vehicles, a Brinks armored car and two military five-ton trucks. They pick up speed. I watch until they disappear into the road's mirage. I wait until I'm as sure as I can be, and then we're back to walking, taking our general direction from the freeway, but not walking directly on it. Our course is a series of zigzags as we angle from one area of potential cover and concealment to the next.

I can feel the pressure of Susan and the kids looking at me, but I have no idea what they're thinking. Maybe they're grateful to be walking an easy pace. I'm more paranoid than usual because the goons might've left someone to watch their back trail, but we don't run into anyone good or bad, and my adrenal glands start to calm down. I'm tired and they're tired, but we need to cover a few more miles.

I'm not happy to be walking in the same direction as the ambushers, but there's no choice in it. I pick up the pace. I glance back over my shoulder and their faces show resentment, but they keep up. The kids were angry at me at first, for not letting them walk a straight line down the road, but they don't say anything now. We only have what we have, no more and no less, and we have no choice but to walk our careful rays and obliques, hoping they lead to something better.

We've gone maybe five hundred yards when we see the bodies. They're below us in the road in their large, medium, and small sizes. I don't want to look, but I have to look, because we need to scavenge, too. Susan and Scotty cover me from the trail. Melanie moves to my side as if she's made up her mind to go with me. She's standing stiffly upright and her fists are clenched. Her mother helped her with her hair this morning, and she shakes her head, and her red ponytail writhes against her back. She's never been one to shy away from doing what needs to be done. She looks as if she wants to find survivors and nurse them back to health. She looks as if she *needs* to find someone alive, to somehow give the gift of life in the midst of all this taking.

"Trust me," I say. "They're worse than dead."

I don't have to pretend that I'm pleading. Her eyes are forest green, darker than her mother's, but flecked with gold. When she feels strongly about something, the flecks are very bright, but I don't look away now. I know it could go either way, my daughter deciding to obey or defy. I've never been good at predicting the outcome of our battles of will. I try to put my arm around her but she sidesteps and squats and I stand like an idiot, looking down at her, wanting to make things better. I stand with her until my silence is too pathetic to bear, then I turn to the task at hand.

I scramble down into the roadcut, my knees bitching all the while. I tell myself I'm checking for survivors, but I hope I won't find any. I feel naked when I step onto the freeway. Dark smears descend from the crown of the northbound lanes. Blood on shaded asphalt is the color of blackberry jam. I look for the wild woman who screamed her righteous cry into the face of death, but there's no way to pick her out of the motionless crowd. The bodies are fanned out like blown-down timber, dead adults shielding dead children. They've been shot to pieces, nineteen bodies, all present and accounted for. The coats and shoes and socks of the adults are gone. The pockets of their pants are turned inside out. They're traveling light now, without the blessings and nuisances of their corporeal husks.

The monsters have won again, if one can make the assumption that mortal sin will no longer be punished. The east-side drainage ditch is lousy with 5.56 brass. I pick up three of the empties and put them in my pocket. Maybe someday I can present them as evidence. I can't deny that I'm pissed off enough to kill. If I were in charge of this sector, I'd insert Force Recon teams into these hills so the ambushes would go the other way, and peace would break out due to a general lack of freelancers.

I look down and see scraps of bubble wrap from the air-dropped package, but the package itself is gone. There's a group of bloody footprints. I follow them. They lead to a big ponderosa pine. A body is stretched out, its head propped against the base of the tree. It's one of the ambushers; I'm sure of it. It's a big bastard and it has a single, center-mass shotgun wound and two gold coins weighting its eyes. There's another bullet hole in the center of its forehead. The body has a baby face. It's the body of a big kid, and it's smiling.

There isn't a blood trail from the road to the tree, only footprints and spatters of blood. I guess the bastard got hit on the road and walked under his own power to the tree. The shot between his eyes came later. I remember the final pistol shot we heard, and it could've been this headshot. It's a reasonable assumption and I tuck it away.

The body's hands are knuckle-down at its sides, and there's a pint bottle of whiskey lying atop its open right palm. It's a bottle of Jim Beam. I pick it up. It's three-quarters full. I unscrew the top and take a sip to rinse my mouth. Maybe I'd meant to spit it out, but I don't. I swallow and a small warmth flares around the edges of my soul. It brightens the sky and makes my shadow stronger. I take a bigger drink and it's one good thing in a world of bad ones.

There's an open pack of Marlboros on the dead ambusher's chest. I drag a pack of MRE matches from my pocket and light up. Holy God Almighty and the Angelic Host, it feels good to stand on the road and smoke a butt. I get a headrush and smoke the cigarette down to a stub, then I use my knife to lift the gold coins away from the dead boy's eyes. I use water from my canteen to rinse them and then I wash my knife. The blood leaves dark fans on the road. I pocket the coins and whiskey and smokes, and then I turn to search the bodies of the victims. I try not to look at what's left of their faces. I run my hands into their pockets, feeling the last warmth of their flesh. My hands are thick with coagulating blood, but I force myself to check them all. My anger makes me strong, and I don't want to puke up the whiskey, so I don't.

All I find is a shot-to-pieces folding knife and a bloody pack of Beeman's gum. I can't waste any more water, so I walk to the drainage ditch and scrub my hands with cold mud. I find a vine maple and wipe my hands on its leaves. I walk uphill to my family. I don't have any food for them or news of the outside world, but the whiskey is a warm gift inside me, and damned if I'll feel guilty about it.

I get back uphill and I hold up the coins and the smokes. I'm breathing hard. Susan's nose twitches.

"Anything else?"

I shake my head. I start to feel guilty despite myself, but I'm committed now, so I put on a poker face.

"Give it to me," she says.

I pull the pint bottle from my pocket. She takes it from my hand and I let it go. Her face is hard. She did a stint in rehab two years back, and she's still on the higher path, and she still has zero tolerance. She lifts the bottle. She measures the fill level with addiction-calibrated eyes, then passes the bottle to Melanie.

"We might need this. I'll know if any is missing, and I'll know if it's watered, too."

Melanie says okay. She says, Don't worry, Mom, then she gives me a look of disappointment to add to the other looks of disappointment she's given me over the years.

They're doing the right thing, of course. A group of Marines or soldiers in this situation would pass the bottle around, a lucky find, a small vehicle of escape, but Melanie correctly puts the bottle in the hip pocket of her jeans.

Susan

We enter a small clearing. It's very cold. I feel more nude than naked. The sky is a mixing bowl of death, but I think up less unpleasant names for its colors. It's sepia with swirls of russet, and our faces are golden in its light.

Jerry walks us south from the ambush. He seems to be towing us against our will. He rarely looks back at us, and I wonder what would happen if we stopped, Jerry chugging away like a locomotive unhooked from its burden and purpose.

The weight of my pack makes my shoulders burn. I bear it. I've borne worse. The underbrush is thin but riddled with poison oak. I point it out to the children. I whisper, "Leaves of three, let it be." They roll their eyes. It's long been their most common response to my words, and I'm glad they can still do it.

We skirt the poison oak as best we can. The trees are gray-green and I remember how I used to love walking beneath California pines at dusk, flying at low altitude, hushed and safe, and the Lord is my shepherd, I shall not want. I try to keep my eyes on the trail, but my neck aches from turning and looking back at Melanie and Scott. Their faces are tight and their eyes have a bulging look. It's very slight, and maybe no one else would notice it, but I do.

I make eye contact with Melanie. She looks away, but then she looks back. I think she's trying to share her horror about our *now*, and thereby dilute it. I'm grateful that she's reaching out, and I return her gaze with the full strength and power of motherhood, and just for an instant I'm no longer pretending to be strong.

Scott sees that I'm not watching where I'm going. He says *Mom* in that serious way of his and he points to a branch in my path. I'm about to walk straight into one of nature's impersonal ambushes. I push it aside with the barrel of my shotgun. I whisper a thank-you, and it's for my son and my daughter and any supreme being within earshot, in gratitude for everything that hasn't been taken from me. I tell myself to be thankful for what I have, even though the molecules of my childhood home are probably circling the globe as fallout, and my own children are on foot in a place where people get shot and robbed, but nobody gets buried.

But still I try to appreciate the Northern California forest, with its half-serious cover and dry, open places. It's nothing like the land of my upbringing, western Oregon, where Douglas firs reach into the clouds and nurse the devil's own blackness below. The underbrush in Oregon will take your skin off—blackberry patches and sword ferns and tangles of vine maple and stinging nettles and God knows what else, nature's barbed wire.

Here, there's some underbrush and a bit of poison oak, but it's only for decoration. It's as if someone prepared the way for us, and provided places of cover and concealment stretched out before us like stepping stones, and I can't help but think that *He* did it, in *His* infinite wisdom, as part of *His* perfect plan.

We walk for two hours before I decide to say something. I catch up with Jerry. He's walking fast again, but I was a race walker and I can catch him, even though he was a Marine. I pull alongside. I nod back at Melanie and Scott.

"They need a break."

"Don't we all."

He winces as soon as he says it. Maybe he wasn't trying to sound bitter, but it's too late.

"Am I annoying you?"

"No. Sorry."

He stops. He wipes his face on his coat sleeve. I can smell the tobacco on his breath and the alcohol evaporating from his pores. He reaches for my shoulder, but I slip away.

"Okay," he says. "I'm sorry."

I know what liquor does to him. When he's first had a drink, he's the sweetest man on earth. It's as if he wants to share the pleasure he receives from intoxication with all the world, but it's all downhill from there. Either he drinks himself wild, or he stops drinking and grows sullen and resentful. I know the highs and lows of it, because for many years we were a perfect match, drinking-wise.

We move into a field of low boulders and slip out of our packs. Melanie and Scott sit down. They're both in good shape, but they're not sure we're doing the right thing, walking out. They think we might be better off holing up and waiting for the government to save us. But Jerry and I both know better. We've seen enough failed federal disaster responses to know that we're better off walking into a future of our own choosing.

Our children, in their new adulthood, don't know whether they should trust us. They've passed beyond the automatic rebellion of adolescence, but they move with reluctance, each step a dragging doubt. I don't want to make things harder for them, so I fight down my urge to quarrel with Jerry. I keep my back to him. I make a show of taking out MRE crackers and a packet of pasteurized cheese spread.

We chew and wash down the thick, military nourishment with drinks from our canteens. A red-tailed hawk circles above. A breeze gives the pines a steady sigh. A large tree branch cracks and falls to the ground. It hits with the sound of a falling body. We reach for our guns. We stand ready, our canines gleaming, our nostrils flared, until we're sure we're not under attack. We put down our guns and sit until the fringes of our sweaty clothes take on a hint of ice glitter, then we resume our march.

The first terrorist bombs were detonated two weeks ago in Washington, D.C., Philadelphia, and New York. Back before people became so untrustworthy, we heard news reports on a survivalist's radio. The survivalist's name was Roger Romain. Nobody thought he was paranoid, under the circumstances. His eyes were blue and sometimes they sparkled. He carried a pistol in plain sight and shifty people came to him for advice about guns and tactics and food storage techniques and improvised explosives, and he must've been in survivalist heaven.

Every morning Roger Romain used his old Underwood manual typewriter to print out what he'd heard on his radio.

The government claimed its investigation had uncovered all the answers. Al Qaeda terrorists had manufactured the bombs with enriched uranium from North Korea. The bombs were thermonuclear devices of Pakistani design. They were smuggled into the country in the holds of oil tankers. They were loaded onto trucks and detonated at ground level. All the facts were so quickly and clearly laid out that nobody believed them. But we believed the government reports about its overwhelming counterstrikes overseas, because the clouds steadily grew thicker and swollen with death.

The cycle continued. We hit them. They threatened us. One day, Roger Romain nailed this note to a tree:

Seattle, Portland, San Francisco? Scratch them off the list.

And then people went all to pieces. There were plenty of guns and not enough food, and so here we are.

But just after the cars stopped, I thought that everything would be okay. Jerry would retire, as we'd planned, and we'd take cruises to Alaska and Mexico and the Caribbean, dancing and dining and walking alone to private cabins that held no kids but plenty of time. The sky was clean and sweetly blue before everything circled back around. I couldn't believe anything bad had happened. There weren't any mushroom clouds and the trees were picture-postcard green, but Jerry was adamant.

"Only one thing could've caused this."

"There's only one thing that can make cars break down?"

"All of them? All at once? Yeah, pretty much."

Melanie said she'd watched a show on the History Channel about mega-disasters. She said we could've been hit by a small gamma-ray burst, flying at us from outer space, but her eyes wouldn't settle on anything when she said it.

"I don't think so," Jerry said. "And listen, what we need to do now is watch the people around us. We need to be ready to defend ourselves when they start going bad."

"You're *such* an asshole," Melanie whispered, and I was thinking it, too. Jerry winced, but he didn't respond. We sat without talking, nursing our glares, and I didn't want to believe that people couldn't be trusted.

In the beginning, the people were fine. It was as if we'd all arrived at a party that didn't have enough parking places. We pulled our coasting machines onto the shoulders of the freeway and we set about helping one another, families emerging from minivans and SUVs, mothers handing out snacks, fathers helping their sons and daughters into their Christmas coats. So many little girls in red and green. Boys in jeans and holiday sweaters. Mothers with freshened lipstick. We were all somehow formal, even the truckers, who slicked back their hair and tucked in their shirttails and offered to help people with their luggage.

All the voices and introductions and smiles. It felt as if we were waiting for something, a church service or a wedding. It caused me to remember scenes of my youth, my mother dressing for a Christmas service. The rustle of her dress. The smell of her perfume and her industrial hair products and the hasty precision of her walk. Our clear, formal purpose. It was then and now and all those times together, but we were all so worried that our politeness seemed like a sweet act of bravery.

I told myself I wasn't worried in the least. The walk to Yreka was long but cheerful. Our numbers grew as we neared town. People streamed into that freeway-elongated town from north and south. Melanie and Scott were perfectly well-behaved. They were no longer merely pretending to be adults. They joked with small children and took turns helping burdened mothers carry suitcases, blankets, boxes of formula and juice packets, and even the silly things that didn't work anymore, worthless digital cameras and iPods and video game players. Christmas presents were opened on the road to placate the children, and the freeway was littered with ribbons and bright wrapping paper. We joked about our early Christmas. We didn't have to merely make the best of it, because it was a lovely day and we didn't believe otherwise.

Jerry was carrying something wrapped in our traveling blanket. I learned later that he was carrying three guns: the shotgun, his Beretta pistol, and Scott's .22 rifle. The long guns were disassembled and rolled into the blanket we'd brought to keep our children's legs warm. The pistol was loaded, and Jerry carried it at the small of his back. All that sunlight. All those jokes and smiles. All that solidarity and politeness and kindness. Jerry knew it wouldn't last, but he chose not to rain on our parade. He smiled and pitched in with the carrying and sharing and encouragement. He tousled Scott's hair and said we were some pretty fine-looking refugees. We laughed because we didn't believe we *were* refugees. But Jerry was watching everything and everyone. He's not a naturally trusting man. Not since his time in Beirut. He was armed and ready during that entire walk, and I don't hate him for it.

He's hell-bent to get us to a safe place. I can see the fight in his brown-black eyes. He holds his rifle in a natural way that I can never quite match. He walks very quietly, just as he must've walked on the training patrols of his youth. This must be a nightmare for him now, to be older and softer and walking here with us. And for the first time ever, I'm glad he served in the Marines and went through the trials and tribulations of Beirut. It's one of the reasons he's suspicious and quick to anger and prone to binge drinking, even in the best of times, but everything has a purpose, and I'm a fool if I don't believe it.

The road climbs again and cuts deeply into the mountains. A rock wall rises on one side, and a cliff falls on the other. Jerry has no choice but to take us onto the road. It feels fine to have hard asphalt under my boots, and we make good time until we come to a tunnel. It's a hole of darkness set in an impassable ridge. A few scrubby pines grow at uncertain angles around it.

It's bad enough to walk the road, but it's quite another thing entirely to march our children into a mountain's dark gullet. But life is still a matter of faith and probabilities, and the demands upon us are great, and it's no accident that we don't have a choice.

I pray for us. Two weeks ago I was agnostic, and the taste of prayer is like an astringent on my lips. Jerry gives one sharp nod. He's not exactly exuding confidence, but our fate stands before us. We walk inside and leave the daylight behind.

I let the children pass, and I take up position behind them. The kids are stumbling beneath their packs and I catch glimpses of the whites of their eyes. I'm sure they're desperate to see only stationary things, nothing but the continuation of rock and road and the corrugated lining of the tunnel. I want to cry that it's come to this, my children walking into a place where even a blind idiot could kill them, but there's no time for crying.

The tunnel is unlit and it makes a shallow uphill turn. We come to a place of thick darkness. We walk blinded through the mountain's guts and there are only our amplified footsteps and breathing and the clinking of our packs and a dripping sound to remind us of the relentless power of erosion. And then after walking through the shadow of forever, we see the tunnel exit. It seems to remain at arm's length for a very long time, but finally we straggle back into the overcast day.

Scotty kneels and kisses the road. Our laughter is weak but true as we put the tunnel behind us. The road winds down from the hills into a small valley. I'm numbed by the rote of walking, but the kids are steady on their feet. There's a lake filled with cattails and tule and thick, exotic-looking grasses. I imagine its mirrored surface was once ruffled by white birds perched on stick legs, feeding. Then we're briefly in oak country. Squirrels' nests decorate bare branches, and bunches of an oily plant stand against the dark sky. It takes me a few seconds to recognize it, but then I do. The plant is mistletoe. I try to resist it, but an image of a long-ago party rises from memory, Jerry as a young man, giving me whiskey kisses as if kissing were an improved way of talking, and me kissing him back, yes, yes, and yes to all his kiss-sent questions, a holiday fireplace warming our backs and all the world in our arms.

I shake my head until my vision blurs. I walk until my vision grows sharp again. Only idiots can sustain that wild kind of love, and even then, after a few years it's false. I miss it sometimes, but what comes up must come down.

I glance at the yellow sky again. It makes me dizzy to look up while I'm walking. Jerry is ahead, just to my right, and I wonder if my position behind him resembles some paternal code of female subservience from another time or place. I can tell he needs to cough, but he hunches over and fights it. That's Jerry, always fighting something. He's fighting for us now, and I wouldn't want to be the fool who stands in his way. I'll back him with my last breath, for the time being, but I might as well admit that my plans for the future don't necessarily include him.

Melanie

Just before dark, we walk around a long highway curve. The litter here tells the local story—crushed Budweiser cans, empty Marlboro packs, Quarter Pounder with Cheese wrappers, and loaded disposable diapers. The highway curve is banked and it takes forever for us to unwind it and then we're standing at the base of a hill that's six lanes wide and disappears into the dirty clouds. It's like one of those "stairways to nowhere" in the Winchester Mystery House in San Jose.

As the road gets steeper, we lean forward and put more muscle into our pace. Every step takes us closer to the clouds. Dad and Mom give each other a look, but they keep walking. They don't stop to talk about what might happen if we breathe the crap in those nasty clouds. They just keep walking, and so do Scott and I, but Scott is shaking his head and muttering to himself, and I think we might have to part ways with Mom and Dad soon.

We climb until dark. I'm an athlete and I'm tired, so I know the others must be just about wiped out. Mom gives us an MRE pouch of fruit cocktail. Scott and I take turns slurping it down. We spend the night shivering in a roadside ditch, then we walk uphill again. It's getting colder and there's more snow. The last gravel spread by the last Caltrans crew crunches under our boots. Lots of cars and trucks died here. The ones that had been going uphill couldn't coast to the side of the road when they died, so they're all over the place, some of them backed into ditches, but most of them stopped right where they lost momentum.

We don't bother to search the cars and trucks because their doors are all open and they've already been picked clean. Dad and Mom and Scott keep their guns at the ready, but there isn't anyone else here. We climb until the cloud ceiling is just above our heads. When we can't smell anything but smoke and toxic chemicals and burned meat, Dad stops. He turns and looks as if he wants to apologize. Mom is crying. Scott turns and walks downhill, but Dad tells him to wait.

"What for?" Scott says. But he turns and walks back to us.

Dad takes Mom's hand and they bow their heads. If other people were here I'd be embarrassed as hell, but since we're alone it just looks sad and pathetic. They pray and nothing happens, of course. We stand in the freezing air and wait for the big head in the sky to pucker up his lips and blow away the clouds. I look back downhill and see some people at the bottom. They're climbing toward us. There are maybe twenty of them. They're carrying guns, and I think they see us. Scott clears his throat. Dad looks up from his praying. He sees the other group.

"Okay," Dad says. "Maybe there's another way around." His voice is very low, and there's a look of disappointment on his face.

But then the wind picks up. It blows uphill from the west and makes the clouds boil and lift. The wind blows the heavy cover up and over the top of the mountains. There's a kind of tunnel in the smoke. It's like the pipeline of a big surfing wave, and we can see all the way across the summit.

Mom and Dad laugh together, her voice riding high over his. They run uphill. Scott and I hesitate, but then we run, too. We run into the place that was choked with clouds, and there are bodies in the road, but the air is okay, for the moment, and we make it across. We pass a yellow sign that reads "Steep Grade Ahead." We run downhill until the clouds are high above us, and we stop and bend down and try to get our respiration rates back to sane levels. The wind dies down and we turn and watch the clouds close in again and cover the road. Dad and Mom don't say the word "miracle," but I know they're thinking it. They're smiling and Dad points at the ground. He says, "Let's have lunch, right here." Mom breaks out an MRE entree of Vegetable Manicotti and we eat it, rich and cold, then we hit the road again.

We get caught up in the rhythm of walking and put some miles behind us. I shoot Scott a look. He shrugs his shoulders and rolls his eyes. I'm totally with him. Maybe it wasn't a miracle that caused the clouds to open up for us, but it *was* some damned good luck, and so we stay with Mom and Dad.

We walk and listen to the bad rhythm of gunshots in the distance. The feeling of being lucky fades a little more with each shot. My teeth are chattering, and not only because of the cold. The clouds are high above us now, but I'm more afraid of the clouds than I am of other people. There must be radiation. There has to be. And I'm worried about the ozone layer. I don't feel any different, but there's a chance that our skin is being bombarded by the sun's UV rays. Maybe tumors are growing on our skin. And I wonder if these nasty clouds cover the whole earth. And if they do, aren't we in for a serious round of global cooling? And then what happens to the crops and the animals?

I want to ask someone about it. Dad might know something more, but he'd only try to withhold the hard facts from me, all evasive and Dad-like, because he's the same man he was when I was growing up. When he's not drinking, my dad is more uptight then anyone I've ever met. I can't help noticing that his whole world is filled with worry, and that he's worried about *us*. Giving orders is his way of showing love, and he's loving us with all he's got, my uptight daddy is.

I haven't seen him relaxed since he was drinking beer with the colonel, the poor old colonel and his cool, wrinkled wife, back in Yreka, that beautiful place in the good time that didn't last. We had a fine time, just after the bombs. The locals put on a crazy food orgy of a barbecue, then the colonel and his wife took us in. They were just about the friendliest people I've ever met. It seemed as if they didn't care about their own needs at all. They gave us their best food and asked if we had room for dessert and if we wanted more blankets or needed anything, anything at all. The colonel gave Dad that black rifle, yeah, but I just thought it was a weird gift at the time.

But maybe they were too friendly. Dad was right to be paranoid, and I'm embarrassed that I wasn't. Groups of hungry people started sneaking around in the night. They stole only food at first—who could blame them?—but then a big armed group came rushing up the freeway. For some reason, no one tried to talk to them. There were gun battles and the outsiders won them all, because the locals were all spread out. The locals didn't band together because they refused to leave their houses, the evidence and trappings of their lifetimes of hard work, and so they died family by family.

Dad keeps up a pace that doesn't seem possible. His skinny legs seem to be moving at an ordinary speed, but we have to keep breaking into a run to keep up with him. Mom was a speed walker back in the day, and she gets her hips swinging and she manages to stay with Dad, but her face is strained because we keep getting all strung out on the trail.

I used to think that walking wasn't really exercise. To a gymnast, walking is only part of the peaceful vacations that come between workouts. But we've been walking for weeks now, and I'm starting to change my mind about the whole walking-as-exercise thing.

"Goggy" was the first word I had for my dad. It was an illogical baby-talk mutation of "doggy" and "daddy." All I knew was that I loved both doggies and my daddy. It lasted until sixth grade before it began to slip, that idea of love without question. I was a very bad girl for a while, but when I returned to Planet Earth after that first big blast of puberty, he was a different, softer Goggy than I'd known back when I was little.

I sprained my arm in my senior year from a flubbed gymnastics vault, and he stayed home from work the day after, joking and bringing me stuff and acting like he was about to explode into a big, mushy cloud of worry. I was taking classes at a junior college and Dad was proud of me and the air was heavy because of all the permanent changes that were coming. My arm healed and I came and went as I pleased, but I was about to leave for good, and I came to see that the threshold of a house isn't defined only by what arrives, but also by what leaves.

Then this shitty thing happened and the world is still turning, but this was supposed to be my big year. The year I went off to Berkeley. My first year of freedom, and I was *so* ready to grab hold of it. Why else would I work my ass off to get a gymnastics scholarship? I was ready to see if anything better existed beyond the hypocrisy of "turn the other cheek" and "peace through strength" and "smite thy enemies." I was ready to join forces with people who didn't believe in an afterlife—and so they had to maximize the amount of goodness they could bring about in the here and now.

But now they're gone. The nuclear-free zone of Berkeley is a graveyard of common sense. Maybe they'll build a memorial there when the radiation cools, but that doesn't help us now.

And, in a way, Daddy and his pride did this to us. He and his kind. The selfish, hypocritical neocons. The armchair war pigs. I love him, but my Goggy is a war pig, and I won't take the gun he wants me to carry. I won't kill people. It has to stop somewhere. It might as well stop with me.

Scott

I don't have to think about things so much anymore. I'm nice to my family but I'll shoot bad people in the head, if I have to. I won't hesitate to shoot them, and I think that soon enough I'll be doing a lot of shooting, and I don't mind it at all. Fighting to stay alive gives people two faces, and both faces are more real and deep and true than our bored, spoiled peace faces. No more of the bitching and whining of the spoiled people we used to be. There's only love of life and family now, and I'll blow the shit out of anyone who threatens us. It's down to love and hate, baby, and I've never felt so alive. It's the purest rush I've ever felt, and I've felt a lot of those.

I don't know what I'll do when the time comes to prove myself, but I want a chance to find out. We sleep in a hole above the road. I stand my watch from midnight until four, and nothing moves. It's hell getting up and staying awake at that ungodly hour, but fear keeps me sharp. I barely remember having stood guard when morning comes. I've never been so tired, and that's saying a lot because I've been able to sleep like Rip Van Winkle since I was about twelve. If we weren't in a dangerous place, I'm pretty sure I could sleep straight through a whole week. It's one of the things I really, really want to do.

We're in a hurry to get moving, so we eat a cold breakfast. When I'm not chewing, I'm yawning. There isn't much to say, so we clean up our campsite, bury our garbage and our shit, and we use pine boughs to wipe away our tracks. It wouldn't fool a decent tracker, Dad says, but we don't want to leave clear signs for anyone, either.

Dad's a trip. It's like I didn't really know him before, the guy who taught me how to throw a curveball and how to play chess and how to be a poor communicator. Don't get me wrong— he's been an okay dad. He doesn't understand me very well, and he thinks I'm still a little kid, but now I can see that I don't understand him very well, either. I guess I didn't think very much about what-all was inside him. I had no idea that he knew all this silly shit about tactics. Sure, he taught me how to shoot, and we had fun doing that, but all the other stuff he knows kind of blows me away. It's kind of obvious stuff, but it took twisted minds to think of it. Don't walk on the tops of ridges, because people can see you outlined against the sky. Walk on *military* ridgelines, which lie just below the summit. Pay attention to the plants and the folds of the earth, in case you need to take cover. The difference between cover and concealment is that cover stops bullets. Flank a group of bad guys and they'll probably have no choice but to run or die. Put out massive return fire when attacked, so the bad guys think they've walked into a superior force. Shit like that. It sounds like it came from the mind of a middle school kid, but Dad says it's all written in the Marine Corps manual. It sounds too easy, but I'm hoping it really works.

All the walking we're doing doesn't hurt so much anymore. My stamina is getting pretty good, even though I was never a real jock. I always had to work hard to keep my place as a starting defensive back in football. I was nothing like the guys who seemed like they were born to block and run and hit, but I got to the point where I could almost keep up with them.

Hard work alone can't make a person great, but it can help you beat lazy, gifted people. The blisters on my feet are turning to calluses, and I'm getting harder all over. I don't have a shitload of foot speed, but maybe I could run down a deer if I used the simple tactic of never giving up.

But still, I'd rather be flying. It's my favorite thing in the world, to break the surly bonds of earth, as they say. And seeing that little bird in the sky yesterday made me happy. It was a Cessna 182 with retractable gear. I'd give one of my nuts to be sitting in the left seat, cruising at 150 knots and flying us somewhere else.

About halfway through the day, we smell woodsmoke. Dad marches us from one place of cover and concealment to the next, until we can see a big column of smoke rising into the brown sky. We pass a barn surrounded by cows that look like they died of thirst. We cover Dad while he searches the barn, but he comes out right away and shakes his head. The gas rising up from the dead cows is about the most disgusting thing I've ever smelled. Melanie looks like she wants to puke again, but the smell is so sick that it makes me want to break out laughing.

We walk toward the smoke, because that's where the road

takes us. It's another killing zone. There's a white house beside the freeway. It's on fire. There's a picket fence around it, and the yard has perfect green grass, but flames are pouring from the house windows. Bodies are lying in the grass. Lots of bodies. More than thirty, and so it wasn't just the people from the house. The people are all dressed up like they just got back from church or something. I used to be a big TV watcher, and I've seen town hall meetings on television. Maybe that's what it had been.

But this is where the meeting ended. Facedown. Old men with white collars biting into their flabby old necks. Old ladies with hair nets and gloves. Parents and high schoolers and a few little kids. The bodies of mothers and fathers wrapped around their babies, but there aren't any survivors. The suits and dresses are shot full of bloody holes. Most of the shoes are missing. There isn't a way to know, but I guess they were good people who didn't deserve what they got. I know I should cry or blow chunks or something, but I don't. I know Mel would think I was a savage if she knew what was going on inside my head, but I'm so pissed off I can barely stand upright. I won't lie. I want to blow away the people who did this. I want to blow them right out of the world.

Mel froze up when she first saw the bodies, but she unfreezes and starts to run. I grab her and pull her behind a tree. It's a big oak with a tire swing. Mel fights me, but I wrap her up and push her against the raspy old bark of the tree. For a second, I kind of like showing her how strong I am. Little brother isn't so little anymore, is he? But now isn't a good time to teach that lesson.

Mel struggles and starts to compare me to all different kinds of vile shit. I shush her and then I try to listen. No running footsteps, no guns being made ready to fire, no commands to kill us. I don't feel any eyes on us—not living ones, anyway. There's nothing but the crackling of the house fire and the wind blowing through bare branches.

I let Mel go, and she stays put. There's some graffiti cut into the tree. Just beside our heads there's a big carved heart with bare places above and below it, where the names were scraped away. A relationship gone bad. A symbol for our generation: *Nobody loves anyone.* But it makes me glad to see that the heart is still there, as if our fates are blank canvases and we'll get another chance, and then we'll be better and more interesting people because we lived through all of this shit.

I look up. The tire swing's rope has cut through to bare wood. I wonder if anyone's ever been hanged from the old tree. I look for hanging bodies but the tree isn't a part of this. I like it then, and I hope that someday it will carry more love graffiti on its old bark, and that kids will play on its swing on some sunny day in the future.

Then a man comes out of the house. He's on fire from top to bottom and he's waving his arms. The fire makes it look like he's shapeshifting. He flops down and rolls in the yard, but it doesn't put the fire out. He says "help" and "please" and then "save me." Dad rips a coat from the body of a fat man and throws it over the burning man and he gets the fire out, but the burned man is making a really weird sound, like he's screaming but his vocal cords are cooked, and it freaks me right the fuck out. I don't know if he's good or bad, but I want the sound to stop. The guy is a melted pile of black slime but he scares the shit out of me. He whispers "please" but this time he also says "end it."

Dad doesn't shoot him because we can't afford to make any

noise. Dad isn't without mercy, though. He stands and butt strokes the man's head until the quiet screaming stops. The thud of his AR-15 butt plate against a stranger's skull. Dad's face is all twisted, but he's never been the kind of man who runs away from dirty work. The work that has to be done because it's the only thing left to do. He picks up a little cotton sweater and wipes the blood from his rifle butt. The sweater is white with pink bunny buttons that stand out brighter than all the other colors in the world. He looks at me, and then he looks away. I turn my back and hope the wind doesn't blow the greasy smoke to us.

Mel bends down and just about pukes up her liver. She straightens up and wipes her mouth and looks at Dad like she wants him to drop dead. Mom and Dad search the bodies, but they don't find anything we can use. We move on. We're tired and cold but we keep our watering eyes wide open. Dad leads us the hell out of there. I keep the .22 at the ready. It's a Ruger 10/22 with a 4-power Weaver scope. It's the gun I used as a little kid to take my first shots. I try not to think about the times Dad took me target shooting, the casual-seeming way he taught me about safety and respect and marksmanship and fun and love and killing on all those sunny days. How tired and happy I was after a day of shooting, when we were comparing our ventilated targets, policing our brass, and picking up our shredded aluminum cans, Dad calling me Wyatt Earp and asking if the Marshal wanted to stop for ice cream on the way home.

And I wonder if he knew all along that I'd end up carrying a rifle in hostile territory. Our trips into the woods to shoot didn't seem, even then, to be all about fun. I don't trust people anymore, and so I'll have to rethink my memories.

But whatever. Right now I wish I was carrying a bigger rifle.

The .22 is accurate out to maybe a hundred yards, but it doesn't pack much of a punch. It won't blow through cover, and even heavy clothes could stop the little bullets, but I tell myself it doesn't matter because I'll be making headshots, when the time comes.

A noise makes us stop. Dad holds up his fist and we drop to the ground. The rifle comes up to my shoulder and I take a look through my scope. I use the magnification to scan a clump of eucalyptus trees, but I don't see anything moving. If I was a praying man I'd pray to God and ask for a good target, one of the people responsible for the killing. We wait. I reach into the small of my back and pull Dad's Beretta out of my waistband. I try to give it to Mel for maybe the hundredth time. She doesn't take it, but her "no" is softer now and her breath barely steams the air.

The noise wasn't caused by people. Eucalyptus trees drop their branches in the lightest breeze, and that's probably what it was. We walk until dusk and Dad chooses a camp in a patch of oaks that stand on a low, grassy hill. We can see for two hundred yards in every direction. There's no higher ground close to us. No higher ground within easy rifle range, anyhow, and so it's a good place to be.

I drop my pack. The blood comes back into my shoulders. It feels good to be sixty pounds lighter, but to tell the truth I *like* wearing the pack. Yeah, it's heavy, but it makes me feel strong and more free than I've ever felt before. The weight reminds me that we're doing something important, that our actions and efforts will decide whether we will live or die. And if there's a God, He'll be mad at me for saying it, but I don't think this is such a horrible thing. Not really. Because I think boredom is worse than fighting, because of the way boredom kills you inside. And that's all I had before, shitty days of school and dull

33

days at the mall or the river, and it seemed like I had nothing but boring times ahead of me forever and ever until I fell into my boring grave. There wasn't any real meaning at all, that I could see, so shoot me if I don't hate this new world. At least this shit isn't boring.

We don't light a fire. I open an MRE pouch of Beef Stew and warm it with a heat tab. I try to share it with Mel. I like MREs just fine, but Mel doesn't. She was a vegetarian, before. She takes a few bites of the stew and then she cleans her spoon and puts it away. Mom and Dad share a Chicken à la King. Nobody had to tell us to sit so that we face the four points of the compass, looking out while we eat. We can't afford to slack off. It's the opposite of boring.

It doesn't look like we're being followed. I'm not sure if that's very good or very bad. But it gets me thinking about how the word "very" has lost its mojo. It doesn't make much sense to use that word because everything is "very" now, after the bombs. Very dangerous. Very different, for us, but I've read enough about history to know that there's nothing new about it. Most generations get their time of war. This is mine. I just didn't expect it to happen here in California.

Dad stands the first watch while the rest of us crawl into our sleeping bags. My last bath was a month ago. I smell like a hobo. I pretend to sleep, but I hear faraway gunshots. I drift off listening to the very new, very old sounds of the world.

Bill Junior

Some crazy bitch shot Ookie in the chest with a shotgun. A day has gone by since we sprung our last ambush, but I still can't get used to the fact that my brother is dead. She shot him and he had his hands over it and he was saying, "She shot me, Billy; come see it," like he'd just found a weird bug or an interesting plant. The other guys saw the blood coming from between his fingers and said, "Yep, he's shot, all right," and they watched me to see what I'd do about it.

Ookie was bleeding all over the place and I could see that he was fucked, but the other guys were watching me, too, and that meant I had to be a certain way. I wanted to scream for a doctor. But there aren't any doctors and I couldn't sound like a pussy in front of the men.

I'm in charge here. I've been the boss since the electricity went out and we escaped from juvie. I was the one to notice that most of the guards had hauled ass out of there, and I was the one who came up with the plan to escape, and I was the one who killed the first guard and led the attack against the others. I've only been alive for sixteen shit-ass years, but I've learned a lot in that time. The weight of leading people isn't so heavy anymore, except that I hadn't counted on losing Ookie.

It seemed like I stood there for a long time, thinking, try-ing to put off going to him, like I was trapped in one of those shitty dreams that you can kind of control but kind of can't. But I couldn't have been standing still for very long because Ookie was only on his second sentence after getting shot. The guys were in a cluster-fuck in the middle of the road. I grabbed Luscious and told him to set up a perimeter with half the guys while the others searched the bodies. I said, Holy shit, dude, you know better than to let down our guard. Luscious has just about every kind of race in his blood, and he's six foot five and almost as wide as he is tall, but he isn't a schemer. He's the kind who'll take suggestions from a leader, as long as he respects the leader who makes them, but God help the man he doesn't respect. He's my second-in-command, and when I said that shit about letting down our guard, he looked embarrassed and then he was all action, giving his orders and the guys were moving like whipped dogs at the sound of his voice.

I had a syringe of morphine from when we ambushed that last little National Guard convoy. We used to have lots of morphine, and we kind of had a party with it one night when we were bored, but I saved a few syringes for the bad times. I took a knee next to Ookie. I set my rifle on the ground and pulled out the morphine and held it up so he could see it, and he smiled his little-kid smile. He was only fourteen, but he was a moose of a kid, and only his smile made him look younger than me. I shot him up with the morphine and his eyes went far away and he laughed a little bit.

"We were really pirates, weren't we?" he said, and I said, "We still are." The drug got to him right away and his lips were bloody and his mouth was like it was made of jelly. He mumbled something, but then he fought the morphine buzz and came hard awake.

"I'm dying, bro."

"Maybe."

"You don't need to blow sunshine up my ass."

It was one of the sayings our usually worthless old man taught us.

"Okay," I said. "I'll just stay here with you."

One of the little Kelly twins let out a yell behind me. He'd found something on one of the bodies. He had a handful of coins and they were gold, and the other guys searching the bodies found more gold coins, and then they were hump dancing and tossing coins and whooping it up. They acted like kids for a while. But then they remembered that Ookie was shot and they quieted down and finished stripping the dead.

I motioned for the Kellys to toss me a couple of coins. I caught them and they were warm and heavy. I held one of them up in front of Ookie's face and he said, Wow, but he only said it to make me happy, to show that he was paying attention to his big bro. He tried to sit up, and blood came out of his mouth.

"Listen," he said. I put my ear close to his mouth. He started coughing and shaking all over, but he pounded the flat of his hand against the road until the shaking stopped. I didn't wipe his coughed-up blood from my ear.

"Listen. I'm no good. I'm all fucked up. But there's one thing I can still do."

"Quiet," I said, but it was a dumbass television thing to say. God knows I'd run my mouth nonstop if I was shot and dying. Ookie smiled a huge smile that was like the smile he had when he was twelve and he stole a bottle of whiskey from our dad and gave it to me for my birthday.

"For you," he said. "I can help you one last time."

"Don't worry about helping anyone, kid."

"It's for me, too. It hurts bad, Billy."

I had some idea about what was coming. Part of me didn't

want to hear it, and part of me was curious to see if I was right. He whispered so no one but me could hear.

"Pop me one in the head."

"No."

"Do it. You know it's the right move."

A gust of wind blew through the trees and set the meadow grass to bobbing. The guys were quiet in their plundering. I heard the clinking of gold coins and grabbing sounds as loot was pulled from pockets. They all had their heads tilted sideways, watching. It seemed like even the animals in the woods were watching.

"Okay," I said, and Ookie smiled his little-kid smile like he'd just gotten the best present in the world.

I was packing the Beretta I took from a dead National Guard lieutenant. I pulled it from its flap holster and unsafed it. The guys were done with their work and they gathered around, even the ones who should've been standing guard. I racked the slide and pointed the pistol at Ookie's head. My brother used the last of his muscles and blood and balls and heart, and he said, "Just remember that it wasn't you that killed me."

The guys probably thought he was trying to be tough when he died, but Ookie gritted his teeth into a smile and gave a nod goodbye. I pulled the trigger before his smile could start to fade. The back of his head busted open and there was a lot of blowback. It was in my eyes and running from my nose and chin. I stood with bits of my brother on my face and hands, and the guys didn't say anything, but they couldn't close their mouths. I tore a piece of cloth from the coat of an old dead guy and wiped the Beretta more or less clean and put it back in its holster. I picked up two of the gold coins and put them over Ookie's eyes. I walked into the crowd of guys and grabbed one of the little drunks and searched him and took a pint bottle of Jim Beam off him. I put the bottle in Ookie's hand and I didn't need to say that I would surely kill the man who tried to take it.

The guys formed a line and passed in front of Ookie. A few of them gave him things as they passed. I didn't watch to see what-all they gave him, even though most of the ones who gave him things were only trying to score points with me.

I turned my back on it. I raised my hands and looked up into the overcast, hoping to catch a last look at Ookie's soul, but I didn't see it go. If I cried, my killing him would be for nothing, so I made myself hard. The memories were killing me. They went on and on, my little bro following me around and bragging about me to his little friends and all the times he'd given me things, like he knew he didn't need to bribe me to get me to care about him, but it wouldn't hurt to hedge his bets. I went kind of blind for a while, and when I came out of it I was holding the Beretta down along my leg, cocked and locked. The guys were backed off toward the trees, even big Luscious, who wasn't afraid of anything, but was stubborn about choosing his own way to die.

Ookie had been right. The guys were sad about losing him, but the looks they gave me after I shot him were different and I knew that I was really and truly the boss of the gang, right then. We're still fighting for a good cause. We're fighting for ourselves when nobody else gives a shit—never did and never will—so we gotta make our own way in the world, and follow our own laws and rules, no matter the price.

I've been wasted for most of the day. I want to go back and bury Ookie, but it would be stupid to go back to that place, and it would also be a sign of weakness. I'll miss him because he was the only person who really knew me, but I can't even pull a blanket over what's left of his head. We're like the opposite of the Special Forces guys in the movies. We *always* leave our own behind. But Ookie's not in such a bad place. He was able to get himself over to a tree after he was shot. It's a strong-looking tree, a cedar I think, maybe two hundred years old. The freeway crosses a grassy field there and the sky is stacked high above him and if the clouds ever break up he'll have a good view of Mount Shasta.

And today's another day. I raise my hand and make a spinning sign in the air. George Washington is our captain of the guard today and he raises our Budweiser flag. The town we're in has the tallest flagpole west of the Mississippi, and the old man can see it from the airstrip. After a few minutes the old bastard calls us on the radio. The sound of his voice makes me want to hit somebody.

"Let's see what's south today," I say.

"How about a day off?" he says.

I turn off the radio and after about ten minutes the old man fires up the Cessna and heads out on a scouting mission. When he's in the air I pick up a National Guard walkie-talkie, but I don't call him. I haven't told him about Ookie yet. I don't want to distract him from today's mission, and I don't want to distract myself, because he might not give a shit that Ookie is dead, and then I'll have to kill him. No. It's better to wait until Ookie's wake to talk to him. The old bastard is a happy drunk and I'll get him a bellyful of liquor and then he'll cry about losing his son and I can pretend that he's not the shittiest father that ever lived. But for now I'll leave him alone because that's the way we both like it.

The overcast is higher today and it looks like maybe the sun might poke through in a week or two. I don't want to sit around, so I tell Luscious it's time to lock and load. The boys climb into the trucks. Usually they're telling jokes and grab-assing around when we go out, but not today.

I take my place in the passenger seat of our Brinks armored truck. It's one of the only trucks we've found that still runs after the bombs exploded, and it figures that the greedy bas-tards who suck all the money from the world would make their money truck nuke-proof. Our other two trucks are five-ton National Guard rigs. They're full of holes from when we took them from the weekend warriors and they look like pieces of shit, but they run just fine.

We haul ass out of town. Luscious hands me one of the gold coins. It's warm from being in his pocket and it's heavy. I tell him to give each of the guys two of the coins.

"We'll put them over their eyes if they get killed, like we did with Ookie." Luscious nods and I can tell he thinks it's a cool idea.

We've hit five groups in the last month and I don't think anymore about the price we might have to pay when cops and soldiers take over the world. I used to wonder about the peo-ple we killed, but not now. I only think they were stupid to lose everything they had. Damned if they all didn't walk right into our ambushes and get themselves killed. They trusted the world when they shouldn't have, and we got some good stuff off of them, and that's all there is to it.

That last group had milk for their rugrats and some cheese and butter, too. They had eight shotguns and maybe four hundred twelve-gauge buckshot shells. They must've been backwoods hippie pot farmers, because they had more than a pound of good Mary Jane between them. They had animals, too—cows and sheep and four lambs. Somehow the animals didn't get shot, and I feel like a rich man from back in olden times, to have them.

I don't know where the old gray-haired farts got that gold. Maybe they were hippie survivalists. Most of the grown-ups had coins sewed into the cuffs of their pants, and they had more in their wheelbarrows. It added up to maybe fifty pounds, all told, and that's a shitload of treasure. In the old days, the pirates had chests full of ducats. Doubloons. Pieces of eight. Some of those old coins weren't made of gold, but I don't know which ones. My education kind of sucks. But whatever. All of *our* coins are solid gold. We have our tricks and our brains and our balls and our guns, and now we have our treasure, too, and that makes us pirates, fair and square.

All we need now are some girls. Yeah, that's just what we need. We've been killing everyone we come up against, lately, but now I think it's time we let a few of them live. The wenches. The guys will love me even more if I can get them some of the other kind of booty.

Jerry

We walk past the time that was previously known as lunch. I feel as if I've made them pop-up targets in some giant outdoor shooting range. I start to develop irrational fears. What if that little airplane is armed with machine guns? What if the bad guys have snipers? Wouldn't this hill be a perfect place to set up artillery to control the area? Would they bury mines along the road? IEDs?

Damn, I'm tired. The worry burns in my guts, but the coals of it keep me moving. A cold wind blows down from the mountains. Before we walk into the flatland I stop us.

Susan says, "Ponchos."

"Yeah."

I should've done it sooner. We drop our packs and pull out our ponchos. Surplus military ponchos in woodland green camouflage, the most useful garments ever issued by a government. We put our packs back on and pull our ponchos over everything, our bodies and all our earthly possessions. The sage and winter grasses are tan and gray, and the woodland camo ponchos make us look like mobile oases. Susan looks at Melanie and Scott, and then back at me.

"We'll be warm. And at least it'll break up our outlines," I say. But I immediately regret the negative tone, the tone of settling for second best. I can't afford to sound that way, not even in jest.

"We'll be fine."

"Sure we will."

I want to hold her hand, but I hold my rifle. I look at the dry fields, hoping to find a flower, but there aren't any flowers. The old world is gone, and the fear is feeding on my insides, and I can't help wondering if I've already made love to my wife for the last time. I wonder if we'll someday return to our careless peacetime ways of being.

Miles of open land stretch before us. Mount Shasta powers into the overcast at our eleven o'clock. A much smaller volcanic cone rises at its western base. I remember driving past it once with a Marine buddy who knew something about this part of the Sierras.

We follow the deer trail out of the hills and descend toward an old lakebed surrounded by volcanic hills. A small town comes into view below us. The kids are skittish when they see it. Susan is giving me looks again that I can't decipher. I decide to tell them a story that my long-gone Marine buddy, Rick Sheffield, told me about that part of the world. I stop and point at the mountain.

"The smaller hill at the base of Mount Shasta is called Broken Top."

They look. Broken Top is the most perfectly symmetrical inverted cone a person could ever hope to see. Its top comes to a sharp point.

"What dumbass would call that hill Broken Top?" Scott asks.

It's exactly what I'd said to Rick, all those years ago. I realize now that the question is very old. Maybe it predates Western history. I try to remember the exact words.

"The locals like to tell an old Indian story. They say that Broken Top was once the summit of Mount Shasta."

I point at the flattened summit of Mount Shasta and move my hand down to the perfect cone of Broken Top.

"In the beginning, Shasta was very proud of her perfect figure. She bragged to the other mountains about her beauty and called them ugly lumps, or something like that, and the other mountains summoned the gods and told them about Shasta's vanity. The gods, being fair, warned Shasta not to be cruel to her sisters. But she was very beautiful and vain and she started to brag again. And so the gods punished her. They caused the earth to shake and Shasta's top was blown off whole and it slid down the mountain to land at her feet."

We stand and look. Our breath steams the air.

"The Indians didn't know *shit* about geology, did they?" Scott says. He spits into the winter-gray sage.

"Shut up," says Melanie. "At least they didn't blow each other up."

"Maybe they would've, if they'd had the bomb."

"I doubt it."

"You shouldn't."

Melanie opens her mouth, but she closes it. She's quiet after that, and I think she's written us off entirely. We leave the last of the trees behind. We walk exposed toward the town, and whatever stories it might hold for us.

I cough, but it's more than coughing. A cough can hide a sob just fine. We walk fields of grass that hide patches of granulated snow. I start to worry about dogs. It sticks in my head that a barking dog could get us killed. I scope the place with my binoculars. The town appears to be abandoned. There's a lumber mill lined with half-loaded rail cars. There's a Chevron station, a Mexican restaurant, Primo Pizza, the Golden Eagle Motel, and a wrecking yard. There's also a good-sized food store. Lane's Market.

We pass a burned-out minivan, its skin blackened and drooping between the ribs of its unibody. It's riddled with bullet holes. Scott stops. He points to the market.

"I sure could use some junk food."

More stalled cars and trucks litter the road ahead. One of them is a shot-up National Guard humvee. Footprints leading away from them are stamped into the snowy patches. The snow has melted and frozen, time and again, and the indistinct tracks seem to lead neither north nor south, but some of them are fresh.

"Later. Let's see what-all else is here, first."

We seem to be the only people alive, horizon to horizon. It's what I'm hoping for, and yes, it's what I'm praying for, but the odds are against it. The town is small, but it's surrounded by volcanic peaks and the old lakebed is wild with grass and I can see cattle grazing. There are deer in the hills and bass and trout in the streams, and I know people who prefer the challenges and gifts of nature to all the operas and concerts ever written.

The highway cuts through the four square blocks of downtown, making two fifteen-mile-per-hour turns. It's the kind of tiny, isolated place that most city people drive through, shaking their heads and wondering who could possibly live there, but I understand its attraction. If I'd chosen to live in such a place, it would take more than distant bombs to convince me to leave.

I'm almost certain that we're not alone here. I'm still worried about dogs. Our scent could give us away. We skirt the gas station, with its shot-out windows. We circle the weirdly intact market. I take out the binoculars but I don't see any bodies.

We circle and I try to keep us upwind of the buildings as long as possible. We trudge along with the fickle mountain breezes that could so easily betray us. We're out in the open but there's no other choice.

The door to the Mexican restaurant bangs in the wind. The service bay door of the tire shop is open. We circle the market and check out the other buildings. If everything is quiet, we'll approach the market again from the front. A black pit bull walks out of the wrecking yard and lifts its head to sample the breeze. It looks directly at us, then trots away to the south.

Susan

We're in danger here. I know we are, but we need food, so I can't very well ask Jerry to bypass it. We walk narrow streets that funnel us into more narrow streets. I see no movement behind the dusty windows of the houses and shops that surround us, but that doesn't mean no one is watching.

I pray while I walk. We need food, but that's not what I'm praying for. I pray to be left alone. Is it such an impossible thing to ask? Just let us be left alone. But no man is an island, as they say. What I *really* want is a safe haven, but I don't have the nerve to pray for that today. We keep walking. No one shoots at us, and that's the very definition of hospitality, isn't it? The odds of having faith in others aren't very good, but sometimes there's no other choice but to bet everything on trust.

Cynical. I'm turning into a coldhearted cow. Mustn't let the others see it. No. I won't. Optimism is the best medicine for this condition. Optimism and sacrifice and whatever courage I can muster. These are the things we need, now. Quiet courage and kindness, even if they're not entirely true. The small things, like preparing meals for them. Tucking them into their ponchos at night, trying to get them to remember the bedtime feeling of childhood, the feeling of snapped-out blankets hovering above them, about to float down and create a magical shell of warmth and safety. Having coffee ready when they wake, and clothes that have been at least brushed off, and something special at breakfast—a handful of wild berries or a stick of gum for after they eat. I can still enjoy that kind of thing, and they can, too.

And we mustn't give in completely to the mistrust that's all around us. The enemy is everywhere, because the enemy is also within us. And so if we can't rise above it—if we can't be decent and kind to each other—we'll lose the fight. It's maybe a silly way of thinking, but I'll see if I can squeeze myself into the glass that's half full. Even if I don't believe we're better than anyone else, I'll fake it like I've never faked anything before. If all life is a stage, then I'm going straight for my Oscar moment, walking with this shotgun in my hands, but quick to smile when the danger passes, and quick to do special things for them. And maybe I'll even be nice to strangers, too, if I ever get the chance.

Melanie

It's a tiny, lonely place, but it feels like a city after being in the hills for all those days. Mom and Dad want to scrounge for food. If they thought about it, they'd see that taking stuff from people who can't protect it is the very definition of looting.

"I'll go in alone," Dad says.

Mom doesn't disagree with Dad very often, but she isn't a submissive housewife either.

"No you won't. All of us go, or none of us," she says.

Dad has the good sense not to argue. We walk around the

community buildings, a Chamber of Commerce with a fresh brick façade, a Methodist church, and a coffee shop called Moody Brews. The town is in a bowl that's like a big navel in the ripped belly of the mountain range. We pass small wooden houses with porches that face the slow highway curves. The shade trees in their yards are bare and gray. A cold breeze blows down from the mountains and rattles bare branches. Either there aren't any people here or they're hiding.

Dad tells us to stay alert, as if we're mentally challenged. I'd get mad, but I know he's worried sick, my poor war pig Goggy. He's always been a reactionary kind of guy, but even the most radical anarchists are probably on his side now, wanting the world to go back mostly to the way it was before.

I trip over clumps of grass and my feet make crunching sounds when I stumble over patches of old snow. The sky is the same color as the snow today. It's dirty and cold. I used to love to see snow under cloudy skies, but I don't anymore. I try to pay more attention to where I'm going so I can manage to stay mostly quiet. It's freaking me out, walking into a place that might be inhabited, but I hate myself for thinking the worst of others. Here I am, making my big pacifist statement, trying to believe other people are just like we are, and worth saving, and worth inspiring to higher causes and teaching the ways of justice, but aren't I really just a member of an armed gang now?

I can't let myself think about that, though, so I try to remember the good times. I used to love walking in crowds. When I went up to visit the Cal campus, I'd make a point of walking the streets of Berkeley. I usually ended up, sooner or later, in a conversation with someone cool. Someone real, like a bus driver or a flower seller or a bag lady or a handyman. Working people. People like the ones who used to live right here.

Just after the bombs, the whole West Coast of the country was on foot together, as if we suddenly got an urge to march together for some great cause. And I think our walking was at least partly a protest. So yeah, I miss walking in crowds in the time when people were sane and helpful and giving and kind. Brave. Noble. Someday, people will be like that again. I truly believe it. We'll be comfortable again, and we'll surely bitch about the things that annoy us, but our bitching will be ironic after this. We'll actually learn from our mistakes this time, won't we? I understand that life happens in cycles, and we need to live through bad times to recognize the good ones.

We're all alone in this place, and the sky is brown and the air is so cold that I can't feel my hands and feet. I'm not sure if I could break into a run if I had to. I feel a panic attack coming on, so I try to fill my mind with something else. Anything else. Something symmetrical and orderly. So I think about the train set Scotty had when he was a little kid. He had a train set and a slot car track, both, and he set them up together, with bridges and banked corners. He had a train crossing for the cars, and he ran the cars and the train at the same time. Most kids would've gotten off on having the train slam into the slot cars, or having the cars slam into the train, but not Scotty. He timed everything so there weren't any collisions. He loved to watch all that perfectly timed movement and energy, and I have to admit that it could be hypnotic. But sometimes I got sick of the sound of those little wheels and motors going around and around and never actually getting anywhere, so I'd sneak up and pull the plug, and everything would come to a halt.

And that's exactly what happened to us on the freeway. One minute we were cruising fast in our air-conditioned, gas-sucking Chevy Suburban, listening to good music on high-quality headphones and looking through tinted safety glass at the beauty of nature, sucking down resources like they were cheap beer, and the next minute the electrons stopped flowing and our truck died and all the other cars and trucks around us did, too.

We coasted without making any sound. We didn't see any flashes or mushroom clouds or anything like that. We were driving in the mountains and our car just quit running. The cars and trucks around us rolled without power for a while and then they all stopped, too. Dad said something. A curse or a prayer. I don't know. No one else knew what was happening, but *he* knew. We were parked on the side of the road, and Dad put on the emergency brake. No lights. No iPod. No cell phones. No engines. Car doors opening, and people walking in the freeway. Voices in the road. Someone lit highway flares, but no more cars came up on us, because that way of life had ended.

"Everyone okay?"

"Yeah."

"What the hell?"

"Don't know."

And then it was like coming to understand a nightmare had come true. There was only one possible conclusion. Dad made it clear.

"No, ma'am, it couldn't be UFOs or sunspots or a government plot. Not with all of the cars, all at once. It's here and we're in it. It doesn't matter who did it. Knowing who did it won't help us, but it *will* help us to know where the closest bomb went off."

He sent a young guy up onto a hill to try to see something,

but the young guy came back and said he couldn't see anything but more mountains.

"There's nothing for us here, folks," Dad said. "There's nothing to do but walk to a better place. The nearest town is Yreka, and we need to get there fast. Let's go, people. Let's help each other get through this."

And the people were amazing. Adults took turns carrying children. The young steadied the old. Black, white, Hispanic, Asian, Native American, rich and poor, we all marched together. Progressives and conservatives shared food and water, rattling off the kind of friendly insults that keep people warm inside.

"I've never marched with a Commie before."

"Yeah? I'm happy to see that Republicans don't goose-step."

And the singing. We sang as we walked, and it wasn't an easy journey, but the time went faster because of the singing. We had musicians in our party, two guitar players and a guy with a sax and a neo-funk singer with his backup babes, their big hair and big voices keeping us going. We had bonfires at the side of the freeway at night. One night we camped near a Safeway truck that was full of fresh produce and good wine. Another night we opened up the trailer of a Wal-Mart truck and chose new wardrobes for each other. We were a model society for a while. No one was better than anyone else. Any hints of pettiness or bullying were stopped by the majority. We had zero tolerance for bullshit. It took a nuclear attack to bring us together, but for a while we were good people. We were frightened, but we weren't ugly Americans anymore. And I was *so* proud of us. I thought it would last, but I didn't expect the government to just leave us alone like they did. When the food started to run out, and people realized they could get away with almost anything, singing was the last thing on our minds.

The buildings here all seem to be empty. There's an old motor lodge with little garages between the rooms. It's freshly painted with redwood stain, but there aren't any curtains on the windows. There's a motel with a big plastic sign that's all patriotic with stars and stripes. The Golden Eagle Motel. There's a smoky fire in its little parking lot. We give it a wide berth. There's a small junkyard just beyond the motel, and I don't want to go near it. All those old wrecks freak me out. Blood on the highways. Blood on the dashboards. The junkyard makes my dirty hair try to stand up straight, and if there's one thing I've learned over the last few months, it's this: If you think you're in danger, you *are*.

Scott

We don't see any more dogs. There aren't any walkers or drivers. There aren't any girls in halter tops and tight jeans. Nothing is moving on the ground but I can hear a jet in the sky, headed to the east. It's probably a bomber flying home after getting some payback. On the day after all the cars stopped running, the sky was full of weird lines and curves and glowing, smoky corkscrews from our outbound missiles. That was the last time I saw blue sky. Now it's just the bombers up there, finishing up. I guess it makes sense, in a hard, no-bullshit kind of way, that the government decided to wipe out our enemies before it started to help us. I mean, what good would it do to start rebuilding if the bad guys could still nuke us whenever they wanted?

The only stoplight for miles around is dead, but the yellow blinker of a construction barrier is winking away on the last of its battery power. Some things are tougher than others. Some things are just in better places or somehow lucky when the shit hits the fan. That's the kind of luck I want for us, too. The wind is puffing my hair and trying to push me around. Broken things are banging against rotting things. My boots thump on old asphalt that's seen better days. The thought of an ambush keeps me sharp.

I put the rifle scope on the tire shop, but nobody's home. We walk along an alleyway that divides the tire shop from the junkyard. I slip on frozen puddles. Dead weeds and grass stick up through cracks in the alley. The junkyard is breathing out the smells of rust and old rubber and plastic. The place is surrounded by a fence with busted slats. I can see gray puddles of engine oil. Wiring harnesses are hanging like guts in the frozen mud. Windshields bubbled out by foreheads. Airbags look like used rubbers on broken steering wheels. Cars that have been in front-end collisions look like people with their lips cut off. Jagged cuts where the jaws of life went to work. All that evidence of the time when people cleaned up their messes because there was profit in it.

We put the junkyard behind us and we don't look back. We need food, and we aren't going to pay for it. We might have to fight for it, because these are more honest times.

Bill Junior

I open my eyes and I have a hangover again. It's like freakin'
Groundhog Day. And God knows it's a bad one. I keep my head
in my sleeping bag and try to rest until the pain winds down
into something I can handle, but it just gets worse. Time stops
and there's only pain crowding out my sleep, so I might as well
get up off my ass and do something about it. I stick my head
outside my motel room and try to wake up one of the kids.
It's barely first light and it's cold enough to hurt. Cold air and
hangovers don't mix. I want to send someone over to Lane's
Market to get some aspirin, but we're all wiped out. The men
are still sawing logs in their rooms. The fire is out. Everyone is
dead to the world, and it's quiet as a graveyard.

I get the spins, so I fall back down into my room and let
the hangover have me. I let it have the sadness about Ookie,
too, and I want to say that I deserve to be hurting. I downed
at least one bottle of Jim Beam last night, but I don't want to
think about it. My body hurts everywhere and it's like I've been
poisoned and then beat to shit by Chuck Norris. My skull feels
like a busted eggshell and what's left of my brain is swelling up
inside it.

I keep seeing Ookie's head exploding and that makes me want
to puke, but then it stops and Ookie gets up and tells me that it's
okay where he is now. He says it's like being a rich kid waking
up on Christmas morning. Every day is like that. He looks right

at me, and he has a deep look in his eyes, like the paintings of the saints that were hung up on the walls of the juvie chapel that we used to go to on Sunday mornings for mandatory Mass. It's a look that has the kind of pity that doesn't piss me off. Ookie disappears and I can just barely sit up before I puke my guts out on the carpet. It's like I puke my soul out. It's like a prayer, and when I'm wiping my mouth I wonder if anyone's ever thought of puking on purpose during a church service, because puking is more real and honest than any prayer can ever be.

I get my skinny ass back into bed. I tell myself that I'll be okay after a while. Time heals everything but sometimes it's too damned slow. Pain can only be fought alone and my soul is on the motel room floor beside me, so I don't have anything to pray with. After a few minutes I fall asleep, and I sleep until midmorning.

Getting a second stab at the day. My head hurts like hell but I don't feel like I'm about to die, anymore. I stick my head outside again. It's still cold. Damned if the men aren't still catching their Zs. I'm still wearing my coat and boots from last night so I stagger outside. There's booze bottles everywhere around the cold firepit. Luscious hears me and drifts out of his room. He looks like he doesn't have a hangover. He looks like he's feeling no pain at all, but I seem to remember him matching me drink for drink. He smiles and he's holding a pill bottle in his big hand. I read Oxycontin on the label. It's about the perfect cure for a hangover. It's about the best way to prevent one, too, as long as you don't take too much.

"Sorry, boss," he says. "I couldn't face another ball crusher of a morning."

"You could've given me some of that stuff, buddy."

I'm hurting and he's smiling and we're alone and I'm not

56

armed. The overcast is like a dirty church ceiling and birds are flying and eating and singing. The birds make me happy, because they're like radiation gauges. Luscious gives me a hard look, then he starts cracking up because that's what guys do when they're stoned and they've kept something from their leader. I tell myself that keeping the drugs from me wasn't like mutiny—it was only like playing a joke. Luscious is getting off on seeing my pain, and I guess it's a good sign, but I look back at the motel and take notice of where I propped up my rifle.

"You look like you crawled from a dead mule's asshole."

"Thanks," I say, thinking, *Why not let him have his fun? Why not let this play out?*

He points to the pill bottle.

"Take some, now. Get yourself wasted and take a day of vacation." He waves his arm at the motel. "I can handle the girls for one day."

Luscious always calls the men "girls" when he's in a good mood.

"Ah hell, I'm awake now. Might as well face the music."

I see another pill bottle on a rock by the firepit. It's empty. That's twenty-five pills, plus the half-empty bottle Luscious gave me. That's enough to give every man at least one dose.

"The men are sleeping like babies, are they?"

"Yep. Every last one of 'em."

"You didn't let them OD, did you?"

"Nope. Rationed out the happy pills myself."

Just after we took over the town, we ended up with lots of drugs we found in the market and the houses and the cars. I had to lock them up in a little safe at the junkyard before the men could swallow and snort and shoot themselves into druggie paradise. I'm not a prude, but I didn't want a bunch of dead or strung-out pirates on my hands. I hold out the pill bottle.

"Did this come from our stash?" I'm still smiling, but Luscious gets serious in a hurry.

"God, no. The hippies had it on them. Our other drugs are still locked in the safe."

"Okay," I say. "So this is just your average, everyday smart-assed conspiracy, all of you guys working together to get over on your boss?"

Luscious lets his breath back out. His smile comes back.

"That's just what it is. I'll make us something to eat while you go clean up the puke pile you laid in your room."

"You heard that, did you?"

"I thought I was gonna have to send for an exorcist."

He laughs his low laugh and he's very damned pleased with himself. I'm glad that he's not so afraid of me that he can't have some fun. Ookie is probably laughing his ass off, too, in heaven. I'm hurting like hell and the pain is my own damned fault, so I guess it's okay that my second-in-command is giggling like a little bitch.

I sit by the dead fire and a short stretch of time comes that doesn't have any pain in it. I know that I'm a sight. It makes me kind of happy that Luscious and the men got over on me. It's a mild thing for them to do after they watched me shoot Ookie. It's the middle road between them obeying me out of fear, like beat-down dogs, and them killing me. They'll be in a good mood today when they wake up, and maybe this will be one of the days we'll remember.

"Someday we're going to say these were the good days, right?" I say to Luscious.

"Yep. It's just like that."

He stands next to me for a few seconds too long, not saying anything about Ookie. I'm weak from the hangover and I start to mist up. I think that Luscious is misting up, too, but I look over and he's only wasted out of his gourd. He's flying high and looking at the empty firepit like he can't remember how to make a fire, so I tell him to sit down before he hurts himself, and I go for firewood.

One of the chores I've made the men stick to is firewood detail. We have maybe five cords stacked in the motel parking lot. We've cut and burned most of the trees close-in, so the men have to walk farther for it, but they've done a good job. It won't be long until we'll need to get a regular logging outfit going, and I've even had ideas about getting one of the town's lumber mills up and running again. It wouldn't be a bad way to put the men to work after the law comes back. The rich city fuckers will have to rebuild the places that got smoked, right? Maybe if I put the men to work doing something useful, something legal that makes money fair and square, the law won't put us back into our cages. Yeah, there's more than one way of taking advantage of bad times, but my head hurts too much to do any planning this morning.

I load up a wheelbarrow of wood that was split from a wind-blown pine. I'm careful when I load the wood, so it doesn't make any noise to hurt my head. I'm standing bent over and breathing hard when I hear the sound of people walking. I think at first that my men are waking up, but it's not them. Then I think it's only the wind or my hangover playing tricks with my ears. But no, it's real. The sound is coming from the road. We have visitors.

I run as quietly as I can back to the firepit. Luscious is zoning out with a blanket wrapped around his shoulders, and I wake him and shush him and he hears it, too, and then we're back in the world that's been left to us. Luscious comes back into himself then. He goes from room to room and wakes the men. They gather around me. They're wasted on downers but they squat on the ground and load magazines and strap on their ammo pouches before I even tell them to lock and load.

There's no way strangers should've gotten this close to us. I'll leave it for another time to punish the ones that didn't stand their watch last night and this morning. I split us into two groups and we move to surround the strangers. The eyepieces of my binoculars are cold against my eye sockets and they give me a monster headache, but I keep looking until I see that there's four of them, one of each kind of human being, man, woman, boy, and girl. I hold up four fingers and the men hunker down without a sound, like the good, stoned hunters they are. The people head for the market, just like any hungry animals naturally would.

Jerry

We're hungry and cold. I'm tempted to go into the junkyard and see if I can get one of the cars to start—one of the big SUVs, maybe, with a good, strong climate control system and seat heaters. But no. Everything with a computer is down for the count, and the fact remains that running vehicles attract death.

We circle the market. Nothing. I take us around again. It takes ten minutes, but peace of mind is worth its weight in time. It's about eleven in the morning and the light through the overcast doesn't quite have enough strength to cast shadows. The wind is blowing over us and a few sick-looking geese fly south. The market overlooks the freeway. It's located between the airstrip and the junkyard. I glass the surrounding area, but I don't see any movement.

I turn and look into the windows of the store. My mind takes me back to past road trips, and I imagine the thrum of the road and the stillness of stopping. The wind is always blowing in places like this. The daylight looks a certain way when it hits freeway outposts. Thick. Weighted. A place that shouldn't matter burrowing nevertheless into memory. The bright signs that draw people to the shabbiness of the closer view. Not mere patina, but barely restrained decay. But there's the temptation of packaged goods. A bargain bin full of things past their shelf lives. "Shelf life"—the sad feeling of those words. The incredible loneliness of such places. Arriving and taking and buying and leaving. Lives spent just passing through, but I wonder what it would be like to stay here.

We finally move across the asphalt of the market's parking lot, taking cover behind cars. The glass door isn't locked. We enter the store. Scotty stands guard automatically. I want to get us in and out as quickly as possible.

The store has been looted, but not completely. It's still a gold mine of packaged chips and cookies and candy, but I hunt for protein. I grab the last packages of beef jerky and cans of mixed nuts. Susan fills the outer pouches of her pack with antibacterial ointment and ibuprofen and multivitamins and Band-Aids.

Melanie opens a two-liter bottle of Diet Coke and takes a chug that brings tears to her eyes and a smile to her face, then she goes for the gossip magazines. She reads us articles about

J-Lo and the Baldwin brothers. The articles she reads all revolve around the issue of stars with big backsides. We're laughing. It's a good day, I'm thinking. The worry is still there, but we need something good to punctuate the other days, don't we?

I find myself in the beer section. I slip a warm bottle of Widmer hefeweizen into my pack for later. There's also an entire aisle of wine, but I walk behind the counter to the booze section. I limit myself to one bottle of Crown Royal. For medicinal purposes, you understand. I'll light a fire tonight and have a nip of whiskey and maybe I'll be able to lighten up for a few minutes. Yes. It's a good day. I want the good time to last, so I don't rush it. I know that high morale is a weapon in itself. The clock is ticking, but I let them shop to their hearts' content.

Susan

We're laughing and stuffing our packs with riches, with life itself, and then bullets are snapping all around us. Melanie is closest, and I pull her to the ground. We get right down on the broken glass and try to push ourselves into the cracks between the tiles. All of us but Scotty. He's standing with his new, proud posture and shooting his rifle at the ambushers. Jerry runs and tackles him and pulls him back from the front of the store. Bullets take pieces of things with them as they pass. Melanie is screaming. I wrap myself around her. Bottles of wine are breaking red and white, and the floor is slick with wine and glass.

I check Melanie but she hasn't been shot. Her screams aren't screams of pain, but anger. People aren't supposed to be like this. People *are* like this. I push the shotgun out around a rack of greeting cards and fire a blast into the parking lot.

Melanie

Stop it! Just stop it! What's so fucking hard about that?

Scotty

I'm sorry, sorry, so sorry I didn't see them before they opened up. I was supposed to be watching and I didn't see them. Are we hit? Is there any blood? I can't see Dad and Mel, and God damn these assholes if they killed them. I end up next to Dad. He's okay and so are Mel and Mom. We're all okay and the shooting is letting up. They shot high. Maybe they didn't want to ruin the stuff in here. But now what?

We're surrounded by shooters. We're surrounded by a parking lot that only has a few cars for cover. And I get the feeling that the shooters didn't just stumble up on us. No. I get the feeling we're caught in a trap. Something makes me look up at the shelves. Rows of chips. Corn chips and potato chips and pretzels and cheesy fish crackers. I didn't notice before that some of the packages are open. The bags are crumpled and crooked on the shelves. Some of them have dirty fingerprints on them.

It's the kind of thing I wouldn't have noticed back when the world was boring, but I see it now, all right. Bait. It's bait and this is a trap and we're in it. The rat eats the cheese; the rat eats the cheese; hi-ho, the dairy-o, the rat eats the cheese. And now we're totally screwed. Unless we fight. Unless we fight and kill and win.

Bill Junior

We pour some fire on them to see what they're like. They pop back at us with a little .22 and one shotgun round. Let's just say that our fire is a lot noisier, and so the situation is clear. I send runners behind us and all the way to the trees to make sure there aren't any more strangers setting a trap for us. I learned how to play chess when I was locked up in juvie, and an ambush is a lot like that mean little game. I know I can't pay so much attention to setting up an attack that I fall into somebody else's.

I send runners to get some of our dynamite. I don't want to blow up the market, but I want to be ready for anything. I hold up my fist and the men stay low and some of them look like they want to get this over with and go back to sleep, but they're watching me and understanding my signals, and I know they'll do whatever I say.

For now we'll wait. We've had good luck with waiting. We've had people surrender after the first few shots. We've had people shoot up all their ammo at us, so we could just walk over and put them out of their misery. One dude even shot his family and then himself while we waited. Ookie said that the dude didn't know what side he was on, and we laughed about that crazy loser for days.

No, these strangers aren't going anywhere. I'll wait for the runners to get back before I make my next move, then I'll think of something that doesn't get anyone but the right people killed. I glass them with the binoculars. The girl peeks out from behind an aisle of soda pop, and she's looking fine, fine, fine, with that wild red hair. She's wearing a ski coat and some nasty-looking blue jeans, but her clothes can't hide the fact that she's one hundred percent female. I hand Luscious the binocs and ask him what he thinks of her.

"So *that's* what you're after," he says.

"That there is a righteous-looking wench," I say.

Jerry

The shooting stops. The kids are quiet, and I crawl to them and check them for holes. I check their arms and legs until they push me away. Susan hasn't been hit, thank God. I remember to check myself. There aren't any holes in me either, thank You, Lord, again and forevermore. Thank You for not letting us die because of my stupidity and greed.

But how did we miss these guys? I don't buy the story that they just walked up on us. No. They could've been hiding in the motel or the wrecking yard, watching us pass. But if that was the case, they could've taken us on the road. Maybe they have hidey-holes. Spider holes, like the terrorists had in Beirut. It doesn't take long to prepare positions like that. And nestled down in the earth, beneath good camo cover, you're very hard to spot. Unless someone steps directly on the position, a spider hole is practically invisible.

But I'm only being paranoid again. They probably just didn't see us right away, and that's a good sign, because it means they're fallible, too. I low crawl to Susan and whisper that we'll wait until dark. We'll melt away into the night, God willing. She squeezes her eyes shut. Her lips move, but she's not talking to me.

I brush shards of glass from her hair. I want to kiss her but I don't. I sweep a place free of glass for us. We roll onto it. I reach up above us and pull a few things from the shelves. I treat the cuts on her forearms with hydrogen peroxide and I cover them with SpongeBob SquarePants Band-Aids. Then she treats my cuts while the children follow our lead and bandage their own cuts.

"Be ready for anything," I say. "We have a long day ahead of us. If these bastards don't have other plans, we'll be leaving when it gets dark."

I want to crack open the Crown Royal and take a long pull, but I don't. We settle down to wait, but the killers don't wait forever.

Susan

They're running across the parking lot. No. It can't end like this. Please.

Scott moves to cover the door to the storeroom. I move so I can cover Scott. Jerry doesn't have to say a word. He crawls to the front door. Melanie sticks close to him. For half a minute we crawl like insects to the places where we'll live or die. I get more cuts from the glass. The reality of our situation is hard to swallow, but I swallow it. We're together in this. None of us is alone, and if we have to go, this is the way to do it. But no. Hell no.

The shooters are close. A voice comes from outside.

"Give it up, people."

Jerry saying, "Sure thing—right after you give us your guns and cook us a steak dinner."

Our attackers talk among themselves, but I can't hear the words. The voice starts up again.

"We know it's you, Hammersmith."

"Who's that?"

"That would be *you*."

"That would be bull*shit*."

They talk to each other again. I can't hear what they're saying outside, but they're saying a lot. Three minutes pass. And then finally:

"I'm coming in. I want to talk, but my buddies say I shouldn't bother. We have a shitload of dynamite out here. If you shoot me, you'll die ugly. Got it?"

"Yes."

"Okay then."

"Okay."

I hear the door opening. It grinds on its hinges and pushes through the debris in its path. I hear careful footsteps on broken glass. I move to a place where I can see both the storeroom door and the storefront. I get a look at the guy. He's holding a big cowboy revolver, but he's keeping it pointed at the floor. I get a look at his face. He's a boy, maybe one year younger than Scotty. He's either afraid or he's a very good actor. I can't bring myself to point my shotgun at him. He sees me. He stops, but he doesn't raise his pistol. I move the shotgun so it's beside me on the floor, almost out of his sight. For a second, he looks grateful.

Jerry stands. He walks to the boy. He walks quickly in a way that could be seen as threatening, but he doesn't have a choice. He's closing the distance between them, so he can keep Melanie out of any potential line of fire. He stops when he's right up against the checkout counter. He keeps the boy at his two o'clock position, so I still have a clear shot. I slide the shotgun up and manage to aim it in the boy's general direction.

Jerry keeps his rifle pointed at the floor. They size each other up, as males of different generations do. Jerry is bigger than the kid, but the kid doesn't seem to be intimidated.

"We're up from Weed. We're looking for a man who kidnapped a girl. You're not him."

"Nope."

Jerry doesn't say anything more. He coughs once without opening his mouth. Seconds pass. The kid loses the edges of his tight posture. He lets out his breath and betrays the fact that he'd been holding it in.

"What's your story?" he says.

"We're coming down from Yreka, headed south. Headed home."

"I heard it was bad in Yreka."

"It was."

"Who's this with you?"

"My family."

Jerry's trigger finger is white against the trigger guard of his rifle.

"Okay," the kid says.

"Okay?"

"You don't have to be afraid of us."

"I don't?"

"No."

Jerry flicks a glance at the riddled store.

"Convince me."

"Well, let's start by taking ourselves off high alert."

The kid uncocks his cowboy revolver and slides it into its cowboy holster. He shrugs his thin shoulders and raises his eyebrows. Jerry nods and slings his rifle so it's pointed muzzle down. It looks less threatening that way, but I've seen him bring it up and fire a shot in less time than it takes me to blink. He doesn't ask us to stand up, so we don't. I have a say in everything else we do, but I'll let Jerry make the decisions about whether we should talk with strangers or kill them.

Melanie

His story about looking for a kidnapper is bullshit. He's younger than I am. He smiles at me, but maybe he's a monster, so I don't give him anything. He has long brown hair and he's wearing a natural grunge look. He looks bright enough. He could be a poet, for all I know, but all I can see is that stupid, so-called Peacemaker on his hip. I hope he's a decent person, but I think he's probably a killer. I want him to leave, but I don't have the nerve to say anything.

He shouts to the other guys.

"It's okay, men. The shooting's over. And for God's sakes, put away the dynamite."

He calls one of them inside. The door opens again and a huge brown kid comes in. He's really big, but he looks like he's about sixteen. Dad treats both the young guys like men. They probably think they are. Dad introduces himself and shakes their hands. They shake, but they keep their serious boy-man faces on. The big one says his name is Luscious. He looks straight at Dad when he says it, like he's daring him to say something. The leader calls himself Bill Creedmore Junior. His eyes are bright and he has the same wild look on his face that my brother has. It's like they think this is some kind of extreme sport. If I thought it would do any good, I'd remind the testosterone-poisoned males of the world that the process of evolution has a habit of weeding idiots from the herd.

Maybe he's a killer, but Bill Creedmore Junior has an interesting smile. It's sad, but there's something complicated in it, too. His eyes do that sparking thing that shows he wants to tell me something interesting. Something that has nothing to do with this shit.

But no. I'm with Dad on this one. Being peaceful doesn't mean you have to be a sucker. Like that old maggot Ronald Reagan said: Trust but verify.

Scott

No way do I trust them. They might have Dad and Mom and Mel thinking they're okay, but not me. Something's wrong with them. They're saying all the right words, but it's like they're reading from a half-assed script. Look. There. The smaller one just apologized for shooting at us, but he's a shifty-eyed bitch. And he's standing all stiff and uptight. If he was really sorry, he'd relax a little bit. Maybe he'd look down at the floor. But not this dude. I know he's lying, the little dickhead. Maybe I can't read minds, but I know when someone is lying. I've spent enough time in front of a television to know bad acting when I see it.

They're still talking, but I keep watch on the storeroom door. I lean the .22 against a shelf of cleaning stuff and take out Dad's Beretta. The pistol packs more punch at close range. I back up so I can see Dad better. There's another dude, a big kid who looks like he's made up of every race and creed on earth. His acting is just as bad as the first kid's. The smaller one lights a cigarette with a pack of Circle-K matches. He doesn't shake out the match. He lets it fall to the floor and then he stomps it with his weird gray shoes. They're walking shoes. They don't have any brand labels that I can see. The other kid is wearing the same kind of shoes. Two more kids come into the store. They're all wearing the same crappy shoes. It's like they're in a cult or something. Like the cult that thought there was a spaceship hiding in the tail of Halley's Comet.

More of them move up and stand at the door, and all of them are kids, and all of them are carrying black rifles. My ears start to buzz and I can see almost too clearly and my face is hot. I try to get Dad's attention, get him to check out the bad footwear and the military rifles, but he's keeping a tight focus on their eyes and hands. I don't think he's bought their story yet, but I'm afraid he will. Unless he's putting on an act, too, it looks like he's already starting to relax. I take the Beretta off safe and wait for the little shits to show us what they're really all about.

Bill Junior

You have to be patient, but also you have to know when to make your move. What's the difference between a player and a bitch? The player knows when to do what needs to be done.

The man's getting old. He was probably a tough mother-fucker when he was young, but he's got that old-man hesitation thing now. Unless it's an act, his ass is mine. But it's his daughter's ass I'm after. The mother doesn't look too shabby, either. She's a project the men could get behind. But the daughter is a natural eight, even dirty as she is. A real stunner.

I give her a smile. It's my mysterious smile, the one I used to practice when I was locked down in juvie and dreaming about girls, the smile that says, Baby I could show you things you couldn't *imagine* learning anywhere else. She tries to look through me, but I think the smile got to her, because she's working hard to pretend I don't exist.

Her old man sees the smile, too, but he doesn't get mad. It makes my alarm bells start to ring because it shows that he's a good salesman, too. He's not afraid of me, that I can see, and he probably wants to blow my guts out for what he must know I'm thinking about his girl, but he looks right into my eyes and asks me if any of my men are wounded. He says he has some training in first aid, and maybe he can help.

"No," I say. "Nobody's hurt, thank God."

I add the "thank God" thing without thinking about it, and I like how it makes me sound like a man with values. The truth is, I don't know if any of my guys were hit. I kick myself inside a little bit for not asking right away. The sales job I've got here extends to my men, too. It takes both carrots and sticks, and I should've at least put on an act and checked on my men, first thing.

Jerry

I don't think they're okay, but I want them to be. Maybe they are. Two more of them come inside. They smell like sweat and tobacco smoke and a night of drinking. Their leader, Bill Junior, is looking at Melanie. He has a good poker face but it doesn't take much imagination to see the lust in his eyes, and it says something that he doesn't hide it from me.

He changes course and takes a good look at my rifle.

"Nice AR. Can it shoot like a machine gun?"

"That would make it illegal."

The kids get a big kick out of that. They're all armed with military M-16s and M-4 carbines. They stand behind Bill Junior and have a good laugh, but Bill Junior doesn't laugh.

"*Nothing* is really illegal anymore, is it?" he says.

"Some things always are."

"Yeah? Maybe you're right."

"I hope so. When people can do anything they want, some of them tend to do the wrong things."

"But what if they're only hungry? Is it still wrong to take what you need to live?"

"I'm still working on that one."

The kid nods and relaxes a bit more. I notice the shoes. Gray walking shoes. All of them.

The big one offers me a cigarette. I shake my head no. Bill smiles and says, "Naw, Luscious, you don't get old by smoking that shit." The kids are smiling, but there's a predatory sharpness to it, and I'm absolutely certain that I'm standing face-to-face with the monsters that shot up the families on the interstate and the people at the farmhouse. I'm a father and a career man and I've learned how to keep emotions from my face, but I feel rage rising inside me. I remember the road ambush, and the woman's high scream, all the horror of loss and the true promise of killing it held. I don't say anything else, because the time for talking is over.

I take mental snapshots. The posture of each of them. The way they hold their weapons. The weapons are filthy, and that tells me something. The kids are wearing serviceable coats, but they're stained dark in places. They're wearing layers of clothing, torn and dirty. They're dirty. We're dirty and the whole world is filthy and stinking, as far as I know. Long hair and as much beard growth as their ages will allow.

One of the new ones looks like a teenaged Jesus. He has hard booze on his breath, and not from last night. The smile on his face contains the opposite of mirth. All of them are smiling and it won't be long now.

They seem to think my silence is a sign of weakness. I can see it in their eyes and in the way they're moving around me. Three more of them come into the store. More gray walking shoes. They stand close to me. Too close. I look over at Susan and give her the look. *Get ready.* She is ready, God bless her. She gets a good cheek weld on the stock of her shotgun and she dials in on one of the new ones. The kids broaden their wolf smiles, and I back up two steps to improve my position. All the fights of my life coalesce into this one.

One of the kids comes at me with a horizontal butt stroke. He's very fast. I backpedal, but he whacks the butt of his rifle across my face. I roll with the blow, and I take a glancing hit.

I go down on my back, but I manage to get the rifle up between my knees and I go to work. I'm in the cocoon of it, muzzle blasts going like flashbulbs, and I have no choice but to serve my purpose. I hear only the voice of my own weapon. Susan and Scott are firing, but I don't hear their shots or the shots coming at me. I don't know if I'm hit, but it doesn't matter because I'll keep fighting until I win or die.

Susan

Lord help us. I fire the shotgun and work the pump, and my life is boom, pump, boom, pump. I'm shooting and some of the boys are hit and some are running. Jerry's on his back but he's banging away with his black rifle. All but two of the little monsters are running away. The two that stay are hit and hurt, but they're on their feet, holding their rifles out like lifted crutches and trying to shoot back. Their faces are twisted and older, as old as they'll ever be, and they're shooting and we're shooting and they're wilting and it's horrible, horrible, horrible.

Bullets pull at my clothes, but I ignore them, and then the two boys are down and I'm outside, chasing the others. The leader and the big kid and a half dozen more of them make it into the parking lot. Boom, and another one is down. Three of them peel off and get behind a minivan and start shooting back at me. Rack, pump, rack, *click*. Running out of ammunition is like running out of oxygen. I kneel in the parking lot and pull shells from my coat pockets. My hands are clumsy but I force them to slide four fat shells into the shotgun's loading gate. Bullets smack the ground around me. I make the shotgun ready to fire. I raise it to my shoulder, but then I hear a snapping sound and feathers fly up from the sleeve of my down jacket.

My left arm stops working. It drops of its own accord to my side. The shotgun swings down and hangs in my right hand. My breath is stuck inside me. I feel very small. When I try to move my arm, it's like lightning hit me there, just below the elbow. I can't move it and I don't want to move it, but then Scotty comes out of the market, firing the pistol. One of the boys lifts his head from behind the minivan. He has brown hair and wide brown eyes and his thin lips are moving. He says something and the three boys stand up and point their black rifles at my Scotty.

I don't remember loading the shotgun. Did I load it? But then I'm up again. I still have one good arm. I walk wide around the minivan to get a better angle. I'm on a mission to kill roaches. I'm bringing insecticide to a hive of vermin, but they keep the car between us. Scotty comes around the back of the minivan and shoots one of them in the chest. I hold out the shotgun with one hand and shoot the thin-lipped boy. The shotgun bucks itself out of my hand and Scotty's pistol is out of ammunition, but the last surviving boy runs away, the gray soles of his shoes flashing left right left. He run across the road and out of sight.

I want to sit down on the asphalt. I want to hold still for a while, but I find the energy to pick up the shotgun and get my boy back inside the market.

Melanie

I'm sick. There's blood everywhere. I knew Mom and Dad and Scott could be assholes sometimes, but *damn*.

Mom and Scott come inside. One of Mom's arms is bleeding down over her hand and onto the floor. There's nothing on her face. No fear or anger or horror. Nothing. She's pale as death, and she walks over to me and runs her good hand all over me. It grosses me out, but then I realize she's checking me for wounds, and I let her. She starts to do the same to Scotty, but Scotty pushes her away and says he's fine, dammit, just give him some space.

Dad is sitting up. His face is dripping blood. When he sees Mom he smiles, and his teeth are bloody.

"Are we okay?"

"We're alive," Mom says.

"Are you okay?"

"Everything's okay now."

"Let me look at that arm."

"I'm fine."

"It's a miracle."

"Yes, it is."

Mom sits down hard on the floor and squeezes her eyes closed. Dad goes to her.

"Help me get her coat off," he says.

I kneel and unzip it. I get warm blood on my hands. Mom hisses when Dad rolls the coat down over her shoulders. She screams when he pulls the sleeves from her shot arm, and then she passes out. I catch her head and lower her face to the floor, where it's bound and determined to go.

Dad tells me to get some first aid supplies. I stand up and look down. It's the wrong place to look. The bodies of two boys are on the floor. I make the mistake of looking at their faces, and my stomach goes crazy. The store smells like burned gunpowder and blood and shit. I run to the back of the store. I get sick. My ponytail swings around and Mom isn't there to hold it back. I barf up the mass-produced food that brought me such happiness only a few minutes ago.

I have no idea what will happen to us. I have no idea what we deserve.

Scott

Maybe I shouldn't be happy, but I can't help it. We stood face-to-face with the little shits, and we're still alive. I know for sure that I centerpunched one of them. My 9mm slug must've hit his off switch, because he dropped like the sack of shit he was. No tears for him. Not from me.

And Mom was a savage. She did what she had to do, and more, but she looks like hell now. I feel guilty for pushing her away when she was checking me for wounds, so I go to her and put my coat under her head. I want to give her a hug, but she wouldn't know about it. I've never felt so happy and so sad. I hold back my tears, but Dad squirts a few. He pats me on the back, then he goes to work on Mom's arm.

I look out at the parking lot. Nothing is moving. No moans. Only bodies. Life's a bitch, right? But I think we've earned a right to stay here. We should take whatever we want. Maybe camp here for a few days.

I pick up a bottle of booze and crack it open. It's Crown Royal. Dad watches me take a sip, then he holds his hand out. I pass him the bottle and he takes a big mouthful, swishes it around, and swallows it. He gets that look in his eyes, the one that gives away the pure pleasure he gets from liquor, as if it's okay that the world has gone to shit, just as long as he can still get his drink on.

I pick up Mom's shotgun. I pick up her bloody coat and pull a handful of shells from the pockets. I top off the shotgun, rack the slide, and stand behind the store's cash register. The Beretta is loaded and riding in the small of my back. I probably look like the last guy standing after a takeover robbery. But I can cover Dad and Mom from here, and I can also cover the door, so it doesn't matter how I look.

Mom opens her eyes. Dad offers the bottle to her. She shakes her head but she doesn't give him any shit when he puts it to her lips. She takes a sip and then another one, then Dad puts down the bottle and cuts her sleeve away. He pours whiskey over the tiny entry wound and over the bigger exit wound, and wipes the blood away. Mom's arm is floppy and loose. It's broken. Mel brings a bunch of stuff from the first aid section of the market, and Dad goes to work with it.

Mel comes behind the cash register with me and grabs a bottle of vodka from the wall of booze behind me. She rinses her mouth and sets the bottle on the counter. She spits and it splatters on the face of one of the dead fuckers. Her pale face goes green, and she runs to the back of the store and does her yerching thing again.

"No need to feel sorry for these cum stains," I say. "Mel?"

She doesn't answer, but I hear her crying, and I don't understand it. Myself, I feel like I've just hit a big lotto. Maybe later I'll feel guilty about this shit, but right now I'm very happy—so happy that the word "very" doesn't describe it. We're alive and none of us got killed and we took some bad people out of the world and we have all this stuff. If Mom hadn't been hit, there wouldn't be any downside at all.

I take another sip of whiskey. It goes to my head, but it's not just the booze that's causing every hair on my head to celebrate.

I'm very tired. I start going over everything that happened. I think I'd be feeling a lot better about myself if I'd have shot more of them. My brain won't stop playing it back to me. If only. Why didn't I? What if? Next time I'll have to shoot straighter, and sooner. Those thoughts go through me again and again until I want to lie down and go to sleep. I want to get wasted on whiskey and go to sleep and dream about nothing at all.

I'm tired as hell, but Dad has work for me to do. Blood keeps running into his eyes, and he asks me if I can bandage him. He has a deep cut above his right eyebrow. I pour booze over it, and the red-gold shit runs all over Dad's face and over his lips, but he doesn't try to drink it. I dry the wound with a paper towel. Part of the paper sticks to the blood, and it's like a huge shaving cut. I put a big white bandage over it, and wrap it with tape. I wrap the tape all the way around his head, and it's just above Dad's eye, so it looks like an eye patch that missed its target.

Dad takes the pistol from me and makes sure it's loaded. He gives it to Mom and she braces herself against a pyramid of motor oil and covers us as we drag the bodies out of the store.

Blood trails. I've never seen a real one until today. Not all blood trails are the same color. Some of them are strawberry-colored. The worst ones are the color of blackberry jam.

I don't look at the faces. I don't feel sorry for them, but I don't hate them either. They lost and we won, and it's as simple as that. We were in the right and they were in the wrong, and now they're dead. Life's a bitch. I don't look at their faces but I'm curious about the wounds. Maybe I watched too many TV shows about crime labs and medical examiners. Maybe I just want to know how well our guns work on live targets.

We drag them feetfirst. Their shirts roll up when we drag them and they show off their new decorations. Mom's shotgun really messed these dudes up. Her buckshot gave them zits from hell. But it's the little holes from Dad's rifle that are the most interesting. Tiny holes in front. Pinpricks. Icepick wounds. But the exit wounds are the size of lemons, tangerines, baseballs. He's shooting hollowpoints. I know my little .22 wouldn't do anything like that. The .22 rimfire is supposedly the Mafia's weapon of choice, but I'd rather be carrying something that blows chunks out of motherfuckers.

We go after the other two bodies behind the minivan. The dude I killed with the Beretta has straight black hair. The one Mom shot doesn't have a face. We drag them over with the others.

I gather up the kids' guns. All four of the dead guys had rifles, but one of them is different. It looks like Dad's AR, but with a shorter barrel and a collapsible stock. That's more like it.

I grab four loaded magazines. Dad sees me with the rifle. He holds his hand out and I give it to him. He points at the rifle, but I can't take my eyes away from his bandage.

"Look here," he says. He puts his thumb on a switch on the left side of the gun. He pushes the switch to its top position. "This is safe." He moves the switch to the middle position. "This is semi-auto." He flicks the switch to its last position. "This is the burst setting. You get three rounds every time you pull the trigger. Don't fire in burst mode unless you absolutely have no other choice."

He puts the rifle on safe and hands it back to me. He nods. I set it against the front of the store. It's mine now.

And then we're only half awake, dragging bloodlines across the white concrete that surrounds the gas pumps. Dad checks out the gray shoes the kids are wearing. Maybe he knew about them all along. He searches the bodies for information. We turn out all their pockets, making a little pile of bubble gum and ammo and gold coins and rubbers. We peel back their layers of clothes and it turns out that the dudes are all wearing the same kind of shirt. It turns out that they were all big fans of the Shasta County Juvenile Detention Facility.

Dad looks at me, but I can't tell what he's thinking. We stack the bodies in the gas station's dried-out landscaped area. They smelled like shit when they were alive and dying didn't make them smell any better. We face them all the same way, their heads away from the store. We do good work. After all this excitement, we still take pride in our work. We stack them with care, like we stacked our firewood back home. I'm not sure if we're trying to show the world what good workers we are, or if we're showing a tiny bit of respect for the dead. It's not a very fun job, to tell the truth, but we're very precise in our work and we make a neat stack, don't ask me why.

We finish our chores. It's getting dark. The American flag is still flying above its Chevron sign. We siphon some gas from a Suburban that will probably never run again. We soak the bodies and set them on fire and then we sweep up the mess inside our bullet-shredded store.

None of us can sleep, so we all stand watch together. The night is cold and hard under the funky clouds. Mom's teeth start chattering, and Dad gives her more whiskey. It's all he can do to treat her for shock. He gives us each a small shot and he takes one for himself.

They wait until dark. When they come again, they come through the storeroom door, in back. They pin us down with their fire. Glass breaking and the juices of shot-up stuff raining down on us. Bullets shred everything around us. One of them takes off the lobe of my right ear. A shooter starts popping off in the aisle I'm sitting in and the bullets are snapping just above my head. I'm trying to hide my whole body behind a box of minibag popcorn, and I'm somehow fitting behind it. I'm praying and making promises to the God that allowed this to happen, but what I really want is a chance to shoot back.

I see a pair of gray walking shoes. I bring my new rifle up but there's a sound and my left hand is on fire, and I drop the rifle. The tip of my little finger is gone. It hurts like a bitch but I pick up the rifle and crawl forward. Mel screams. I crawl as fast as I can, and I see movement and I put my rifle sights on it, but all I see is Mel reaching out with her arms as the fuckers drag her by her legs out the back door. I crawl after her, but then a wall hits me. It's an explosion moving through the wine section. Glass breaks and wine hangs free in the air, bottle-shaped.

Bill Junior

We use three sticks of dynamite to blow the place on the way out and then I post a guard and gather the rest of men around the fire. The girl is at my feet. She's duct-taped with her hands behind her back but her tits are naked and free and they look great in the firelight. The men circle and get eyefuls, and her green eyes are spitting fire and the men are laughing and pretending they're falling in love.

Having a girl can be dangerous. It's like having money or booze or drugs, and I need to set some rules so the men won't be fighting too much. That, and the only other girl we managed to take alive didn't last very long. It was my own fault because I didn't make any rules about how they used her. If anybody needs rules, it's these men, so I call for Luscious to bring me the guard duty list. I stand up straight and let the men babble for a while after their victory, but they know they can't tear into the girl until I've had my say, so they quiet down.

"Here's the deal," I say.

I hold up the guard duty list. All our names are on it, including mine, because we all stand our turn at watch, no exceptions.

"We might be pirates and outlaws, but we share and share alike. After each man stands his watch, he'll get a turn with the girl."

I wait and let the idea sink in. Some of them nod, and I go on.

"Just remember the rules. Rule number one: Hurt her so we can notice it, and you get twenty lashes. Not easy lashes either, but hard ones from Luscious. Rule number two: Kill the girl and the penalty is Hunt Club. No exceptions, no mercy, and only a five-minute head start. Rule number three: Every man gets one cum, and no more."

Some of the men are nodding, the smarter ones that can think beyond the reach of their peckers. I know how I want my words to sound to their ears. I want to sound like a man they'd follow into hell.

"Other than that, boys, you can do whatever else you can think of."

A cheer rises up from the ranks of them. It's what they used to call a round of huzzahs, and it warms my heart.

"To get the ball rolling, we'll start with the watch that just now ended."

Little Donnie Darko lets out a holler because he just came in from his watch. Some of the men grumble something about why should that little peckerhead go first, but I hold up my hands.

"If anyone has a fairer way to do it, let me know right now."

I watch them hard and they stop their grumbling. Biggus says that at least little Donnie won't tear her up none, and he pities the man that gets a turn after he plows the field. They're laughing then and grabbing their nuts.

"Okay. Stick to the rules. That's the way it's going to be." I smile and even the smallest one of them smiles, too, because they all know they'll have a turn. "There's one more thing, though. We need a proper whorehouse. See to setting it up."

They're really hyperactive then, and they run over to the old junkyard office shack. They push everything outside, including the dog-chewed body of old Junkyard Jake, and they drag the girl in there and Donnie runs through the crowd and the men give him about a hundred high-fives and then he goes to the shack to claim his prize. The men surround the place. Some of them are carrying torches and it looks like a wedding in one of those places where people aren't civilized.

Donnie Darko goes inside and closes the door. The men quiet down and listen for the sounds they'd like to be making themselves, but there aren't any sounds. No screaming or ripping of clothes. No pounding or slopping around in paradise. Someone says that little Donnie is soooo romantic, and that gets a laugh, but after that the men get bored.

Donnie isn't more than a half hour before he comes out smiling. The men cheer. He bows. "Best piece I ever had," he says, and his buddy Stumpie says, "Yeah, because it was your first, not counting your hand," and the men hoot and whistle and Donnie joins them and they lift him on their shoulders and carry him to the fire.

I grab Luscious and a Coleman lantern and we go into the shack. It has a garage door and I open it so the men can see that I'm not taking my turn early. The girl is on the floor face-up with her pants down. Her hands are still taped together behind her and her mouth is gagged and her jeans are pushed down to the tape around her ankles. Her legs had to have been closed when Donnie slipped it to her. Maybe Donnie didn't do anything, but that's between the two of them.

I take the cloth out of her mouth. It's a sock with old blood and lots of miles on it, and I expect her to scream when I take it out, but she doesn't.

"My name is Melanie," she says. Her voice is low but strong, and I want her to last a while, so it makes me glad to see that she's okay.

"Glad to meet you," I say.

"You're Bill Junior."

"Yep."

"Are you the person I talk to about getting a bath?"

She's not happy, but she's keeping her shit together. It kind of surprises me.

"I'm the person you talk to about getting *anything*."

She doesn't cuss me or break out crying. She looks right at me with her steady green eyes, not talking down to me or trying to kiss my ass. It's like we just met in a park somewhere and we're equal in every way and maybe we'll get to know each other better and maybe we won't. I don't know whether to be disappointed or impressed with the girl.

"Well then, I could sure use a bath," she says.

"Yeah? You don't want to eat first?"

"No."

"Okay. I'll see what I can do."

She doesn't thank me and it kind of pisses me off, but I let it go. As I walk away it comes to me that she didn't ask about her family, and it says something about how smart she is. How in control of herself she is. I tell Luscious to keep someone watching her because people like that can be dangerous, don't ask me how I know. People like that make plans and they keep the promises they swear to themselves.

The men drag the girl over by the fire and then they get to work sprucing up the whorehouse. I doubt if any of us has ever been to a real whorehouse, so they only have television to go on for inspiration, but they do a good job of it. They line the walls with leather cut from the upholstery of cars and they lay down a carpet of optional floor mats from Toyotas and Nissans and domestic, made-in-America what-all.

While they're making their love fort, I send Luscious to see about heating up water for a bath. It's high time we all had one, to tell the truth.

Jerry

Dear God, protect and keep us. Keep us breathing, every breath a prayer, every heartbeat an oath. Susan is shaking my shoulder and saying it's time to get up. The new explosion mixes with my memory of the explosions I heard in Beirut.

I sit up and only Susan is here, her lips moving, her arm in a sling. I don't know where the children are, and then it's worse than just another bad day. I come out of it in stages. My legs are rubber, but I get to my feet. No telling how long I've been out. The sun seems to be no lower in the sky. I can hear only a solid tone—the sound the television used to make at night, back when television stations went off the air.

I unwrap my face so I can see better. The blood flows again, and I let it. The roof is down in the back of the store. Scotty is alive but unconscious. His pulse is strong and he's breathing okay. I drag him behind the checkout counter. Susan starts in on him, cleaning and bandaging the ear, wrapping what's left of his little finger, finding a pair of tweezers and pulling the glass from his face.

I call for Melanie, but there's no answer. Susan gives me the look. I find a length of two-by-four and I pry up layers of tarred roof and sheetrock and snapped framing and blasted merchandise, but I don't find her. She's gone. They must have her. I pick up my rifle and start after her. I get outside and work my way almost to the gate of the junkyard but then I stop. No. The horrible logic of it. I can't afford to waste my life, no matter how badly I want to pour fire into the bastards.

So I go back to the store and stand watch over Scotty. His face is red meat, and I cry like I did on the day I pulled Marine bodies from that barracks in Beirut. I cry in the same way I cried then—praying for God to allow me to get some payback. I hold Scotty's head up and pour a bottle of distilled water over his face to clear away the grime. He coughs but he's not coughing blood. He's alive and I'm here for him, but our Melanie is gone and I can't live with that.

A flash from another life comes to me, Melanie the four-year-old running on the beach. Square little feet. Tiny toes. Huge smile. The sun going red, the same color as her hair. Her bangs cut straight across the front in a pixie cut that sways back and forth when she moves. Perfect rollers are coming in from the Pacific. It's a good day. Perhaps it was the best day of family we've ever had. The day after I was promoted to VP. Money was no longer a problem. Scotty was there, too, and he was walking and flopping down on the soft sand and laughing his baby laugh. He hugged my legs and looked up at me and beamed pure joy. I can still hear the recorded-voice sound of toddler happiness and his sister Melanie saying, "Put me on your shoulders, Daddy," and me lifting her high and running fast on the wet sand and Melanie laughing nonstop in my memory from that time until just right now.

Susan

Jerry and I are crying. Scott sits up and then he lies back down.

"Can you see me?" I ask.

"Everything's blurry," he says.

"Oh no."

"Shit," he says.

"Please."

"Sorry, Mom."

"That's okay."

"I've been telling myself I could take whatever happened."

"It's a shitty thing," I say. "It's a damned shitty thing."

The old words feel clumsy in my mouth. I don't tell him about Melanie. He reaches for my good hand and gives it a squeeze.

"Pray with me?" he says.

"I thought you didn't do that anymore."

"Well, maybe now's a good time to start."

There's something in his voice. I know he's doing it for me. He doesn't really want to pray. He wants *me* to feel good about something. He wants to give me hope, and I'm proud of his nobility. My tears stop flowing.

"I'd like that," I say.

"Okay then. Let's get it done."

Melanie

I'm on the floorboards of a shack. My hands and feet are bound. It's dark away from the fire, but I can see its flickering light through cracks in the walls. The boys pulled down my pants after they tied my hands and feet. I scrunch across the floor, trying to get my pants back up, but it doesn't work.

A boy comes into the shack and closes the door behind him. He's holding a lantern, and all I can see of him is the crazy shadow he casts against the wall. He comes closer and he isn't much over five feet tall. He looks about thirteen. I think he probably has black hair, but I can't be sure. He stands and looks at me like he's making mental notes about female anatomy.

I have no idea what he's planning to do. If he tries to rape me, I'll have to fight him. So I get ready, but he squats down beside me and tells me his name is Donnie. He stays far enough away from me that I don't feel so threatened. He tells me he's not going to hurt me. He asks me my name. I tell him. He tells me that just because he isn't going to do me, others won't. I can't answer him for a while after that, but then I ask him about my family and he won't look at me. He says he isn't sure, but he thinks they're toast. I cry for a few seconds and he wipes my nose with a nasty handkerchief and I thank him before I can stop myself. He asks how I'm feeling and I say, "How do you think?" He stands up like he's about to leave. Then I ask him how he's feeling and he says, "Don't worry about me." I ask him to tell me the truth about what they'll do to me, and he leans in and feels my forehead as if he's checking my temperature. He tells me that his crew had captured another girl, right after everything stopped working.

"She lasted less than three days, but she was hurt bad before we found her, and the guys didn't cut her any slack. I couldn't save her."

I can't breathe when he says it. I want to cry and I want to scream, but somehow I don't. He says he's sorry, and he hopes I'll last longer, and wouldn't it be great if all the guys just came in here and talked to me and didn't do anything else? He says there isn't much chance of it, though. He turns up his gas lantern and his eyes are brown and red-rimmed and I can see that he isn't happy about my situation. I tell him I'm okay; I know the score, but thanks for telling me the truth. Then we talk about things that have nothing to do with this place.

I ask him what he wants to do when things get back to normal and he says I'd laugh if he told me. I promise not to laugh and he tells me that he's always dreamed about being a doctor, ever since he could first remember being alive. He moves forward into the light and I can see his face, a gentle face with a button nose and full lips.

"Do you think good people would let me be a doctor?"

"I don't see why not," I say, but he can tell I'm only humoring him.

"No. I don't think they would, either. But maybe I'll lie about my age and join the army or navy. I could be a corpsman. I'd be a damned good one, too."

"If it's what you want."

"Yep. It is. I've been fixing up hurt people and animals for a long time. I've seen all different kinds of hurt and I've patched it up. I've only lost one of my patients, but she was all fucked up before I got to her. Let me take a look at you now."

I'm bound, so it's not like I have a choice. His hands are gentle as he takes my head in his hands and runs his fingers over the lumps that rose where the boys kicked me. He seems to relax when he examines me. I hear his small breath going in and coming out. He holds the lantern to my face and checks my eyes, and then he runs his finger down my ribs. He's not just copping a feel. He finds the exact part of my ribcage that's hurting, and he pulls my shirt up, careful not to bare my breasts, and binds my cracked ribs with duct tape.

He asks me what I think about his chances of getting into the military. I don't say anything about his wanting to join. He's interested in helping people, yeah, but maybe he'd be helping the wrong people. I only tell him I hope things will work out for him, and maybe someday we'll run into each other somewhere on a sunny beach and I'll buy him a beer or something, and he says he'd like that.

I know I should be pumping him for more information about my family and the other boys, but I find myself telling him about my luxury hotel fantasy. I can see his teeth in the dark when I tell him. He says he'd sell his soul for a slice of pizza. "Extra pepperoni with hot, stringy cheese and a cold bottle of Coke. Not a can. A bottle that's wet on the outside because it's so perfect and cold."

He asks if I've had anything to eat and I try to remember, but I can't. He takes off his coat and puts it under my head. With my head up I can see that his hair is black as ravens. I'm bound and hurt and crusted with God knows what, but it feels good to be able to look at him without straining my neck. Donnie's voice is low and gentle and I can imagine him trying to nurse a wounded animal back to health. He reaches into the pocket of his coat and takes out a package of turkey jerky. He breaks off a piece and puts it in my mouth. I don't tell him I used to be a vegetarian. I chew and he smiles like I'm a sick dog or cat he's found and soon I'll be all better. He feeds me more, a handful of M&M'S and some salted cashews with pocket lint in them, then he gives me water.

"I never had a sister," he says.

"I have a younger brother."

"I hope you still do."

"Thanks."

He leans in again and runs his hand through my hair, then he leans back and sits again.

"You won't tell them I didn't do you, will you?"

"No."

"Because if you tell them, I'll never hear the end of it. They'll say I'm a fag, and maybe I'll end up in here someday."

"I won't tell. When will I see you again?"

"There's sixteen of us. Each of us gets a turn after we stand our watches."

I can't hold back, and I let loose all the profanity I've ever heard, and then I scream straight into the world's horrible face. Donnie starts to leave, but I stop screaming. I want to ask him something. I'm not sure about the question floating around inside my head, but then I get my mouth to work.

"How long are your watches?"

"Four hours," he says. "I hope I can talk to you when my turn comes around again."

I hear my voice say, "Me, too," then I kind of pass out.

When I wake up, I'm alone. I try not to think about anything. People in hell shouldn't think too much. I breathe my way through a monster panic attack, then I focus my eyes on close-up things, the spiderwebs that cover the inside of the shack. Their silk is white and heavy with dampness in the warm room.

They kicked me very hard when they took me, and I keep drifting off into some unreal place. I cough something up but it's not blood. My memory of talking to Donnie is still clear, but my memory of Bill Junior's visit is a fluttery thing that I can't trust. I know I'm in bad shape. I try to sleep.

When they took me, they dragged me by my hair. If it hadn't of hurt so badly, I would've laughed at them for being so cliché. They threw something into the store and pulled me toward the wrecking yard. There was a huge explosion behind me. I saw the orange blossom of it above me. Pieces of lumber and roofing shingles fell from the sky. The boys stopped to laugh and high-five. I looked back. The rear of the store was completely flattened by the explosion. I started to fight them. I did it without thinking and I'm not proud about it now. I scratched and kicked and punched, and I didn't quit until they kicked and punched me to sleep.

I drift off for a while and then another boy comes into the shack and closes the door behind him. He's much bigger than the first one, and he's not there to talk. I scream, then I fall again into the blackness. Fighting my way to the surface and staying awake long enough to witness the rape. My own.

When daylight comes they lock me in the trunk of a car. I have no choice but to curl up on moldy carpet and rusty metal. Dark and alone. Torn flesh trapped inside twisted wreckage. Then there's the sound of approaching footsteps. Laughter. They pull me out for more. Like a snack, I think, but then the blackness takes me and I'm grateful.

Scott

So dizzy. Dad says I have a concussion. I can see light, but the world looks like it's not put together right. I don't tell anyone. I don't want to jinx anything. If I ever get my sight back, I promise God and man and the devil himself that I'll use it in the cause of justice. But right now the things I see best come from my memories, and it's not the same, and I wonder if I'll ever see anything new again.

My circadian rhythms are all screwed up because I can't tell what time it is. Anyway, I don't want to sleep ever again. My missing fingertip hurts like hell, even though it's long gone. I keep trying to see something. Anything clear. If I fall asleep, I might miss my chance to see something. I blink about a thousand times, hoping to open my eyes to a clear scene, then I stare like I'm trying to read a license plate from a thousand yards away. Maybe if I try harder, my vision will clear up. I've always had good vision, 20/15 in both eyes. Pilot's eyes. But now I'm getting a panic attack. Going suddenly blurry feels like being locked up in a box, underground.

My hearing is all screwed up, too, but I can hear my heart going like a speed metal drum. I think I'll either die or explode. Mom kisses my forehead then cleans my face with some kind of cloth. It feels good, but it freaks me out to be touched without being able to judge when the touches are coming. She works with tweezers. I feel tugs and pulls as she gets the glass out of my cheeks. I try to hold still. She tells me to take a deep breath. She plugs my nose and dumps about a gallon of water over my head while she runs her fingers over my eyeballs and I scream. She stops and I quiet down, but I can't get rid of the feeling of her fingers on my eyes.

"I didn't find any glass in your eyes."

I blubber for a while and then I get some of my *me* back.

"That's good news."

"We think you have a concussion. Are you still dizzy? Do you have a headache?"

"Yes, yes, and yes."

I don't want her to worry. She tells me to rest. To try to calm down. I say okay, but I'm thinking, *Yeah, right.* I drift off, but it's not sleep.

I can see more light when I wake up. It's colder when I come back into the world. I'm pretty sure it's dark, and what I'm seeing is the moon above the clouds. Dad and Mom are doing something. Mom's arm is in a sling, but she doesn't let that stop her. They're loading stuff into our packs, probably the junk food and supplies we fought for.

I remember the times I woke up early when we were on vacation, lying still in a motel bed, my eyes closed and listening to them pack supplies for the day. Something important is missing, but I can't figure out what it is. I just know it's something that will make me feel stupid or very bad.

Dad walks up to me. I can tell it's him by the sound of his boots. He shakes my shoulder and stands me up.

"Can you travel?"

"Sure thing, Captain."

I fall down and he stands me up again. I thought I'd gotten past the dizziness when I was stretched out on my back, but standing brings the real message home. Dad puts a pack into my hands and helps me put it on. He puts my poncho on me, too. I'm swaying back and forth and he takes both of my hands in his and holds my arms straight out.

"Your sister's gone."

"Dead?" I'm already winding up to cry like a little girl.

"No. I don't think so."

"Is she hurt?"

"Maybe. Probably. They have her."

"Well, let's go get her back."

"Let's get out of here first."

"But this place is *ours*."

"There isn't much left of it. And I'm sure they'll come again."

"Well okay, then."

And then I'm sneaking away in the dark with my parents. Mom holds my hand, but the whole thing feels like a long sobriety test. I stagger with my hands held out in front of me for more than an hour, then finally I learn to trust that Mom won't lead me into a boulder or something. I finally stand tall and put one foot in front of the other. My hearing is slowly getting better. I can hear us stumbling in the grass and on the shoulder of the road. I can see well enough to know that it's dark and we're all blind now. We walk forever and ever, it seems. I can't tell which way we're going, but whichever way we turn feels like the wrong direction. I can't see Mount Shasta but I know it's somewhere above us. I try to use the breeze to guess where we're going, but it changes direction too often for me to guess anything about anything.

Bill Junior

First things first. I send Luscious and four sober men to go search the bodies in the store, but Luscious comes back and says the bodies got up and walked away. It's the worst mistake I've made since Ookie got shot. Shoulda, coulda, woulda, yeah, but I was so happy we got the girl that I didn't finish the job.

Luscious shrugs his shoulders. It's getting dark, so I'll have to wait until first light to put together a team to go after the old man and his ball-and-chain and their smartass-looking kid. But the more I think about it, the more I'm kicking myself in the ass for thinking they were killed in the explosion. The girl's daddy isn't someone we should fuck around with. He's pretty damned good with that rifle of his, and he'll want to take the girl away from us, but she's ours now. I need to make him understand the facts of life and death. Tomorrow I'll take my best shooters with me, and some dynamite, and if we can't find them fast, I'll get the old man up in his plane to spot for us.

I wake up without a hangover for the first time since Ookie died. I get up before it's completely light, but I let the men sleep. There's only me and one other man, George Washington. George still has an hour of guard duty left to stand, but he sees me and I wave him in from our little sandbagged bunker on the highway. He slings his rifle and walks over on his skinny legs. He's carrying a book. It's an old paperback copy of *To Kill a Mockingbird* from the high school. I don't like my men to read when they're standing guard, but I let it pass.

"You're relieved from duty, George," I say. "Go ahead and take your turn with the girl."

"Thanks, Bill," he says.

He has a deep voice, and I like how our conversation makes us sound like professional soldiers—salty fuckers who know exactly what we're doing. George nods and walks across the parking lot, whistling. He disappears into the junkyard shack, and I hear the girl's voice say, "No, no, no," and then rise into a long scream.

She quiets down after a few minutes. I stoke the fire and make a pot of coffee and watch the sun come up, what's left of it, behind the shit-brown clouds. I don't much like the feeling of being alone. I sit in front of the fire and watch the world take shape in the light of morning. A breeze blows down from Shasta. It's cold and it smells like pine and black lava rocks and the snow that fell when all of us were locked up in juvie.

I look over at the junkyard shack. For some reason, I don't like the idea that another man is with the girl. When George comes back out, I have to fight the urge to pay her a visit of my own.

When everyone is up and out of their motel rooms, I pass word that we'll be having us a Hunt Club adventure. I watch the word spread and some of the men think that maybe *they'll* be the animal we'll hunt, but Luscious tells them the girl's family isn't exactly room temperature yet. Looks of understanding come onto their morning faces. Normally, the men get happy when we have a hunt ahead of us, but now they get all shifty-eyed and mumbling and then they do a really bad job of pretending to be happy.

"Okay. What the hell's the matter? Somebody speak up."

They hem and haw and then one of the Kellys stands up.

"I do love me a good hunt, boss. You know that, right? It's not that I don't want to take care of business. It's just that if I go out hunting, I'll miss my turn with the girl."

The other men nod. Just about all of them. It doesn't make any sense because sixteen men are taking turns with the girl. I've done the math. Each man gets a turn every four hours, so it's sixty-four hours between turns.

"Well, shit."

I don't know what else to say. I could order them to go hunting, but they'd be really pissed off at me. I could ask for volunteers, but what if none of them stood up?

A wind blows over us, and it's so nose-hurt cold that it makes my eyes water. The fire flares and then almost goes out. We turn our backs so the dust won't blind us. The gust picks up even more, and it gets ahold of the Golden Eagle Motel sign and lifts it into the sky and takes it away into the sky, spinning. The sign crashes into a tree and comes apart, its plastic bits of red, white, and blue spread out on the highway. Things settle down for a second, but it seems like it's ten degrees colder.

"Well, that just cooks it. Okay. You men want some R&R? You got it."

They smile, but some of them look at me like maybe they're coming to understand they weren't thinking straight, back when they feared me. I walk away. I start to wonder what the girl is doing to them. What the hell could a little hundred-pound girl do to cast a spell over my pirates?

Jerry

We walked about five miles south last night and came to an airfield. The ground was in shadow, but I could see low structures against the sky. A cyclone deer fence lined the perimeter, but the gate was open. We headed for the nearest building, a steel hangar for light aircraft.

A dog barked. I heard the sound of an animal trotting on dry grass. We waited, but there wasn't any more sound. We crossed the tiny flightline and I opened the sliding door and peered into the first hangar. I couldn't see anything, but I was tired and as fatalistic as I've ever been in my life. I walked straight inside. I held still for ten long seconds but I didn't draw any fire, so I lit my butane lighter, hoping that the Big Guy was still on my side. Apparently, He was. The place didn't hold any airplanes. It was stacked half full with hay bales. At least we'd be comfortable.

I pulled off my poncho and dropped my pack and put my poncho back on again. Susan's face was stone pale, and I cut open three of the bales and made straw beds on the steps of the other bales. I vowed to myself that soon we'd be making beds for four. That, or we'd be in a better place.

I grabbed a handful of hay and put it to my face and inhaled the smell of old rye grass. In spite of the fact that I was once addicted to Western movies, I'd never been this close to so much hay. The most I ever saw was in the elephant exhibit at the zoo, but there were more than a hundred bales in the hangar. It didn't smell sweet, but that might only be because it was old. There was something like the smell of fermentation in the air.

"It might be a little rotten, but it should make for a nice place to sleep," I said.

"Why shouldn't it be rotten?" Scotty said. "Everything else is."

Susan gave him a quick hug, her arm splinted and in a sling between them. Her head barely reached his chin, and their size difference surprised me. Scott's been taller than his mother since he was fourteen, but once I got used to the idea, I guess I stopped paying attention. Now the height difference is enormous, even though he's more dependent upon us now than he was when he was fourteen. I said a silent prayer for him, but I couldn't keep the accusatory tone out of it, as my opinion of God's mysterious ways isn't what it used to be.

We got situated. Hay isn't as soft as you might think, but we were insulated from the ground and protected from the wind and it felt very good. And our relative comfort made me feel guilty because one of us wasn't here, so I stood the first watch. I stood all the watches, in fact, and let them sleep. But they didn't sleep, and I didn't, because it was simply impossible.

At first light I leave them and walk back to the north. A gust of wind comes out of nowhere and alters my course. But I keep walking. I find a small rise and I put my binoculars on the place we left. Right away, I see that the kids have the market surrounded. One of them goes inside. He comes out, holding his arms up, a booze bottle in each hand, and the others stand and shoot into the air. Melanie isn't with them. I scope the motel and the wrecking yard and the Mexican restaurant, but there's no sign of her. One of the boys seems to look directly at me. He's well out of rifle range. It has to be Bill Junior, but he doesn't lead the boys to the attack. Maybe I imagine it, but I'm sure he's smiling at me. He enters the store with the others, and they cart off as many supplies as they can carry, a line of dangerous ants carrying away their plunder. I watch the figures from a thousand yards away and they aren't human, but enemy, and I feel no guilt for what I'm about to do.

Rocking on my heels and holding it all in. Holding my head in my hands, greasy hair and skin, my long fingernails biting into my scalp. I squeeze until I feel blood oozing into my shirt. The gash in my face from where the kid clubbed me opens up, too, and I have myself a good, cleansing bleed. Rocking and bleeding and praying for guidance and wisdom and a temporary transfer of vengeance from God to me.

I return to the airfield. Susan heard the celebratory gunshots and she comes out of the hangar and stands close to me. She leaves and comes back holding a shirt we took from the market. It's a "Get High in Weed, California" T-shirt and she also has the bottle of Jim Beam I took from the dead kid. She tears the shirt into strips and cleans my wounds. She offers me the bottle, but I find enough strength to wave it away. She kneels with me and holds me, but she isn't crying. She feels hard to me, inside and out. Her hug feels like a goodbye hug, and maybe it is.

I don't know how much time passes. I know I can't go after Melanie until after sunset. The wind is blowing from the west, so I'll make my approach from the east. But not yet. Not just yet. It's going to be a long day.

*   *   *

Scotty is as listless as I've ever seen him. The lines in Susan's face have deepened. Scotty bled in the night and the bandages around his head are stained dark. We unwrap him. Before the last wrap is removed I get an impossible image of him, healed, smiling at me with his bright, young intensity. His clear blue eyes both sending and receiving.

But no. His face is cut to ribbons. Jagged cuts line his cheeks and jaws, welded into a sort of jigsaw puzzle by clotted blood. His eyes are swollen and red. I spark up my lighter a foot from his face.

"Anything?"

"I can see shapes okay, but I can't really get them in focus."

"Well, it's up to God."

"That's what I'm afraid of."

"Don't give up on Him. He hasn't given up on us."

"How can you tell?"

"We're still breathing."

"Whatever."

Susan cleans his cuts with whiskey and tears the last of the tourist T-shirt into strips. She wraps his head. I give his shoulder a squeeze and he flinches.

"I know it's not fair," I say.

"Just leave me alone, please."

"I'll be leaving soon enough. How's your hearing?"

"It's getting better. Why?"

"You'll need to take care of your mother."

He's quiet for a while. I know he wants to go with me, but it's impossible.

"Okay," he says. "I'll stay with Mom."

I pick up his carbine and press it into his hands. He runs his fingers over the selector switch to make sure it's on safe.

106

"Okay, then.

"Good hunting," he says. "Good luck."

There's a lot more of him behind his words now. He's growing to fill the position he's been forced into. He hasn't completely accepted his wounds yet, but he's not out of the fight.

"Thanks."

It's all I manage to say, even though I want to say more.

I drift away from him and stand close to Susan. We try to come up with a plan, but we keep coming back to the old standby—fight or die. I walk away before the tears can begin—hers, mine, I don't know the difference anymore. I walk to the other hangar. I go through the door, holding the Beretta close to my belly. There's a Cessna 182 inside. The engine compartment is open, but the tires are fully inflated. I look at the engine and everything seems to be in working condition. I open the pilot-side door and turn the wheel and push on the rudder pedals, and everything moves smoothly.

Scotty was about to get his instrument rating, just before the bombs. He was flying VFR all over California and taking lessons for his instrument rating and talking about getting his multi-engine rating. At night he screwed around with flight sims on the computer. He swore he didn't know what he wanted to do with his life, but it was no mystery what he loved.

But yeah, Scotty's not up to flying right now. So it's too bad I never learned how to fly myself. I very much wanted to get my license when I was younger but something always came up. And then I got too old, too cautious and comfort-seeking, to want to crank and bank, even though it would've been a cool thing if I could've learned to fly with Scotty. But I can't afford to open that box of regrets just now.

One wall of the hangar is lined with pegboard and neatly arranged tools. The place smells of bare metal and solvents and scrubbed concrete. It's the kind of place that always made my own father happy. Metal and order and work. There's a tiny office area. The only chair in the office is empty. Yes, it's all clear. I look at the shop area and then I get an idea.

I go back to get Scotty's .22 rifle. He's still holding his newly acquired carbine and he says something about how it might not be such a good idea to give Stevie Wonder an automatic rifle. It makes me smile, but then I stop and I give a little laugh that sounds pathetic even to my own ears. He shrugs, but he keeps the smile and it makes me proud.

I return to the shop area and I prop the .22 in a corner. I find a scrap of two-inch-diameter aluminum tubing. I lock it in a vise and use a hacksaw to cut an eight-inch piece, the sound of my work filling the shop and making me feel useful and vulnerable all at the same time. A nudie calendar hangs above the workbench. I ignore it for as long as I can, and I have other things on my mind, but I'm a man so I have no choice but to admire God's creation. The model is wearing nothing but a big smile. Her breasts are magnificent, and I have to lean in close to see if they're real. It takes me a few seconds to realize that some of the days of the calendar are crossed out with black felt pen. I try to remember what day it is today. If I have it right, the last day crossed out on the calendar was yesterday.

I hear a nightmare sound. The sound of a single-action revolver being pulled to full cock. Someone is behind me. Stupid me, stupid day, stupid life cut short by stupid haste. And my family, too? Will they pay for my idiocy?

"Whatcha doing, boy?" A phlegmy voice. "Put down the hacksaw. Let's see your hands. Move away from that little rifle. This ain't television and I ain't fixin' to shoot warning shots."

Matter-of-fact tone. I turn. I get a look down the muzzle of a Ruger .44. The light of day goes slow. Looking up into squinty eyes the color of wastewater. Knowing it's no good, but moving my hand to the small of my back. Getting my fingers up underneath my coat and onto the grips of the Beretta. His gap-toothed smile.

"No need for that." The muzzle stays in my face. "Unless you're overly eager to leave this world."

"Okay, then. What next?"

"Well, it might be that I want something."

"Hope you take credit cards."

He cackles at that.

"Got any smokes on you?"

"As a matter of fact, I do."

I move my hands slowly to my coat pocket and pull out the pack of Marlboros I took from the dead kid.

"Good news, good news. Guess I won't hafta quit after all." His cackle again. "Let's say we take ourselves off high alert, huh?"

"Okay."

He lowers the .44 and decocks it and slides it into the worn gunfighter rig on his hip. For a while it feels fine just to stand and breathe in and out in the presence of a stranger. He takes the smokes and pulls one out and lights up. I pick up the section of pipe I cut. He watches me, but the revolver stays in its holster.

"This your shop?"

"Yep." He points at a hand-painted wooden sign that hangs above a workbench. *Bill and Sons*. "I'm Bill Senior."

"Bet you're a good fabricator."

He looks at my hands.

"Best one standing here."

I know he can't be trusted. In this new reality, there are only two groups of people: good people who can't be trusted, and bad ones who need to be avoided or shot. The good ones don't hesitate to offer their hospitality, but this guy hasn't offered me anything. He might later, but it's too late. I've already put him in the *bad* category, and there's not much he can do to change my mind.

He's one of the bad ones, but I don't think he'll shoot me for no reason at all. I go back to working on my project and he figures out what I'm doing and he joins in. We cut disks of aluminum plate that fit into the small cylinder I'd cut. The old man gathers up the disks and he brazes the first disk into the tube, to form a compartment. I epoxy a strip of high-temp muffler wrap into the inside circumference. We make four lined compartments, then he welds thicker caps on both ends and locks the gadget in a vise and uses a battery-powered drill to bore a small hole straight through the sandwiched assembly. I ask him why he's here.

"Couldn't see any reason to move on," he says.

"Are there any others here?"

"You've already met them, I think."

I can't trust him. I won't. I haven't had a conversation with a non-hostile man since we fled Yreka, and the careful chitchat is making me grind my teeth. No time for it. I'll need to get started soon.

"Are you alone here?" I ask.

"Well, I got my girls." He looks up at the nudie calendar. "And before you decided to trespass on my property I was about to make the acquaintance of a certain black dog. Keep him or shoot him, I don't know which I would've done. But I sure wouldn't mind having a good dog around here."

"Sorry we scared him off."

"Well, he was probably a flesh-eater anyhow." He spits. "Could be you saved me from having to put him down."

"Are you okay, otherwise?"

"I'm fine. Saw it coming. Laid in a good stock of supplies, too, except for the cigarettes. Had a full case of Marlboros on order, but it didn't get here in time. But I have food and booze, both."

He gives me a look from his watery eyes.

"When we're done, I wonder if you'd have supper with me? I figure it would be healthy for me to socialize more."

I don't trust him and he doesn't trust me. I like the idea of dining with a stranger, but no.

"Maybe later."

The quaver in my voice gives me away.

"You got a pressing engagement?"

"Yes."

"It's the boys, isn't it?"

I pick up the .22 and unload it. I unscrew and remove the front sight while he rummages through a drawer filled with oiled taps and dies. We cut good, sharp threads into the outside diameter of the muzzle of the rifle and then we cut matching threads inside the mounting flange of the device. We attach it and I test the balance. There's a slight muzzle-heaviness, but it's not bad. I sight through the scope and the suppressor doesn't cut into my field of view. I load the rifle and lean it against the workbench and leave it alone to let the epoxy set up. The old man goes out and I put my hand on the Beretta's grips and watch to see what he's up to. He comes back with a bottle of Johnnie Walker Black. He fills two shot glasses that are marked "U.S. Navy." He offers one of them to me, but I don't take it. He shrugs his shoulders and takes both shots. He lights up another cigarette.

"Sure glad I didn't have to shoot that dog today."

"Me, too." I don't mention that a gunshot almost certainly would've caused the boys to run straight at us.

"Yep. Here's to not having to shoot."

He watches me to see how I respond.

"I can't drink to that, just yet," I say.

"No?"

"Tonight of all nights, I can't."

"You should ask me if I'll help."

"I know you won't."

"Maybe you're right." He walks closer. "Tell me about that young kid, Bill. Is he healthy?" he says.

"Seems to be."

"Is he still wearing his cowboy rig?"

I nod.

"Well, I rue the day I bought it for him, just so you know."

"They took my daughter. Will you help me get her back?"

"Sorry, no. But thanks for asking."

He pours himself another shot and lifts it to his squirming, old-man lips. While his head is tilted back, I reach in and grab his revolver from its holster. I pull back the hammer and point the gun at his chest. He coughs whiskey breath into my face and then backs away.

"You going to be a problem?" I ask.

"Nope. You?"

"Peace is the answer, right?"

"Damn straight."

I point the gun in a safe direction and lower the hammer.

"Okay then. Tell me about those boys."

"You've seen 'em. Words alone can't tell you more than their actions already have."

"How many are there?"

"Less than twenty now. There used to be more, but they're in a dangerous line of work."

"I want to know about you, too. Why aren't you over there with them?"

"Because I'm not suicidal, is why."

"Okay. I can buy that. But maybe you spot for them in that Cessna? Maybe you help them and they let you live, but you have to know they won't let you camp out here forever before they decide to charge you rent."

"Oh, I'll be fine."

"How?"

"The Lord will provide."

"There's not a lot of that going around these days. You've got an angle. What is it?"

I point the revolver at his left knee.

"Maybe I have an angle, maybe I don't. Maybe I'm just a crazy old man. But I'll not tell you a damn thing more. No sir."

He smiles and I swing the gun fast and the barrel catches him across the temple. But he doesn't fall like people do in the movies. He just says, "Ow," so I hit him harder and he goes to his knees. My next swat gets him to go down and I drag him to the lone office chair and use a roll of duct tape to strap him down.

Bill Senior

Bastard blindsided me. Didn't see it coming. And he's going after the boys, for sure. I could've shot him right off, but I'm glad I didn't. No, maybe it's for the best that I didn't. I think

I'll let this play out, see what happens. He'll go after his daughter. He's got no choice. Then maybe this dude will set me free, somewhere down the line, if he's still breathing after paying his house call on those boys.

Yeah. The more I think about it, the more right it seems. One way or the other, I'll be fine. Serves the little shits right, too. Bill Junior doesn't know when to stop. He won't stop until someone gives him a dirt nap, and nobody knows the size of the body count he'll rack up before that day.

I can't say I haven't thought about taking him out myself. Call it "for the good of humanity." I'm not much of a father, but I'm the one who knocked his mother up, God rest her soul, and I can't bring myself to put a stop to what the good Lord allowed to survive. But it looks like he fucked with the wrong daddy this time. Yeah, this dude seems to be just the one to teach him the lesson he's been begging for. And even if this daddy gets himself killed, the boys will find me here, gift-wrapped in my chair, and I'll be fine.

Anyhow, the boys would've been out here after this family soon enough. These people are eyewitnesses to God knows what, and sooner or later the cops and soldiers will be here, and there'll be hell to pay for the ones that didn't cover their tracks. No, the boys *have* to get this man, one way or another, and it suits me just fine that he'll be taking the fight to them, instead of holing up here and getting my place all shot to hell.

So let whatever happens happen. I wash my hands of Billy and the others, and it's high time I did it. Those boys are pure evil. Their time in the juvie hall only gave them ideas and got 'em more fired up. Lord knows how many people they've killed of late. And it looks like this good man and his family are next, God help them. I wouldn't bet money on this dude winning, but I can wish him well, can't I? Truth be told, I hope he takes a crapload of the little bastards with him.

Oh well. Life's a bitch, et cetera, et cetera. Mother Nature has a way of finding her balance again after we crap in her shoes. There'll be fewer people around here soon enough, and the fewer hostile people in the world, the better, is what I always say. Just give me my freedom back, some good weather, and a clear runway, and I'll take my little bird for a walk in the sky. It's ready. I'm ready. It's all fixed up and ready to fly, and then this shit happens. But first chance I get, I'll fire up my little freedom bird and climb to an altitude that takes me out of rifle range. I'll fly my bony ass to a place where it's warm and not quite law-abiding and the women aren't trapped inside pinup calendars. I'll find me a well-seasoned, hard-drinking gal and we'll have us a time.

Susan

"I found something," Jerry says. "Come take a look. Tell me what you think."

I follow him into the other hangar. I see an old man duct-taped to a chair. He has blood in his hair. He's breathing, but his gray-bearded chin is down on his chest. He's knocked out cold.

"Did you find him like that?"

Jerry lets out a sudden unexpected laugh-cough.

"Not hardly."

"What will we do with him?"

"Beats me. He's got an interesting family history. He's Bill Creedmore *Senior*."

The boys are coming for us tonight. They can't let us go. Someday this will be over, and bad people will be brought to justice. They're monsters, but I don't think they're stupid. They're cunning, like all scavengers are. They're cunning like we are. If they don't know right from wrong, maybe it's our fault, the fault of our old society, but now there's nothing left to do but kill them, if we can.

I get Scott ready to go. I make fresh bandages from rags I found in Old Bill's office. I don't trust that old man, and I'm glad Jerry took precautions. I don't let myself think we're starting to resemble the bad people in the world. No, I don't mind that Bill Senior is taped to a chair, and I'll take things from him whenever I get a chance. His monster of a son has taken our Melanie from us. Maybe the old man isn't to blame for the way his son turned out, but I firmly believe that I could take Old Bill's *life*, and we still wouldn't be even. No. Not in my book.

So I wrap Scott's face in paisley cloth from one of Old Bill's clean rags. It beats me how that man can be as dirty and stinky as a bum but still have clean rags. He made some noise and struggled against his restraints when I took the rags, but he quieted down when I pointed the shotgun muzzle at his crotch. Why old men place such value on their sexual organs, I'll never know. Hope springs eternal, I guess, even if it doesn't spring often. But according to my way of thinking, Bill Senior has fathered enough children.

Scotty reaches up and unwraps the bandages from his eyes. He picks up the rifle he took from one of the dead boys. His hands reach without hesitation or fumbling and he ejects the magazine and tops it off with fresh ammunition. It takes me a while to realize that his vision must be coming back.

"These boys are country boys, and they'll track us. They'll hunt us," he says.

He points his crosshatched face toward me.

"What will we do with the old man?"

I shrug my shoulders and he nods.

"Okay. Now you're making sense."

Melanie

Cold and stinking. They throw bags of corn chips and bottles of water at me before they lock me back in the car trunk. I hate them and want them to die, but then my brain starts to work again. At first I can only scream, but after a while I try to talk to them when they take me out. They only laugh at me. Power. They are power and I am meat. I could have power, too, because I found a tire iron in the trunk. But no. I won't. This is Gandhi. This is Martin Luther King Jr. and Jesus of Nazareth and Mother Teresa. This is all of them, with me.

But that's bullshit. Maybe the only thing I have in common with those people is stubbornness, and I haven't used even one percent of what I have in that department. They haven't seen anything yet.

So I stop talking to them. I don't say anything when they come for me, and I try to stop screaming. I give them the same silent treatment I once gave my dad.

They don't notice at first. They're too busy going after my body, but after a while some of them start talking to me, after. And talking is my mission and also my chance to survive. I can't preach to them. They've been preached to all their lives by cops and judges and the people in juvie, and just look where it got them. No. I can't preach, but I can tell stories, can't I? I can tell lies about how rich my family is, and maybe the power of greed is stronger than the power of lust.

Not all of them are monsters. Maybe none of them are, given enough time and caring and therapy. There's Donnie, for instance. He could just be playing with my head like the others play with my body. And if that's true, then it would be okay for me to hate them all. Then it would be okay for me to wish them dead, if not kill them myself.

But Donnie seems to be a good kid. He looks like he's about thirteen, and he brings me things. After the first rapes he brought me baby wipes and a clean set of boys' underwear and a fresh apple and a Pepsi and two pills that turned out to be Oxycontin. He's a really super-white little kid, with his sad eyes and black hair, and he can't look directly at me when he gives me stuff. He's nervous and he wipes his nose on the back of his sleeve. I didn't notice it before, but he has a speech impediment. He says, "Here," but he pronounces the "R" like a "W," so it sounds like "Hew." And I think it isn't very good advice, but what should I expect from a wild boy with unrealistic goals?

I didn't thank him that first time after the hell started, because I thought he'd been sent by someone else. But it was all him that time, and the times that followed, and now I hope he'll sneak over and give me things, and he does. He gives me a fur coat that smells like old people and mothballs. He gives me a granola bar and a pillow that's slightly damp, smelling of laundry detergent, with a single bullet hole in the middle and only faint bloodstains remaining.

He doesn't say anything this time, but he looks at me, then looks away when I meet his eyes. I ask him about getting a bath, and he says they took baths last night but forgot about getting me into the tub. He says he'll remind Bill Junior. I thank him and I reach out to touch his arm, but he pulls away and walks all hunched over back to his comrades.

The other boys taunt him when he comes out of the shack. They say, "Donnie's in loooooove. He wants to issy-kissy the itchy-bitchy, dooooesn't he?" They have a good laugh, but then the mean ones start talking about what they want to do to me, and *will* do to me, soon, and I bite my lip to stop the screaming, and sometimes it works.

Scott

Dizzy. Feels like a truck ran over my head. If this crappy little settlement had a pharmacy, I'd be tempted to load up on drugs. But no, I'll limit my drug of choice to Motrin. Mom stands over me. Her shot arm is in a lumpy, dirty sling, and she uses her other arm to offer me a bottle of booze. I refuse it. I think she's trying to get me wasted so I won't know when the little shits come for us and it's time to die. I'm grateful and pissed off about it, both.

Dad is still away, but Mom isn't pacing when she prays, so

I know he hasn't left to get Melanie yet. I don't know how he'll do it. There has to be more than a dozen of the little bastards left alive. I've never been able to believe in God, some huge eye in the sky that loves us and watches over our every move, and not only *lets* things happen, but sometimes *makes* them happen. I wish I could believe it. I wish I could look right into that supernatural eye and ask it to help my dad, but then I feel like a hypocrite and I cry a little bit. I cry and I tell myself that I'm only washing out my eyes, and fear has nothing to do with it.

But yeah, right. That's what I used to say about most things—*Yeah, right.* Everything before was bullshit. But not now. This is them and this is me. No more flying around on trips to nowhere, smoking weed and buzzing through life at low altitude. No more playing computer games at night, waiting for my life to start. The bombs jump-started me, and that's a good thing. I never would've been this alive without the bombs. God help me, I like it. I want to get back into the game, and if I was a praying man, that's what I'd pray for.

And I can't afford to ignore the possibility that He or She exists, because He or She is my last hope. I want to believe that my gramma is in heaven. I want to believe it so much that it hurts, so I kind of *do* believe it. At least I don't rule it out, the heaven she believed in without doubt.

Maybe hope is God and God is hope. Maybe it's as simple as that. Yeah. I can pray to that. Please help me, whoever You are. Give me the wisdom to figure out where I stand with people and with myself. Even if You've moved on, or You're dead, or You're only make-believe, I still think I'll talk to You. Dad needs my help. He's going out to kill or be killed. I think he's planning to trade his life for Melanie's. But then what? Then

Mom will be stuck in hell with a half-blind son and a pacifist daughter. We'll be easy prey for the vultures.

So let it come back. Let me see again. A single person isn't worth much these days, but another gun could make a difference. I know I'll be making a lot of promises to You soon, and here's the first of them: If You get us through this shit, all of us alive and whole, I'll give the rest of my life to You. I'll dedicate my life to some holy cause that You see fit to tell me about.

I'm serious, here, Mr. God. I'm every bit as serious as one of the heart attacks You use to kill billions of people. I'm as serious as a lightning bolt or a tornado or the blast of a volcano. Take us through this and I'll be Your faithful servant. Amen.

I drift off for a while, then I open my eyes. I start to feel like a fake asshole, because I was praying, and meaning it, and other people might say it's just a coincidence, but when I open my eyes again, I can see better. My vision isn't all the way back, but I think it will get there. And He's got me, then. I stumble outside and I can see faraway ridgelines, darker against the dark sky. I can see the enemy's bonfires, too. The world is like a wet oil painting, but it's fine art, to my eyes, and He's got me in His service now.

I go back to my bed of hay, my little manger bed, and I dream in Technicolor.

Bill Junior

She's a fine one, all right. I can't get her out of my head. Part of me wants to take her for myself, but the men probably wouldn't stand for it. Pirate leaders are always making hard decisions, because their men don't want to be led at all, right? Isn't that the whole point of being a pirate? Sure, a little bit of assholishness is called for, whippings and Hunt Club, and all of that. I need them to fear me. They *want* to fear me, but I also want them to think of me as a fair man. A little assholishness goes a long way, but no, I can't take the girl for myself. If we find more girls, maybe I'll take her then, but I can't do it now.

But she's still in my head, so I go to see her. I arranged a bath for her, with hot water and fresh bars of soap and five different kinds of shampoo and our two queer dudes standing guard. It's two hours before the next watch ends, so she's had some time to get her shit together. I walk into her shack. It's warm inside. There's a propane heater glowing red in the middle of the floor, but I leave the door open, like I did before. She's sitting in a chair. There's a little desk in the shack and someone brought her a mirror, and she's combing her hair. I walk to where I can see her reflection, and she's combing her hair without looking into her eyes. I look at her eyes myself, and they're green and steady, and I'm glad to see it.

She doesn't turn around. She doesn't say anything, so I clear my throat. I feel almost like I don't know what I'm doing.

"I'll get you a bath every week."

"Good."

I'm quiet for a while. I want to ask her how she's doing, but I have a pretty good idea. Then she surprises me. She asks me how *I'm* doing.

I tell her not to worry about that. There isn't anything else to say. I want to tell her I'm not such a bad guy. I want to say I'd like to get to know her, and wouldn't it be nice of we'd met some other way, but damn that shit sounds lame.

I walk away. When I turn to close the door, she's looking straight at herself in the mirror, and her eyes are like the eyes of a pissed-off angel.

Jerry

Seems as if I haven't slept in years. I might go crazy or I might drop dead in my tracks, but I can't sleep. Even if I suddenly grew tired, I couldn't sleep now.

I sit with Susan on a hay bale. I put my hand on her knee and she stands and then she paces.

"You can't go alone."

"There's no one else. There's you and me and Scotty and Melanie. We're not leaving without her. And we can't leave Scotty here alone."

"I could be the one who goes after Melanie," she says.

I love her for saying that. She doesn't show a shred of fear, even though she's offering up her life. She's like me and I'm like her and we're like the other people in the world who only reveal what they're made of when everything goes to hell.

"No," I say. "Your arm, for one thing…"

"Look. You're the only one who can lead Scotty to safety. You could carry him, if it came to that. I couldn't."

"No."

"The boys wouldn't be as afraid of me as they are of you. I could walk straight up to them."

"And then what? Be their mommy? Try to kill them all?"

"The children need you more than they need me."

"Nice try, but that's simply not true."

I want to give her whatever she asks for. Anything but that. I want her to know I'm the right person for the job. I'm afraid for Melanie, but I'm so pissed off at those little monsters I have no qualms about killing them. The worst of human depravity. Cutting and separating that which was joined. Looking into eyes and shooting, hitting, crushing until the lights go out. Maybe even stopping the bloodflow and bandaging wounds to keep them alive, and then starting over again. The only thing worse than being dismembered is being dismembered by a vengeful father with a dull knife. It almost makes me smile.

But I don't want Susan to remember me this way. I don't want her to know I've fallen so far. I hold her and she holds me and we shiver together without tears or arousal. The path before us isn't of our choosing. I have no choice but to go. We're in the right, and that should count for something. Good people lose, too, but I don't intend to be so good that I reduce my chances. I'll be good and I won't torture the little fuckers, but I know from personal experience that good people can be ruthless, too.

I take the warmth and strength Susan is giving me, and my animal anger turns gradually into something quiet and patient as death itself. She isn't crying. She gives me a stiff, last hug, her splinted arm between us, and then she moves away. I have no idea what she's thinking, but this is probably our last goodbye, and I don't want to ruin it by asking.

Susan

Stubborn man. But I'm stubborn, too, and if we weren't so stubborn, we wouldn't still be taking up space among the living.

But if he doesn't come back? I'll have my freedom then. Maybe I can handle it. But now I don't know if I *want* to handle it.

Maybe I was thinking about leaving him, but I still want him to be alive in the world. I shouldn't let him go alone. Any idiot knows not to go out alone these days. And I'll feel alone without him, maybe for the rest of my life. He's not a big talker, but I hate the way the world seems to shed possibilities when he's gone, its colors growing duller and nobody else around who cares enough to have even his limited ability to understand me.

My arm throbs without end. The sharp bone-broken throbs are coming less often, but my left arm will be worthless for at least another month, assuming the wound doesn't get infected.

I breathe carefully in and out while Jerry pulls out his folding knife. He walks up to Bill Senior. He cuts the old man's legs free and then his arms. He helps him stand and Bill Senior stumbles around as the blood flows back into his skinny extremities. He seems to be in pain, but he doesn't complain. Jerry gives him a canteen of water and he guzzles and spits and belches.

"I wondered whether or not you'd turn into a decent human being," Bill Senior says.

"Decent human beings are in short supply these days. I have a proposition."

"Figured you might."

Jerry runs his hands over the Cessna.

"Will it fly?"

"Bet your ass it will. And yes, I can fly it. So what's the deal?"

"Take a guess."

"There's not enough room for all of us. Not if you get your girl back."

"I know."

"Okay. What then?"

Jerry walks over and stands very close to Bill Senior. He points at me. He points at Scott.

"You take two passengers."

"Where?"

"Fly them to Sacramento. My wife and son will put in a good word for you there. You should be able to get a fresh start after that. I'll be walking or driving out with my daughter. But if these two aren't safe and sound in Sacramento when I get there, I promise I'll see you dead."

"Well, I've made a few bad deals in my time, but I guess I can play along. The question I want to ask is, what do I get out of it?"

126

"The boys struck gold. That last group they ambushed was carrying gold coins."

The old man's eyes go hard.

"How much?"

"Enough to set you up just fine if you were to get, say, half the take."

The old man snorts.

"So you want me to believe you're gonna rescue your daughter, steal the gold, and then meet up with me in Sacramento and give me a fortune? You see a dunce cap on my head?"

Jerry points the cowboy revolver at Bill Senior's groin.

"Care to see what's behind door number two?"

The old man holds out his hand and Jerry shakes it. Jerry speaks over his shoulder to me.

"Don't trust him."

"Don't worry."

"But first things first. You're going for a walk," Jerry says.

The old man looks at Jerry as if he's only curious. Jerry picks up Scott's .22 rifle. I see the silencer Jerry told me about. He puts it to the old man's temple.

"Nod if you plan to go peacefully. If you don't nod, there's only one other choice, and I'll do it right now."

The old man nods. Jerry marches him outside and points him toward the highway. He moves his hand to point out a northerly direction and then points to a small creek.

"I'll have you in my scope the whole time. Make tracks in the grass. Clear tracks that lead to the interstate. Walk the stream back."

"Think they'll buy it?"

"I only want them to wonder. If they spend any time looking for you, it'll be time they don't spend hunting us."

"I bet you miss watching reality shows on television."

"Shut up and walk."

The old man shrugs and ambles off and we watch him. The overcast is thinner and the moon gives a wan light. Jerry sits to adjust the sling of the rifle. He makes it very tight and then he crosses his legs and snaps his body into line behind the scope. He tracks the old man every step of the way. The muzzle of the rifle doesn't waver and I have no doubt that Jerry will shoot without hesitation if the old man tries to run.

It's a weird scene, husband and wife watching quietly, the husband using an invisible string to control this old boar as he circles. Remote control, the line of the bullet untraced, but heavy with promise. Bill Senior walks through the alpine grass without looking back. He isn't in very good shape, but he doesn't mutter or curse us. He's lived a long time, and longevity isn't something that happens by accident. I watch him make his controlled circuit, and when he reaches his most distant point, I don't see him as an enemy anymore, but only an old man staggering in the wilderness. I see him as an alter ego to my own father, who didn't make it to old age. I see Jerry himself in some distant time, gray hair lifting and fluttering in the wind. A man is about to step onto the road. He'll turn and signal that everything is okay, but he turns and it's only Old Bill. He stands on the road and gives us the finger, then he steps into the creek and lets our invisible bullet-string reel him back to us.

Scott is sleeping on his bed of hay. Away in a manger, no pillow for his head. I should've fed him before he fell asleep. Well, we'll have a snack later.

We enter the hangar, all of us walking together. We leave the door open to let the moonlight dribble in. I sit down with Scotty and the old man while Jerry loads the plane with the barest necessities. The shotgun and ammunition. Bill Senior's cowboy revolver. Ponchos. That's it. Jerry tells me to take the food, but I take only a package of crackers and a pouch of peanut butter. I tell him we'll only need an in-flight snack, at the most. He smiles at me, and I hate myself because I love him so much now, just when I'm most likely to lose him, and maybe that's *why* I love him now.

Jerry and Bill Senior open the hangar door as wide as it will go and push the little airplane outside. Bill Senior is talkative.

"I was gonna sneak off soon enough, anyway. I always meant to leave at night. Can't risk letting them shoot me down, now, can I? You think *cars* attract bullets, try flying in a low and slow *airplane*."

I tell him to shut up. He says, Is that any way to treat your savior? I tell him that God is my savior. In God and my shotgun do I trust. And then he's quiet.

Jerry and Old Bill fiddle with the airplane and I have time to sit and think. God, don't let Jerry be killed. They have to be ready for him, but let him slip through, Lord, and come out the other side whole and with what he went to get. Let him bring our Melanie back to us. Keep him strong if there's a fight, but please, Lord, don't let it come to that. One of our children is half blind and the other is kidnapped. Probably raped. I've been shot, and that's neither here nor there, but please help Jerry make things right. The ledger must be balanced, Lord. I don't claim to know the mysteries of Your plans and intentions and calculations, but don't let this injustice stand. Let Jerry kill these servants of Satan. I can't believe You won't set this wickedness straight. So thank You, Lord, in advance.

Melanie

Someone is watching me. I can feel it. Most of the boys are getting ready to go out on a raid. It doesn't take a genius to know they'll be going after Dad and Mom and Scotty. But I've been telling everyone about how rich my family is, and how good deeds won't go unrewarded, wink-wink, so maybe they won't be so quick to kill them.

Little Donnie is one of the boys that were ordered to stay behind. He has a fire going, and he's roasting three rabbits he shot with his slingshot. Two older boys are with him. One of them is taking shots of liquor and spitting them into the fire and making it flame up. There's no kindness or hospitality in the other boys, that I can tell, but Donnie is there. I hope he stays kind and decent, because he has more power over me now that the others are gone.

The roasting rabbits smell very good. I hope Donnie will share. I'm wrapped in the old fur coat he gave me, and every once in a while the oldest boy comes over and takes a sniff of me and says pee-you and laughs. I admit to myself that I want to see him dead. Forgiveness is divine, but I'm not.

The mean boy keeps me in his field of vision when he walks back to the fire, but I feel something else, too. It feels like there's someone behind the shadows. I know Dad will come for me soon. There isn't any reason on earth to feel optimistic about how things will turn out, but I do.

Scott

Mom and Dad start talking again and I'm wrapped in my sleeping bag with my poncho pulled up over me. I'm listening to the sound of their voices. They're disagreeing about something, but they're working it out like they usually do. They're keeping their voices so low that I can't hear the words, but I think I can pick out the curving tones of disagreement, suggestion, consideration, and then agreement. Two voices, one low and one high, the conflict gradually turning into a duet.

I don't know how they do it. It's freaking amazing, really. Most all of my friends' parents are divorced, and I feel like a lucky freak sometimes, to still be on my original set of parents. I wonder how they can stay limber enough to do all the bending it takes to stay married. I wonder if there's a difference between compromise and just not caring enough to fight. Between being a good person and being a flimsy one. But the power each of them has is somehow balanced out in their relationship. Dad is strong as hell and quick to act, but Mom is better with words, and she's a clever lady, so Dad knows that by sharing power, they're both better off.

I start to wonder if I'll ever meet a girl who wants to fight *with* me instead of *against* me. But I'm stretched out under the stars in time of war, listening to the voices of my parents, so I manage to keep my mind off of girls for once. I drift off, then I'm younger and riding in a car at night with friends. I'm sitting alone in the backseat of a car. We're driving through a place near Gramma's house in Portland. I'm with friends. I don't know which friends they are. All I can see are the backs of their heads, but I know they're my friends. The sky is dark and low. It's drizzling and the streets are shiny. We're driving up a hill on this dark, quiet road. I've just made some kind of philosophical or political point about the place we're passing through. What I'd said was deep and serious and we're quiet as we approach a place of lights. They're security lights, because the stores are all closed. The first store is a gun shop and it's all lit up inside and out, and it somehow serves as exhibit A for the point I just made.

I'm happy that I'd been so right, so damned right about something, and I look into the store, with its lit-up rifles and shotguns, rows and rows of them. My eyes are drawn to the guns because we need firepower. But then I notice shapes standing around outside the store—animals standing like Christmas trees at a charity lot. Stuffed animals, but they used to be real. Deer and elk, their fake eyes glittering in the night. It's very weird, and I know it will get even weirder. The next shop is also a lit-up gun store and it's bigger than the first one, and there are more animals out front, but they're all bears. Stuffed black and brown bears standing on their hind legs like they'd just gone out for a smoke break. They're lined across the storefront, forming a sort of pocket that you couldn't help entering as you approach the store.

But we don't approach it. We keep driving in that slow kind of way that gets you places in real life, but doesn't get you anywhere in rainy dreams. We pass another gun store, and another and another, but they keep getting smaller, with fewer interesting animals, and it's like shopping for a good place to buy a Christmas tree, because people always pass the best lots in search of something better, before they admit that the best is behind them.

We keep driving, and after a while I stop being so freaked out. The sky lets go of the danger it was holding, and then it's just another soft Oregon night. The car picks up speed and takes us away from there. I'm with my friends in some strange Oregon place that probably never existed. We stay quiet as we drive up the long hill. We leave the gun shops behind us, and I'm getting the start of a feeling that might be something like hope.

Bill Junior

I swear it's getting colder than I can ever remember it being. I almost wish I hadn't taken a bath, because the oil and scum on my skin kept me warmer. I was thinking about getting one of the guys to give me a haircut, but I'm glad I didn't, because the long hair keeps my neck warm. We're all growing our hair out now, and we're starting to look like what we are. I try to think of the words people use for guys like us, words that aren't really insults. Pirates, cutthroats, outlaws, and killers. Thinking about those words makes me happy. I'm clean and I have a new set of clothes that don't have any bullet holes in them, jeans and a flannel shirt and just about the last clean socks inside a hundred miles. We'll need to set up a laundry soon, and that gives me an idea and an excuse to visit the girl.

One of the alcoholics is coming out of the shack when I get

there. He's a skinny dude with bad teeth. We call him Chivas because that's his favorite scotch. I had to start rationing the booze, and he's shaky. He stands with his back to me and it takes him a few tries to get the door closed, then he turns and sees me and it's a strange time. He looks proud and happy, but he also looks kind of afraid. We act like two dudes who just found out they were about to rob the same liquor store. I say, "Nice night, isn't it?" and he says, "Sure is." He stands there like his brain just ran out his ears. I give him some room and he walks away with his hands in his pockets, whistling.

I go inside and close the door behind me. It's too cold not to. I tell the girl that we'll try to take her people alive, but it sounds like bullshit, even to me.

Bill Senior

We push my birdie to the north end of the runway and turn it into the wind. The bitch wakes up her scarface brat and walks him to my airplane and they climb aboard. It's my airplane and so who could blame me for being upset about it? They're sitting in the back seats now, and I'm supposed to be their chauffeur? What if I tell 'em to go to hell? Tell 'em I'm not flying today? No. That bastard daddy would shoot me, sure as shit. But will the bitch shoot me when we're flying at five thousand feet?

So off we go. For now, anyhow, I'll go with the flow. I've

given the bird a pre-flight inspection every day for the last two weeks, but I give it another one. We're playing for all the marbles this time, so I don't rush it. We get strapped in. I turn on the master bus and I only have ten volts in the battery, but I think it's enough. The bastard is standing at the wing spar with his rifle unslung. He's traded his silenced .22 for an AR-15 and he looks like he was born holding that rifle.

I get everything set to go. I tell them *all aboard* and then *last call for alcohol*, but my passengers are crying. They're crying, but it's that stupid, half-happy crying that weak people do, and I don't want to hear that shit, so I crank the engine over and she fires right off. The bastard backs away. He moves so I can't nail him with the prop, but I'm still a good target for him. I don't have all day to check everything, so I let her warm up just enough to get the temp needle up off its stop, and then I stand on the brakes and push the throttle forward. I work the flight controls, and the cables move like they're lubed with KY Jelly, which some of them are, God bless personal lubricants. The power is fine, too. The little bird shakes and strains at her brakes, and I've always loved that feeling. It's like foreplay with a hot young babe. I let her shake for a while, then I let up on the brakes and let her do what she wants to do, and we roll out and rotate and we slip the surly bonds, as they say. I keep the throttle nailed until we're flying at eighty knots, then I pull it back a notch. My eyes aren't what they used to be and I could use some more light, but the altimeter is working and I know the elevations around here for any distance and direction that this little girl can fly.

They're not crying behind me anymore. Going flying usually gets people's attention. It can pull people out of themselves, the rush of it. The memories of other flights. They start whispering to each other but I don't bother to eavesdrop. I look down and

I see the changes a-coming. The boys have torches and they're already making a beeline for the airfield. The bastard daddy is circling back around behind them to go after his slut daughter. He's gotta be down there, but I can't see him.

So now it's my turn to try something. I bank over the town and turn back toward the airfield. Daddy's gone and the boys are coming, and maybe I'm in control again. The bitch cocks my gun and sticks it in my ear, but I stay the course. She tells me to turn back toward Sacramento. No ma'am, I say. Go ahead, I say. The brat says he'll cut my head off as soon as we're stopped. I say "Okay then—I'll fly us into the ground and take my chances— see if I'll be the one who walks away." They're really pissed off, and I think it's stupid because it shows they actually trusted me. People that stupid don't deserve to live.

I think I have them over a barrel, but then the brat unbuckles and wiggles himself into the right front seat. Little shit looks at me and winks. He can see me just fine. Shit. His bitch mother still has my gun stuffed into my ear. The kid straps in. He puts his feet on the rudder pedals and takes the yoke. His mother pushes the muzzle of my gun right into my ear hole and tells me to get off the controls. The kid takes the aircraft away from me, and he seems to know what he's doing. He adds power and turns back toward Sacramento. I remind them that it's my airplane, but it doesn't matter to them. Maybe they're not as stupid as I thought they were.

So they hijacked my girl, the plane I sweated over for hundreds of hours. Believe that shit? I'm so pissed that I push forward on the yoke, but his mother swats me in the ear with my own pistol. Steel on ear cartilage puts tears in my eyes. The kid gets us leveled off. It's dark and we're slow and heavy with fuel and flying at about fifty feet. There's some power lines coming up and the moon makes them shine like the lines of a spiderweb. We don't have enough airspeed to climb, so damned if the fucking kid doesn't fly right under 'em, slick as shit.

Too bad for me, the little bastard seems to know what he's doing. Maybe he's just lucky, but being lucky is the same thing as being good, isn't it? He tells me to keep my fucking hands off the controls and I do and he's got it then. He's not as smooth at the controls as I am, but he's not too bad, either. The bitch takes the gun out of my ear. I relax for a second, then she puts a knife to my neck. It has the scratchy-cold feeling of a very sharp knife, like it just can't wait to take a bite of me. I look down at it without moving my neck. Try that sometime. But I manage to do it, and the knife looks like one of those Ka-Bar knives the Marines like to use. She leans into my field of vision and she's looking right at the side of my face, my still presentable face, and her little turd of a son is driving.

"You sit quiet until we get to Sacramento or I'll cut you into pieces and throw you out, one chunk at a time. I'm sure there are other scavengers here, besides you and your son, and they know just what to do with rotten meat."

The kid laughs at his mother's little tough talk and it really pisses me off. I put my hands back on the yoke.

"No ma'am," I say. "You'll do no such thing."

"I think I'm going to enjoy this," she says, and she gets set to put her shoulder into it. I crank my head around and she has a little smile on her bitch face, and then I know she's got what it takes, so I lean back and relax. I'm bleeding from my ear from where she whacked me. I'm leaking from a shallow cut in my neck, too. I try to think of nothing except *fuck 'em*. I listen to the smooth-running engine, *my* engine, and I try to enjoy the feeling of flying at night, but all I feel is the old familiar feeling of falling out of the frying pan.

Jerry

God knows I've always loved the sound of light aircraft. That friendly sound from long-gone summers. The plane sounds like a happy toy, but it's carrying most of everything I will ever have, and ever be. The Cessna screws itself into the dark sky. Its navigational lights are off but I can see the small blue flame of its exhaust and the white of its wings against dark clouds. Thank You, thank You. Bless them and keep them. If I make it through this, I promise to take those flying lessons, Lord. I'll remember this feeling always, and whenever I fly I'll remember this fine *this*.

I let the sweet feeling of hope shoot through me, but then I'm walking toward the other thing, and who knows how it will turn out? Maybe it only *seems* like suicide. Maybe we'll come out of it okay. God make it so. God willing, or *Inshallah*, as the Muslims say. But that's neither here nor there. This is my fate, so off I go. One man against a pack of armed sociopaths. May age and treachery win the day. I remember watching a History Channel show on TV about the Texas Rangers. They had a saying: *You can't stop a good man who keeps a-coming.* And that's just what I hope to be and do.

So goodbye, wife. I'll be out late tonight. Hugs and kisses. Only time for a quick sendoff. Say goodbye to my turned back. Feel free to wait up for me, but I can't make any promises.

But then the airplane circles around and heads back toward

the airfield. I squat in the grass and watch. The plane dives and the wings are waggling like the plane is about to go out of control, and I don't know whether to watch or turn away. The old man is trying something, but it's a mistake. He thinks they're weak because they're not monsters. I watch and I don't bother to pray. The little bird puts on more power and it rises and turns and putters away to the south. I stand and get moving again. I tell myself that the fight goes to the ones who most need to win.

I hike to the highway and walk straight down the middle, southbound in the northbound lane. Then I go off-road and begin to curve around to the east of town. There's no moon in the overcast sky and the boys are coming in their trucks. They're laughing and grab-assing around as if they're about to have a night on the town. They're making so much racket that I don't worry about the sound of my bootfalls. A big bonfire is burning in town and their trucks are on the road, making their way to the airstrip. They pass behind me and then it's just me and the ones left in town.

I'm carrying the silenced .22 rifle. The AR-15 is slung on my back. I have enough ammo to turn a herd of cattle into beef stew. I'm on the side of justice and decency and light against darkness, and the anger flows from the furnace of my being, arms to fingertips, legs to toes, and I have no intention of giving them a fair fight.

I circle upwind and take as much time as I can afford. I whisper a thank-you when I reach the outskirts of town. A group of boys is guarding the motel and the adjacent wrecking yard. I watch their fire-cast shadows bouncing against the dark earth and the looming buildings, then I work my way closer to what has to happen.

Close enough to crawl. Down on my belly. Oil-soaked

ground. Damn it's cold. Move, dammit. Okay, I'm moving now. No choice, for better or for worse. Am I the bad guy here? Doesn't matter. The stalk seems to last forever, but I'm making good time.

Closer now. Not forgetting the possibility of spider holes and dogs and booby traps and bad luck. I find a trail. A human trail. It leads into the wrecking yard. I smell crap and I crawl past an outhouse. I'm quieter now that I'm out of the dried grass. I look down a row of wrecked pickup trucks. Melanie is close. I can feel it but I don't see her. The little bastards are down there, too. They have a cooking fire going. I still count three of them. Is that all there is? Are others behind me, waiting for me to show? If it were me, I would've put a few guys back in the shadows to wait. I don't know what kind of leader Bill Junior is. Don't know. I care, but that won't stop me. Must be patient, though. A force of nature. Stalking is hard work. Low crawling should be an Olympic event measured in time/distance/decibels/level of concealment. Too old for this shit, but that's okay because either I get what I've come for or I leave this world of pain.

They're saying something. One young kid and two older ones. The young one tests the water, and says it's ready. He pours bubble bath into the water and splashes it into lather. The older ones say that they're ready, too, and they grab their crotches and laugh with their froggy voices. I know what they're laughing about, and then I'm not fighting the urge to be patient anymore.

Stalking closer still. No moon and I'm low and the world is one big shadow, so I don't cast one. Snake in the grass. No. Better than that. I'm two-dimensional. The older ones go into the junkyard office shack and come out dragging someone. There she is. My baby girl and the woman that grew up around her. Hands taped to ankles. Hair clotted with muck, and clothes torn. They cut her free. She unfolds herself and rises. It takes her a while to get to her feet, and I'm cheering her on. You can do it, baby, I think. As if she's doing something important. As if she's showing the little monsters what she can take. I can't see the expression on her face, but her shape against the fire is about the most determined thing I've ever seen.

The kids pull her along a row of Ford F-150s and I lose sight of them. On my feet and really moving now. Moving to the head of the aisle of wrecked Fords and setting up shop. I get an angle on them and drop to a steady kneeling position. Crosshairs on first one boy and then the other. Finger straight against the triggerguard until the time is right. I've always had good timing that way.

They throw Melanie to the ground and pull her shredded clothes away and one of them holds her down. The timing isn't of my choosing, but it's something a father can't endure. I get a good cheek weld on the stock. One of the boys lowers himself between my daughter's legs and I squeeze the trigger. The .22 slug barely makes a sound as it passes through the suppressor. Clack of the little bolt as it cycles, the tiny bullet sent to discover its purpose. The tiny snap from its barely supersonic flight sounds loud to my ears, but the bullet does its work before the kid gets a chance to figure out what's happening. The round takes him through the back of the neck. The kid drops instantly. It's the spine shot I was praying for and I thank God and put another of the bastards in the crosshairs.

The other boy isn't used to being on the wrong side of an ambush. At the sound of the bullet's impact he stands and spins around, trying to spot me instead of trying to take cover or holding Melanie as a shield. He gets off three loud rounds from his pistol before I put two quiet rounds into his head. He's not a sociopath anymore. I look for the smaller kid, but he isn't so stupid. He's gotten the hell out of Dodge and Chevy and

Ford, too. I hear him running though the gate and toward the airstrip, and then I'm alone with her.

I'm standing over her before I realize I've taken a step. I want to hold her, but I give her space. Space to sit up. I pull the last of the duct tape from her hands and then she's up, barefoot on the cold ground. I pull the boots from the feet of the headshot boy and then we're running. It's killing cold and she's dressed in nothing but torn-up underwear, and I'm running behind her as she runs up the aisle of pickup trucks and turns into the foreign car section and stops at an old Volvo. She pops the trunk and pulls out a pile of clothing, pants and shirts and coats. I want to help. I want to apologize and comfort and promise, but I watch her choose an outfit from the trunk of an old Volvo. Some of the clothes are riddled and bloody, but she finds a T-shirt and boxers and a boys' pair of overalls that are stained with cow shit instead of blood, and she gets dressed.

Not much time left. Flickers of firelight in their empty camp, but it won't be empty for long. The pistol shots were huge in the night, and the little kid has to be running away to tell his big buddies what happened. The sound of stiff denim being pulled over tender flesh. The sound of my breathing and the sound of hers. I lean the .22 against the Volvo. I rummage in the trunk and find a pair of cheap wool socks—socks intended for a short winter day of sledding, a snow day that wasn't expected to last long, and so the socks won't last long, but it's what we have.

She puts them on and pulls on the boots I brought. She stands and looks at me, and I know we have to do this looking thing before we make our escape. She looks at me and I look at her. There's nothing to say, but everything to mean. Her face is covered with slime. She looks as if she's been behind enemy lines for weeks. She can focus on eternity, but she can't quite focus on me. Not right away. But then she does focus on me, and her eyes are steady. I smile and take her into my arms. We're out of time, so I back away and hold her at arm's length. I let her go and my hands feel empty. I pick up the .22 and hold it out to her, and she doesn't take it, and then I know she's really okay.

I take her arm. We jog back to the domestic section and then we break into a run and we're running through the last of the Detroit iron, headed for the gate. Razor wire lines the top of the fence, but the gate is wide open and we're coming, dammit, because we're leaving this place. Closer still and we run in the dried ruts of tow trucks and dragged death cars and we're there, at the gate, and it's open enough for us to run straight through without slowing down, and then we're through. She's running fast in front of me and we're through and I'm broadcasting a prayer of thanks because we're out running in the open night, but just when I want to cry tears of praise and start giggling, and the shrinking of my fear is getting me as high as I've ever been, something takes my head off.

Lights on, lights off, earthquake and calm. On my belly, on my back, trying to find enough traction and strength and balance to stand, but I can't tell which way is up. The small kid comes into my field of vision. I'm in his field of fire, but he's in mine, too. I raise the rifle and the kid pulls back on a wrist rocket slingshot and lets fly. And that's all she wrote for this old man. I hear the impact. Rock or marble or ball bearing against something brittle, not me, but yes me. Thwack of projectile on skull but I don't feel it; I hear another rock popping against siding or particle board or some damn thing, a kid shooting up the neighborhood with a slingshot and nobody around to stop him.

Susan

Scotty is flying. He can see and he can fly and I'll always accept forevermore that miracles happen. It's cold in the plane and Scott tells the old man to turn on the heater. I push the knife against his leathery neck and he leans forward and turns a knob and throws a switch. Dust streams from the vents and we cough, but then a wave of engine-heated air brushes against my arms and face and begins to sneak inside my clothes. It's the best feeling I've had in a long time. Sure, our campfires warmed the front or the back of me, but this heat is something else. It embraces me from all directions and I shiver, remembering how it feels to be comfortable. Remembering how it feels to receive a gift. Surrounded by heat. Something as simple as that is magical now, after months of living at whatever temperature Mother Earth preferred.

I get drowsy and I wonder if any other simple pleasures are in store for us. I don't know if we'll make it to safety, if such a place exists, but the heat has me in a good mood. The sweet womb of heat and Scotty is whole and well and I'm even grateful for the knife and the big revolver God has seen fit to provide for me. Loaves and fishes and heat and a knife and a cowboy gun to bring justice to the world. A healthy son and, God willing, a safe husband and daughter. I pray for them as we fly at night above volcanic mountains. I'm grateful that I'm in danger, too, because it makes me feel less guilty about not being with Jerry and Melanie. I have no doubt that Jerry will kill some of the boys. Maybe he doesn't want to, but it isn't a question of choice.

When I almost begin to drift off, I open a packet of MRE instant coffee and take a pinch of the dry crystals into my mouth. I give some to Scotty, and I can't see him very well in the glow of the instruments, but I imagine that his lips are blackened with the instant coffee, and his teeth and his tongue, and that reminds me of when he was little. He'd get a kick out of eating Popsicles, purple grape was his favorite, and then sticking his tongue out at us and chasing his sister, trying to lick the back of her neck with his stained tongue, laughing his way through a summer day. What a joker he was. How long ago that was.

Old Bill pulls a bag from under his seat and starts to dig through it. I tell him to stop, and he does. I tell him to hand the bag to me, and he does. It's a cloth book bag and it's filled with music CDs. Bill points to the instrument panel.

"I jury-rigged a sound system. Figure I might as well have some music while I'm being kidnapped."

I look through the music and it's all Southern Fried Rock from the seventies, Lynyrd Skynyrd and the Allman Brothers and Molly Hatchet. It's the kind of music that delinquents in Oregon used to listen to when I was a kid. I give the bag back to him and he chooses a CD and pushes it into what looks like a car stereo. The sound of twangy voices and guitars brings thoughts of Oregon into my head, and I have to fight an urge to tap my foot to the music.

Now that I'm not fighting for our lives, the thoughts come. There isn't any way to steer them in pleasant directions. What have we done? We were supposed to be better than the Baby Boomers, more grounded and levelheaded and respectful and less selfish. We managed to survive long enough to inherit the world, but just look what we've made of it.

It wasn't us who nuked our cities, but we allowed it to happen. We didn't mistrust terrorists and dictators as much as we mistrusted each other. We forgot about Pearl Harbor and 9/11. We pulled out of the Middle East, finally, and threw money at it. The money was supposed to work like fire retardant, but it didn't. All those billions and trillions to Israel and Egypt and Jordan. AIDS relief. Poverty relief. We gave and gave and gave, and what do we have to show for it? Somebody nuked us and who's helping *us* now?

It's all on our heads and hearts now, another unremarkable generation that wanted to change the world. And we have changed it. Oh *my*, yes we have.

We're following the highway. That damned road is still our guide. Scott flies low, but even then we lose sight of the ground for tense minutes at a time. We're in clouds and then we're in dark sky. I hope the clouds aren't radioactive. We've been lucky, so far. The jet stream flows to the north of us, and that's what kept us out of the death clouds. But poor Oregon. The clouds are almost certainly stacked up over it, as they always are this time of year, but now the clouds are hot, hot, hot. I hope someone lives. I hope the trees remain, at least. The flowers and crops of the Willamette Valley and the deer and elk in the Coast Range and Cascades. The black bear and cougar and salmon and trout.

My mother is gone, God bless her, but I hope the mud of the Willamette Valley is still fertile. I've always wanted to retire in Oregon. I haven't ever told Jerry, but part of me always planned to end up back there. Back home, where I could visit the old neighborhood where people knew the unsavory parts of my history, yes, but also the basic goodness of my family. Americans have shallow roots, but I miss the sweet, sad feeling of being a Northwesterner. The feeling of being strong and reliable when I'm four months into a nine-month rainy season. The feeling of wearing flannel without irony and driving up old logging roads into wilderness that has no street signs or lights, traveling to places where you could die of exposure if you weren't careful. Nameless clearcuts and roaring campfires. The luxury of feasting on trout pan-fried with butter and salt and dill in the midst of the dark temperate rain forest. Toasting marshmallows after. The smell of beer on my father's breath as he told us scary-funny tales about Sasquatch. The glow of my mother's eyes in the firelight, smiling. The feeling of being in the wilderness, but being safe as I said my prayers and climbed into my sleeping bag.

That's the part of Oregon I hope is left.

We almost fly into a series of big power lines then. They're right in the windshield and Scott adds power and pulls back on the controls and it pushes my guts down into my lap. Both Scott and Old Bill are swearing their heads off, but we come through the other side just fine. They swear for a while longer and then they laugh as if they're old friends. But then the silence gets heavy again, and we drone on into the night.

I'm looking forward to daylight so Scotty can take us up high and we can fly in a straight line. The Lord said in His Good Book that the most honorable roads were intended to be straight and narrow. God brings the moon out from behind the clouds for us. It's the first time I've seen the moon since the bombs went off. Maybe our Lord and Savior is showing off. Maybe He thinks it's the least He can do, considering.

So I watch the milky glow of the moonlit road beneath us.

The dead cars and trucks look soft beneath us, and I imagine they're already beginning to decay. Snowy patches on the ground give a hint of our speed. That sweet, man-made heat keeps blowing from the vents, and it smells like hot metal and progress and freedom and the luxury of peace. All of my being wants to begin the celebration of our survival, but I know it's too soon, and so I push the joy back into its bottle and save it on a shelf in my mind, for later.

Melanie

They have him and he's here with me now. That's a curse for him and maybe an improvement for me. He killed two of them to get here. There are only sixteen boys now, and they're so pissed off about Dad's attack that they're ripping their own hair out. They're also beating on Dad. But Bill Junior won't let them kill him.

Bill Junior says something and the beating stops and they drag Dad over to the fire. I'm handcuffed to the steering wheel of a wrecked cop car. Bill Junior uncuffs me.

"Help your old man. If you run, he dies."

I don't say anything. When I was a little girl I always thanked people for everything they did for me, but then I learned about the power of silence. I get up and try to find the right wrecked car, and then I do. I open the trunk. The boys use the trunks like drawers to stash their plunder, and I was lucky enough to

see where they put the medical supplies. I pull out gauze bandages and antibiotic ointment and Ace bandages. There isn't
any medical tape for the bandages, but there's no shortage of
duct tape.

The boys don't visit me anymore. I'm slightly more than meat
now, probably because they want me to get my dad to give them
millions. It's all bullshit, but my Goggy is with me now, sleeping, I hope. Most of his head is wrapped in silver duct tape.
The boys get drunk and they get into another of their stupid
fistfights, two of them fighting in the firelight, and the others
placing bets, and then one boy gets knocked out cold and the
rest of them leave one by one and pass out in their motel rooms
and cars and shacks.

It's been years since I spent time alone with my dad, but it
doesn't seem that long ago. We were a busy family that really
only came together once a year, at Christmastime.

"This isn't much of a vacation, Dad," I say.

He doesn't answer, not that I expected him to, but I keep
talking. He's unconscious, maybe in a coma, and everyone who
ever watched TV knows that people in comas might be listening for friendly voices to guide them back into the world. So I
give him one.

"Do you remember it, Dad—the good things? I'm pretty
sure you remember the time I got busted smoking pot. I told
you it was the first and the last time I tried it, and I loved that
you pretended to believe me when I told you that. But listen, it
was the last time. I don't know why I'm telling you this, but I
thought you should know. It wasn't your fault that I tried weed.
I know you and Mom must've gotten high when you were
young. I've seen the pictures of the eighties. Greed is good. A

person couldn't walk down the street without getting propositioned by a coke dealer, right?"

His breathing speeds up and I think maybe he can hear me.

"But it's not your fault that the world was a shithole when you were young, just like it's not your fault that this happened."

His eyelids flutter and I keep talking.

"Do you remember when I rode a bike on two wheels for the first time? When I won the all-around in varsity gymnastics? Do you remember my first boyfriend?"

I tell him about things that happened in my childhood to see if he remembers them. His eyelids don't flutter again. I imagine he's trying to remember, but when those things happened, he wasn't there. He was always at work. So I trick myself into believing he *was* there. And then I start to make up memories, just to guess what his answers might be. Remember when I hit that line drive in softball and beaned the pitcher? He sends out a vibe like, *Sure. Who could forget that?* I know he's lying, but I don't give him *the look*. The "you're full of shit" look.

It never happened. I never beaned any pitcher with a line drive, but I wish I had. Nope. It didn't happen, and even if it *had* happened, my dad was at work. But I can't stop lying, and neither can he, even though he's in a coma. I tell him lies and he sends out untruthful vibes until our lies become wistful what-ifs and apologies. Remember when...? Sure I do. And the time when...? That was a great day, wasn't it? And so on, until we make up this wonderful, wonderful life that never happened, my dad always right with me to cheer me on, no matter what.

But then I can't help myself from being kind of mad at him. He's a mess and I'm a mess, and we have all this baggage. But sometimes we can break through all of that. He surprises me sometimes by being not so uptight. Sometimes he doesn't drink too much, and he isn't an asshole, and sometimes I can appreciate it. I haven't thought about it forever, but there was this one time when we really broke through the crap.

When I was thirteen, I argued with him so much that he stopped opening his mouth for a while there. I don't know how many times I told him I hated him, but he didn't run away from me. He didn't lock himself in his study or go for long drives like some dads would've done. No, he sat next to me on the couch. Not too close, but not too far away, either. He wouldn't look at me and his face was serious and he didn't talk, but he was sending out this vibe that I couldn't understand. At that age, I was pissed off when I woke up in the morning and pissed off when I went to bed, so at first I took his silence for criticism. So I'd sit there for a while, then mutter a few vile things and stomp away to my room.

But it made me curious, the way he kept sitting next to me. He might've had a small drink before he sat down, but he didn't keep drinking, like he usually did. I stopped muttering at him when he squeezed himself onto the opposite end of the couch. I stopped running to my room. I stopped looking at him, too, and he didn't change his game, so we sat on opposite ends of the couch. We didn't say a word and we didn't look at each other, either, and it was like some kind of contest. We sat and we sat and we sat. Isn't that something from Dr. Seuss? But that's what we did, and it was like a competition. We'd sit after dinner and watch whatever was on the tube, the news or cartoons or PBS. Whatever. And we wouldn't bitch or change the channel. We'd just sit and work very hard at ignoring each other, even though we were only about three feet apart.

We became very good at it. I could go into a state that was close to a coma. Dad would let his eyes narrow to slits and he'd breathe without sound through his mouth like he'd just fallen asleep. We were like cold-blooded animals, dormant right there in the living room. Maybe we were mediums channeling the emptiness that existed before us, and after us, and always. We sat for hours and I could never tell who won the competition, but after a while it started to crack me up. When he puts his mind to it, Dad is pretty good at cracking me up. He'd do weird things to get me to laugh, and that was one of them. And I *did* start to laugh at his game, but I couldn't let it show. I'd sit like a corpse but I'd be laughing my ass off, inside. Weird or disgusting things would come on TV and Dad would be looking right at it, but he wouldn't move a muscle, and that cracked me up. We watched ads for erectile dysfunction, and we didn't flinch. We watched ads for products that treat vaginal dryness and diarrhea and genital warts, but we didn't break our silence, and so we showed each other just how we felt about the culture of television, and how we felt about life in general, and maybe how we felt about each other, all without saying a word. Genius, huh?

For about a week we did that almost every night after dinner, and Dad was stubborn as hell, so I couldn't quit, either. We sat and we sat and we sat, but I was laughing inside, and I knew he was laughing, too. And then one day Mom finally stood in front of us and asked us what in God's name was going on, and Dad looked at me and I looked at him, and we laughed our asses off. The look of love he had in his eyes cut right through my anger and I'll never forget it, all the things about life that were better after that.

And he's here with me now, doing his quiet thing. I sit three feet away from him and I play the Ignoring Game with him. He's playing it, too. I listen very hard to make sure he's breathing, and then I hear his breath. His eyes are closed and his mouth is open. Yeah, he's good at this game, so I have no choice but to go to that place inside me where I used to go.

I become a rock. A hibernating squirrel. A smartass ghost. I send vibes to him and I think he's doing the same, because if I ever thought he wasn't scheming in some way to make me laugh, or to feel better about my life, or to give me orders and commands, then I don't know what I'd do. I remember every single argument we ever had, before and after we played the Ignoring Game, and I don't know what the hell I thought I was doing. He's my father, for Christ's sake. If we make it out of here, I'll be my own person, steady in the world, and maybe someday I'll thank him for that. I'll leave home, but when I visit, I'll never go back to the way I was before we played the Ignoring Game. Never. When this is over, I plan to retire from my career of giving him shit. I'd tell him about it now, but he wouldn't believe me.

I have to prove myself first.

Scott

We're flying over mountains and we bounce into the burned-smelling clouds sometimes. I hope we won't get sick. I don't know the terrain. It makes me nervous as hell, and it shows in the waggling way I fly. Old Bill begs from the left seat for fifteen minutes before I let him take a turn at the controls.

"Thanks, kid," he says. "You don't know how much I've

been looking forward to this flight, present company excluded, of course."

"Shut up and fly."

I don't trust him, but it turns out that he's a good pilot. He's smooth at the controls and he keeps the plane on a steady course through updrafts and crosswinds. But we don't fly more than one single mile before he starts giving me shit. He puts his fat finger on the artificial horizon indicator.

"See that instrument right there, the one with the little airplane on it? That's how I know we're flying straight and level. And don't you worry, I'll keep us out of the trees because I know this country. I know every hill and bump and ditch better than you know the chancres on your boyfriend's dick."

"Maybe you should get out and *join* all that nature down there."

He laughs and keeps trying to show me how a daddy drives his car. Fuck off and die. That's what I want to say to the old dickhead, but I don't. He's right about the flying. He looks at his watch and at the compass and altimeter, and he knows where the mountains are. If I would've kept flying, I would've ended up with a mountain in the windshield. But I don't have to take his shit.

"Hey," I say. "Shut up or I'll put it down on the road and give you a tune-up."

I don't know where I got that "tune-up" shit. I heard it on TV, probably, but it works on Old Bill. It's a language he understands. And so he does shut up, mostly. He smiles at me and wags his head to his old-fart music. He whistles along with "Free Bird," which I shouldn't like because it's the music of rednecks and Joe Gut Six-Packs, but I kind of *do* like that song. I wouldn't have figured Bill Senior could keep a tune, but he's one of those guys who can really whistle. He whistles better than the Lynyrd Skynyrd lead singer sings. It pisses me off. Everything he does pisses me off. I decide to stop thinking of him as Bill Senior. I'll just call him "BS" from now on.

So BS flies and I let my thoughts wander to the time just after the bombs. The people of Yreka took us in. They barbecued all the fresh meat in town, and we feasted like I'd never feasted before. Then they set us up in tents in store parking lots, and after a few days the local families "adopted" us. They did the decent thing, out of the goodness of their hearts, and made up a blind lottery. Each "unhoused" family was given a number and each local family that was involved drew a number, and that was the way they did it.

We didn't see the drawing. We used duct tape to put our number on our tent, and then we waited. Our number was 007. They did everything at city hall or somewhere, and we didn't see it, but it wasn't long before the locals started showing up, greeting people, taking families out of the tents and into their houses. It was damned nice of them. I'd like to think that we would've done the same thing in their shoes, but I'm not so sure. That kind of goodness doesn't seem to be in the world anymore, but maybe someday it will come back to us.

I was hoping that we'd be adopted by a family with a hot daughter. Can't blame me for hoping. But that's not what we got. A retired military guy and his wife drew our number. The man had been a colonel in the army. He was as uptight as Dad, and he was in his seventies, but he was also the nervous type, like I am, with maybe some kind of social anxiety disorder. But he had some good ways to deal with the wobbly-ass world. His hobby was brewing beer. I liked him right away. Gray dude.

Gray hair and gray eyes and gray skin, but he took us into his house and gave us mugs of tasty beer at night.

His wife was just plain great. She was one of those old ladies who makes you feel special. She reminded me of my sweet, dead gramma, and I fell for her right away. When I smiled at her corny jokes, I was really smiling. But I don't want to think about that time anymore, because it's gone.

Right now my dad is fighting what might be his last battle. And Mel—I have no idea what they did to her, and I don't want to guess. Maybe she'll take a gun when I offer one to her, if I ever get another chance. She *needs* to pick up a gun and get to work. The thought crosses my mind that if I give her a weapon, she'll turn it on herself. But no. She wouldn't do that.

Me, I've been healed for a purpose and a cause, and He has revealed His plan to me, clear as the clearest day. I plan to get a group of people together. Young guys like me who want to make the world a better place, and aren't afraid to fight. Call it revenge or justice or taking out the garbage, I don't care. Mob or posse, it doesn't matter. He has spoken to me, and He told me that I am to be His instrument in this time, His perfect weapon, and He will work His miracles through me. I'll get Mom settled in Sacramento, and then I'll get a group of guys together and we'll do whatever it takes to save Dad and Mel.

But we won't stop there. We'll stay in the wild places, fighting to bring goodness back into the world. Maybe we'll call ourselves marshals, but whatever we call ourselves, we'll go wherever the assholes live. We won't steal or kill people who don't deserve it. We'll be strong, but nice as anything, like the way I remember my grandfather, who fought in Hue City in Vietnam, but we'll also be as hard as my grandfather was, and we won't hesitate to kill the bad people, the people who need to be killed to give goodness and decency a chance. We'll be the law and we won't allow ourselves to become assholes. We'll be everywhere and nowhere, blowing the bad shit right out of the world, and then we'll settle down and enjoy the peace we've brought.

I'll meet a girl who maybe won't know about my history, but maybe she will. I'll buy or build us a place to live and we'll make love anytime we want, in every room of the house, and I'll learn how to brew beer and we'll be good neighbors and we won't miss church on Sunday morning. Maybe I'll run for sheriff or mayor, or maybe I'll get into some kind of business, but I won't let my work take over my whole life, because family is the thing that matters. We'll have kids, sons and daughters, and we'll raise them to be strong and good, so this kind of shit will be less likely to happen again.

Below us the mountains are dropping down into plains. Redding is okay. There isn't any electricity, but we fly over hotspots of campfires and the light of lanterns and candles glowing through the windows of all those unelectrified houses and hotels. There's a halo of smoke over the town. It looks like an old town from maybe the early 1800s. I can't see much, but I can smell the woodsmoke and a hint of something that smells like horses and shit. It might be a safe place, but I wouldn't be surprised if it isn't. BS adds some power and climbs higher. I almost decide to take the controls from him, but then Redding is behind us, another mystery.

We fly farther south until we must be over Red Bluff. There isn't much old-timey sweetness about Red Bluff. It's on fire. The whole town is burning. We fly over and the thermals take us up to eight thousand feet before BS can take us into cooler air. There isn't much oxygen up here, but there's us. Us and the heat and smoke, all that's left of a sun-dried little town I barely remember seeing from the windows of Dad's now-dead car.

But then someone outside of town is flashing a light at us, a good, strong light. I take the controls from BS and circle us back down over the southern part of town.

"I wouldn't do that," BS says.

"Yeah. I know," I say. "But maybe that's the trouble with the world."

"Okay then. Don't say I didn't warn you."

He sits his old ass back in his seat and crosses his arms. I take us down to three thousand feet AGL and we take a look. It's two hours until sunrise, and we can't see very much, but the person on the ground keeps flashing that light at us. It probably isn't the time or place to be curious, but I take us down to two thousand feet. I'm thinking that maybe there's some kind of order down there. People who are official, and only not self-elected assholes. Maybe the National Guard is down there, finally helping the people who need helping and killing the ones that need killing. But then a brighter light locks onto us and I see a shitload of flashes on the ground and bullets reach up into the sky. Big bullets. I take us into the thermal again to get us back to a safe altitude. We take the elevator of heat and destruction back up into the sky and I know I won't be indulging my curiosity about the good of man anytime soon.

Farther south we drone through the long, flat grind of the Central Valley. I get a cramp in my leg, so I let BS fly again. No lights. No cars are moving, but sometimes I can see reflections from their dead headlights. Sometimes when the moon almost manages to break through, I see the cars and trucks lined up like some kind of museum exhibit, or some kind of advertisement for alternative energy.

We get down into the long, open places. Rice fields and the marshlands that the environmentalists restored and the edges of the Sacramento Delta. The dim moonlight shines against all that standing water.

I remember flying over this country when I was first learning to fly. I was flying only to build up hours and I took Candi with me, my first real girlfriend, and she thought it was a beautiful place. As we flew over the wetlands, birds rose up from the water like we were in Africa or something. I kept us high enough to avoid a bird strike and Candi leaned over to look out my side of the aircraft and her breasts brushed against me. I was in heaven then, and she was the hottest thing I'd ever seen and done and I remember wishing the flight school's old Cessna 152 had an autopilot.

But now isn't a good time to have a raging hard-on memory. It takes less time to travel the length of the Central Valley than I'm used to. Cruising above Interstate 5 at 130 knots. The Cessna 182 is a faster bird than the flight school's old 152, and I like it. There isn't any other air traffic, needless to say. No left-lane hogs or traffic jams down below. I take the controls from BS and he falls asleep in about ten seconds, flat. I fly and fly and fly. I try not to think. We finally fly over the farm towns north of Sacramento. Marysville and Olivehurst. I see a random sheen of light from a community swimming pool. Rooftops seem to be flat in the night. There isn't any electricity, but I take us higher because of the power lines I know are strung all around here.

The sky is gray at first light. I fly over grazing land, and there are shapes down there. Cattle, their hides rotten. There's smoke rising in the distance. We get to the outskirts of downtown

Sac, but that can't be right. Fires are burning everywhere and it takes a second for my brain to figure out what my eyes are seeing.

I fly over maybe a half mile of fire, then I get to a place where there's nothing left to burn. There's a black hole where the Capitol Mall should be. Nothing. No streetlights or neon or random city lights. It's darker down there than it was in the mountains, and it smells like burned meat and plastic, then it smells like roadkill and old charcoal at the bottom of a barbecue.

I fly a long circle around the place we once called downtown. The sun slides above the rim of the Sierras and I can see better. The bomb made a huge hole in the ground. It probably didn't go off high above the city like the bombs we dropped on Japan. It must've gone off right on the ground and it made big crater that makes an almost perfect bowl in the ground. It looks like something from a disaster movie, and I don't want to believe it's real. It's a Hollywood set, a practical joke, an advertisement, or a sick antiwar protest. But it's not. I waggle my wings and go into a tight turn and Mom wakes up. She yawns and takes a look. She looks for second then jerks up straight in her seat.

"Oh *no.*"

It's just about the biggest understatement I've ever heard, but she says it in the sharp, hissing voice she uses when the shit hits the fan, using the voice that always freaked me out when I was a kid. The voice I heard once when we were driving cross-country at night, and I was maybe nine years old and drowsy, and a car crash happened right in front of us, and Dad slammed on the brakes and swerved and we slid off the road and headed toward oncoming traffic and we didn't know if we'd make it, and Mom said exactly that same thing.

Oh *no.*

I fly us back through and out of the smoke. I leave down-town Sac behind us because downtown is death, and death is still hot and hungry. I fly toward our neighborhood because I want to see if anything is left of the house I used to call home.

Bill Junior

Her old man might make it, and he might not. I take Melanie out of service so she can help her pops. My men bitch like crazy when I do it, but I put a guard on the shack, and I check the place myself every few hours, and so far my pirates are keeping their swords in their scabbards.

I'm not sure why I'm being so nice to the girl, but it's some-thing I need to do, no matter why. I watch her helping her old man, and it does something to me, because I can't imagine any-one doing that for me, staying up all hours and holding me and changing my bandages and crying and worrying. It makes me jealous, but I'm also hoping that someone will care that much about me, someday, and right now it doesn't seem completely impossible.

And of course maybe her old man really *is* rich as God. And if it's true, maybe I'll find a way to get the fuck out of here in one piece, with Melanie and the gold we found and hopes of even better things.

Susan

Dear God, why did I let myself believe that our city might still be okay? And now I'm not sure of anything. Home was the prize—the point of all of the walking and risking and praying and fighting and flying. But I knew it was a possibility that the city was ruined, so there was nothing left to do but see it for ourselves.

At first I don't believe it, but I'm a believer these days, so I try to look down at the hole like an anthropologist, a surveyor, an engineer, an insurance adjuster. I'm a FEMA official looking for survivors, then I'm a funeral director with pre-cremated clients, then I'm me again, the claws of anger beginning to pierce the shock.

I ride out a long wail that scares the bejesus out of me. Even while I'm screaming, I know it doesn't help anything, but I scream like a raging baby, expelling all the air from my lungs, winding down and then taking a deep breath and doing it again. My face is hard and hot and I can feel my veins and arteries worming their way to the surface of my skin, but I can't stop myself. Scott and the old man turn to look and then they turn back. They hold their heads very still and let me wail.

And then it passes, and I can breathe in and out. My wounded arm is throbbing to the beat of the airplane's engine. Scott skirts the bomb crater and flies toward the eastern suburbs. He leaves the hole where the Capitol once stood, and heads for our neighborhood, our home. It's the worst nightmare of *Fail-Safe* and *On the Beach* and duck-and-cover and the documentaries about nuclear war. Red circle in the center. Bright orange ring for the unsurvivable blast. Dark yellow rings for the zones of fire and lethal radiation, and so on, out to a radius of dozens of miles.

When I was a little girl I used to sit on the warm wooden floor of my childhood home and draw red and orange and yellow rings over my coloring book pictures, not understanding what they represented, but loving the symmetry, the rings circling my home and saying, *This is where you live; if you get lost, this is the way home.*

We fly out of the smoke, and I recognize the buildings below. The Methodist church, the elementary school, the Wal-Mart. Scott circles our neighborhood. Our house would probably be in one of the medium-dark yellow rings. There wasn't any fire here, or fallout, but it's too close to the blast zone, and I know we won't be able to go back. Not ever. My garden, with my plans for tomatoes and bell peppers and lettuce and sunflowers. My kitchen with its new granite countertops. The oven that cooked all those meals. The potholders that Melanie made in the third grade. The baby footprints and pictures and the documents we thought were important enough to store in a fireproof safe. All the memories now poisoned unto death.

Scott turns us away and climbs higher. The radiation must be passing into our bodies now. I don't feel anything but I can't slow my breathing and I start to hyperventilate. Dizzy at low altitude, and it doesn't help to look out and see the road crowded with cars and trucks that will never run again. I begin to see bodies, their feet facing the blast. My head hurts. My uterus hurts. I get tunnel vision. But I'm sick of thinking like a victim. Like prey. We've been at the mercy of others for far too long, and I can't take it anymore. I don't want peace; I want justice. I'm dizzy and then I'm not myself at all. The pain fades into the background and I break through the clouds in my head and fly fast and straight in the sunlight. I'm hard and without emotion, and I feel free to do anything I want to do. Why should only ambushers and rapists and killers be allowed to indulge themselves? It's my turn now.

I cock Old Bill's old gun. It makes four clicks when I pull back the hammer. I grind the barrel into the place where his spine meets his brain. I feel nothing at all for him, and I almost forget that my son is close enough to touch. It was people like Bill who did this to us. Bill didn't bomb our city, but his kind did. His foreign counterparts in crime and sleaziness and greed, and the mean and fearful masses egging them on. He might be at the bottom rung of people who do things like that, but he's one of them, no doubt about it, and one of them needs to pay. It might as well be him.

He reads my mind.

"Wasn't me that done this."

He turns and I pull the gun from his spine and let it wander up to his brainpan. He turns his head until the muzzle is pointed at the corner of his forehead.

"I didn't have nothing against Sacramento. I thought it was a fine old town. It had all kinds of hookers, you know. Tall ones and short ones and whores of all colors and persuasions and talents."

He laughs his phlegmy, horny old-man laugh. "And speaking of *fucking*, hey, look on the bright side—the state of California won't be taxing us up the ass anymore. Not for a while, anyhow."

He's enjoying himself. I finally catch my breath. He offends

me. If thy eye offends thee, pluck it out. My finger is moving from the triggerguard to the trigger. My finger is on the
trigger and I'm down in the charcoaled city center. I've been
cremated and the wind is mixing my molecules into the
great mounds of ashes. I'm down there mixing with friends
and acquaintances and strangers and children. All the children, their dust and dead promise blowing through the remains
of the city.

The muzzle of the gun wanders away from Old Bill's ear
and then back and away again. We hit a patch of turbulence, or maybe the turbulence is only in my mind, and the
gun bucks and roars in my hand. The air is blasted and bitter
with the smell of spent gunpowder. We sit with our mouths
open. Scott's lips start to move but I can't hear what he's saying. Old Bill puts his hands to his ears and opens his mouth
to scream but I can't tell if he's making any sound. He turns
and his face is livid. He grabs the barrel of the gun. I pull the
trigger, but I hadn't cocked the gun again after it fired, and
nothing happens. My fingers lose their strength and Old Bill
has it then. I reach for it, but I only have one functional arm,
and he bats my hand away. He cocks the revolver and points
it at Scott's head. He's shouting, and his words dribble into
my wounded ears. He's calling me bad names and then I can
hear again.

"I've had just about as much as I'm gonna take," he says.

He points the gun at my face.

"Sit the fuck back."

I do. He points the gun at Scott again.

"If you try anything, we'll only have one pilot on this flight.
Understand?"

I nod. Scott keeps us straight and level, obeying Old Bill's
command to fly us back to the north.

Melanie

My Goggy is still alive, so things could be worse. But we're in the hands of people who make it their business to make things worse. They let me give him water, but he's not *with it* enough to swallow.

I get a cloth and clean the small part of my dad's head that isn't bandaged. Scalp wounds bleed like crazy. He starts bleeding again. It takes me half the morning to get his head wound to clot, while the boys sleep off their hangovers. The kid on guard duty watches without saying anything. He doesn't tape up my hands and I don't do anything that might make him want to.

The boys are mean bastards when they wake up. I make coffee for them and watch them moan and groan and glare at my dad, and it makes me happy to see their pain. I wish they were in a lot more pain, but then I wonder if that idea violates my vow of pacifism. No. I'm not a saint. And even saints and heroes must've had bad thoughts about their oppressors. Don't you think Gandhi wanted to bring pain to his enemies? Maybe even Christ looked down from the cross at the laughing Roman soldiers and thought about how nice it would be to shoot some fire and brimstone up their asses. It's only human.

Bill Junior soaks his head in cold water and then walks over to us. He walks with his feet turned in and his head down, like he's walking across the stage of a Western movie set.

"Will he live?"

"Yes."

"How do you know?"

"Because he's my dad. He's tough and he's going to live. Get used to the idea, because that's just the way it is."

"Good."

He walks away and organizes a burial party for the two boys Dad killed. I try not to look at them. I don't care that they're dead. Not a bit, even though I was partially responsible for their deaths. If I hadn't let myself get kidnapped...If I would've fought harder or run faster or hidden myself better—if, if, if—then those boys might still be walking the earth and joking and grabbing their crotches and standing in line to pull a train on someone.

Yeah. After a few minutes of wallowing in that thought, I can look at them. The living ones don't bother to cover the bodies of the dead. They leave them staring up into the overcast, their eyes glazed with the stupidity of death. The living boys pile a stack of lumber into a shoddy funeral pyre, then they strip the bodies. They save some of the clothes and they fold them carefully, and then they toss the corpses onto the pyre.

One of the dead ones was called "Rick the Prick" because he had such a big one. The first time he raped me, I bled for a long time. The other kid was Ralph, just Ralph. He had a weak chin and he liked to hit me. They look too small to have been as dangerous as they were. They look pathetic, but I can't stop watching them burn.

Bill Junior doesn't say any words over them. The fire is low and smoky and he throws a cup of gasoline on it and walks away. The fire blossoms into the sky and seems to hover above the bodies, then it gets right down into the evidence of their existence. I don't feel good about how they died, my responsibility for it, but I watch the fire feed on them until they look just exactly *right*.

Scott

I look at the gauges. There's a big hole in the instrument panel. I hear a steady tone in my ears, but it's getting quiet enough that I can hear other things, too.

"Fuel's getting low."

My voice sounds like it came from down a hole. BS shakes his head.

"Just keep us headed north, boy."

"Why are you going back?"

"I think I might've left the oven on."

He smiles but his eyes are as black as the hole in the muzzle of his revolver. He looks back at Mom and tells her not to touch the other guns. Mom moans. I should be pissed off at her, but I'm not. I feel bad for her. I wish she would've shot BS in the head. I wish I had pieces of his skull and brain in my hair and the windows were splattered with the last of his sicko thoughts. I think I'd be happy then.

He keeps the gun to my head. I start to panic but I squeeze the control yoke until my fingers burn. I'm flying VFR at 130 knots and I have to *maintain*. Mom cries for a while.

"It's okay," I say. "Everything is okay."

BS says, "That's the spirit, boy."

I turn to look at Mom. I've never seen her so pale. Even back when I was a kid, after the surgery she had on her knee, she had more color than she does now. Pale, wan, ashen, drawn, waxen. I want to pull her out of the hole she's fallen into, but I don't know how.

She cries and wails again. Her voice rises like an old air raid siren. It keeps going up and up and it reaches a peak and I can't get the sight of nuked Sacramento out of my head. The panic builds inside me again, still. The yoke is a bloody bone in my hands, and I can't feel my feet on the rudder pedals. My heartbeat gets out of synch and I'm dizzy in that sick way that feels like dying. Her voice reaches the end of its breath and she's quiet. She has no air in her lungs, but she doesn't take another breath, and that's even worse than the wailing. My vision starts to tunnel and gray, and I have to slap myself hard across the face. I slap and slap until the panic is replaced with pain.

BS tells me to get my shit together. Mom pulls out of it. She takes a breath. She grabs my shoulder and tells me no. No, no, no. She apologizes and asks for forgiveness and protection for us from her imaginary god, the one we've all been praying to, and then we're finally quiet. I turn off the heat because it picked up the smell of the dead city, but it gets cold fast in the mountains, and I have to turn it back on. I try to get comfortable by not paying any attention to anything that's not directly in front of my nose. The little engine spins its two-bladed prop and we climb into the Sierras.

We've been in the air for three hours and we didn't start with a full load of fuel. The bullet that passed through the instrument panel did some damage. I smell the beginnings of an electrical fire. The smoke starts then, and the rest of the instruments go dead and something behind the panel is starting to glow red.

We're high in the mountains and I can't set it down just anywhere. The smoke makes it hard to see, but we luck out and see a highway below us. I dive down as low as I can go without smashing us into high-tension lines. It's Highway 341. We're southeast of where I thought we were. We missed Reno, but maybe, just maybe, we'll make it to Virginia City.

And we do. The trees thin out below us and we fly into the saddle of a big, grassy valley, with the old Comstock Hills all around. I open my window to clear the cabin of smoke and get a blast of freezing air. The smoke clears for a second and I see old wooden buildings under us. Main Street. Dead cars clog the road, but puffs of woodsmoke are coming from some of the chimneys.

With the window open, the fire flares up in front of me. BS tries to beat back the flames with one of his gloves. I think about trying to take the gun away from him, but I'm too busy to try it. I fly over the main drag and nobody shoots at us. Thin, cold air. Unsteady gusts of wind in the valley. Flames are licking at the windshield. I have a hell of a time keeping us straight and level, but I do. I try to drop the flaps, but nothing happens. I chop the power and we descend. I stick my head out the window and find a part of the road that doesn't have any dead cars on it.

I come in hot and mostly blind. I flare and ease the little tires onto the cold asphalt of the highway. Small screech of rubber and the thump of the struts compressing. Ten toes heavy on the brakes. I kill the engine and roll out. I get us stopped. We're on the highway just east of town.

The instrument panel is burning for real. We don't wait for an order to get out. We cough the smoke out of our lungs, then BS goes to work. He tosses the shotgun and my rifle onto a patch of dead grass. He tells us to move away from the guns and sit down. He takes the rest of our gear from the plane, then he stands in front of us. His airplane is burning behind him and he's really pissed off. He holds the revolver on us and scratches his face. His beard is like gray pubic hair. I have no idea what he'll do. Mom takes my hand in hers, and I don't pull away.

I turn and look back at the town. We're maybe five hundred yards from the first buildings on Main Street. I don't pray, exactly, but let's just say I'm really hoping to have some witnesses. And then yeah, a door opens and people step onto the boardwalk. My eyesight isn't one hundred percent, but it looks like one of them is holding a pair of binoculars on us.

BS winks and lowers the revolver.

"Well, guess I'll be seein' ya. Can't say it's been a slice of heaven."

He picks up Mom's shotgun and unloads it and field strips it and throws the parts far out into the grass. He slings my carbine and takes both of our packs and walks away to the north. It's a hell of a walk to Reno, but I'm very glad he's going, and I don't wish him well. The truth is, if I had a gun right now, I'd shoot him right in the middle of his fat back. I'd kill him if I had a gun, and I'm looking forward to the day when I can, because this shit isn't over for him.

He walks away and we don't have anything left. No food or weapons or poncho liners, but my hair is tingling because we're alive and free. I try to find the parts of Mom's shotgun. I find everything but the bolt assembly. I look everywhere, but it's gone, so I put the slide and barrel and trigger group back onto the receiver, so it at least looks like we have a working shotgun.

We put some distance between us and the plane. It's burning like crazy. It's av-gas, so it's like a big Molotov cocktail. There's a big bang. The heat flares against our faces, but we're okay. The plane takes its last flight, rising into the air from the explosion, and then it settles down and starts melting into the ground.

BS is about a hundred yards away. He turns and shakes his head, then he gets back to walking. The smoke spreads in the valley. The wind blows it flat, but it's really black, and clear for all to see. The air is cold as hell and the fire feels kind of nice. We start to walk toward town, walking a game trail that leads through chaparral, sage, tumbleweed, whatever it is. I've never had time to learn about botany and stuff like that, but someday I plan to learn it.

I can't feel my hands and feet, and I try to ask Mom how she's doing, but my mouth doesn't work. There isn't any cover, and smoke is blowing like a signal behind us, and we have no choice but to walk straight toward the mercy or violence of strangers.

Bill Junior

Damned if her daddy didn't wake up. He hasn't said *shit* to me, and that's good for him, because if he does, I'll put his daughter back into service. He seems to know it, too.

The girl got some candles from somewhere, and she's got about a dozen of them burning in the shack. She's sitting with her old man's head in her lap and I wouldn't mind trading places with him. I like the way her red hair shines in the candlelight. It makes me happy that I let her take baths. I don't think I'll be able to give her the thing she wants most, her freedom, but while she's here, I can be her sugar daddy, with good food and baths and all that shit.

I walk into the shack like I own the place, because I do own it. When I get inside, I pull off my watch cap and just stand there. Melanie looks at me, then looks away. It makes me feel good to see her. It's kind of beautiful in here, the candlelight making the leather and cloth and carpet of the place look all rich and soft, the way even craphole bars can look kind of special in dim light. I'm almost proud, because I'm the guy that made this cool-looking place possible.

"How's he doing?" I say.

The bastard lifts his head and looks at me. His head is all bandaged up. His eyes don't have anything in them, no hate or begging. I keep my eyes on him, but he doesn't look away, and if it was anyone else, I'd put him down like a dog. I can't have anyone making me look like a pussy, so I send my men out of the room. The girl told them all about her rich daddy, and now it's time to find out the truth.

Jerry

I rise into pain and the kid is there. My shirt is pulled up. He's tapping the flat of his hand against my belly. My belly is jiggling.

"So. Tell me about yourself, old man."

"You want a date or something?"

My words are mush in my mouth, but I get them out.

"Ha. You're funny."

He pats my belly harder and my bladder is full and I have a new, urgent pain to add to the other more patient ones. I try to sit up, but I black out. I wake up when my head hits the floorboards.

"What I want to know is—what can you do for me and my men?"

"Give me a rifle. Let me show you."

He smiles a sharpened smile. I'm drifting, almost submerged, too tired and hurt to have any inhibitions. I'm about to tell the boy to go fuck himself when I feel a pinch on the meat inside my upper arm. It's Melanie. She's using her fingernails and giving me a hard, twisting pinch. It occurs to me that she's been running some kind of game with the boys. I fight down an urge to vomit. I somehow have the presence of mind not to look at her.

"I'll say it another way," says the kid. "Why shouldn't I end you—right here, right now?"

"I told them about the money, Dad," Melanie says. God bless her for throwing me a line.

I sigh. Bill Junior looks into my eyes, and I look away. I roll onto my side and curl up with my pain. There's a hint of triumph in Bill Junior's voice when he says, "Okay. We'll talk about the details later."

He leaves without letting us know anything about his plans for us. Melanie is still in the world and we're together, but when I sit up the pain takes the top of my head off. She helps me when I get sick into my canteen cup. I'm in a flat spin even though I'm only kneeling on the ground. Head wound. Concussion. I've had almost every other kind of wound in my life, so why not that?

"Are you okay?" she asks. "Are you still *you*?"

"I'm fine, baby."

TBI stands for *traumatic brain injury*. My voice sounds like the growl of an animal that has learned a few words. I say nothing about how she looks, and she doesn't say anything about how I look. I want to give her something but I have nothing to offer. I don't ask her if she needs anything. I can't escape into the safe territory of father-as-provider, so I hold out my arms and we hug. I want to lift us above the clouds and fly us away, but I don't squeeze her very hard because I don't know what-all might be broken inside us. I have no idea what these little monsters have done to us, and I can't let myself think about it.

"Don't worry," I say. "We've got these boys right where we want 'em."

"Ha," she says. "How do you get that ego of yours through doors?"

"Doors are for pussies. We Sharpes walk through walls."

She gives a bark of a laugh that turns into a cry. I smile from the surface of concussed blackness, then I sink back under it. I drift in and out through the morning and afternoon. Despair and regret and pain and fear for the well-being of what still remains of us, but when I wake up at dusk, I find the kernel of hope that I so badly missed. I've carried it with me on four continents and it hasn't ever left me completely. Determination, for whatever reason, comes around when the world goes to complete shit. Maybe it's only a figment of my desperation, but my mood lifts and I groove along in the hard, rebellious feeling of fighting pain. Family. God. The certainty that things will turn out as they're meant to turn out. And if things don't improve, we'll be in a better place, so there's no need to worry about a little pain.

I drift with the current, then I rise through a hole in the ice. She gives me water. It's sweet and cold and I get greedy and chug down half the canteen. She was our first baby, but she's my nurse now. She once wore shoes that barely fit over my thumb, but now she tells me "Good Daddy" and pats my hand. My stomach clenches but I keep the water down. I was getting dehydrated, and when I get the liquid inside me, my head starts to bleed again. It runs down the side of my face and joins with the tributaries from the cuts in my brows and lips. Melanie is trying to swab it away with a filthy towel when Luscious walks in with a group of boys.

"Damn," he says.

"That's just what I was thinking when I saw *you*," I say.

He squats on a dirty Cadillac floor mat and looks into my eyes. I look back. He doesn't have his gun drawn, but I feel like a small animal that's been hit by a car.

"You still bleeding like a pig? I thought you were done with that."

"Don't worry. I'll heal up just fine, but you'll always be ugly."

He laughs, but then he slaps my head and it's all I can do to stay conscious.

"Your daughter says you're a rich bastard."

"She said that?"

"She says you shit money. Was she lying?"

"No."

Melanie kneels beside me and Luscious moves close enough to grab her.

"Well, that's why you're still alive."

He points to the gaggle of boys. They look at me with the hatred of enemies.

"They want to have some more fun with you, but they aren't very bright. We don't have an airplane to spot for us anymore. A lot of us got killed in the last few weeks. We were barely holding on as it was, so you got to understand our mood. I can protect you for a little while, but I want you to think about how you're gonna pay us."

I sit up and look at him. I have no choice but to force myself into the Alpha mode. I've always hated it. It's stupid and obvious and without humor or the possibility of grace and it reminds us that we're animals, walking fists and cocks, and that we can never forget the politics of the playground. I have no idea why the illusion of dominance works so well, even when it's clearly an act, but it does work, and sometimes there's no choice but to use it.

I look straight into his eyes. The vertigo makes me sway, but I manage to keep my eyes locked on target. Luscious's eyes are hooded like the eyes of someone who has plenty to hide. Like a gangster. Like a terrorist. Like a bad little kid. He tries to return the hard look I'm giving him, but young guys generally can't pull that off with their elders. Older men simply know too much about youthful male depravity. He looks away, then he turns his eyes skyward and grabs his chin and crams himself into a thinking pose that must seem pathetic, even to him.

"Rich people know how to protect their shit," he says. "The world comes to an end, but rich fuckers still have their money."

I sit. I look. Here it comes.

"Don't tell me there ain't no way for you to get it."

"Okay. Sure. I'll call my accountant."

He moves over to Melanie. My stomach muscles tighten and my quadriceps flex and I'm up on my feet, but then my legs give way and I'm sitting on the ground in front of him. He grabs Melanie's arm and pulls her close to him. He squeezes. She gasps and then she rolls her eyes as if she's embarrassed that she reacted to the pain.

"I'll give you some time to heal up. Then you'll tell me about my payday." He looks at Melanie. "It's that, or we'll stop being so damned polite."

"Okay."

When I say it, I try to convince myself that it's a lie. I was never a POW before, but Mel and I are POWs now, and survival is all that matters. What I say under threat and duress doesn't mean a thing. My words to him have only one interpretation: *I will survive you.* I know it and he probably knows it, too, but I need to keep my defiance in the background. I can't push him too far in front of the others, but I can't bend over, either.

"Okay then, kid. If you want me to help you, you'll need to show some manners. Go back to your little circle jerk and maybe later I'll show you how the big boys make things happen.

Classes start as soon as I stop bleeding. Get some sleep. You're going to need it."

He picks up his rifle then he shakes his head.

"You talk to me like that in front of my men, and I'll shoot you on the spot."

"I know it."

He squeezes his rifle and hesitates. I know I'm about an inch away from being executed. I nod at him, the most respect I can muster, and he nods back and takes his leave.

I fall back and sleep for a long, unknowable time.

Susan

Scott walks tall beside me. His face is cracked with blood lines, and it makes me want to cry, but he's walking with purpose. I have the nonfunctional shotgun in the frozen claw of my right hand. My left arm is itching beneath its splint and bandages, and I hope the itching is a sign of healing, and not infection.

We walk without hesitation toward life or death. Scott is unarmed. I have two cold coins in my pocket, the coins Jerry took from the dead boy. The sky is a flat-bottomed, endless yellow cloud. If I saw it on television or on a picture postcard, I would say it was a *transitional* sky, the kind of sky that makes a person think, because it's neither storm nor calm, but could certainly become either, in time. The world is frozen and glittering in the strange light. We're half wet with perspiration and we have no idea what we're walking into. Wind through the grass. So much rotten winter grass. I'll be happy when the snow buries all the grass and footprints and empty cartridge cases and blood trails and corpses. I'll breathe easier when the world can at least pretend to be clean and whole.

We walk the shoulder of the road, then straight up onto the pavement. Bootfalls on cracked asphalt. Flutters of wind in my ears, and we haven't had our hair cut for weeks and we're all dirty and aflutter.

The thought of Melanie makes both of my arms ache, and I'm about to start thinking about Jerry, too, so I push the fear mostly away and concentrate on the *now*. The mountain wind is tricky and we're half frozen and it's not easy to walk a straight line, but we walk in the approximate center of the road. The buildings of the town grow as we approach. It takes hours or minutes or seconds, but soon enough we're walking on the main drag of Virginia City, Nevada.

We stop in front of the Bucket 'o Blood Saloon. Dark shapes move behind red curtains and I feel eyes watching us. Scott takes a side stance and puts his hands on his hips. I manage to sling the shotgun over my good shoulder. Scott turns to face me, and he gives me a hug. I'm too cold to feel it, but I hug him back with all the motherhood that's ever been inside me. We stand on the main street of town and we present its inhabitants with a public display of mother-son affection. It's brilliant of Scott, and heartfelt, and I love my son and my love is plain for all the world to see, no matter what the world has come to. It's an offering of sorts, and an opportunity to say goodbye. We say the usual things. Love you. Love you, too. Proud of you, whatever happens. We hold each other in the cold hug that could be our last.

We stand under the weight of watching eyes. Scott pulls away and puts his arm around my shoulder. We're both almost to a point beyond shivering, and I know we can't possibly survive without shelter. There's nothing left to do but throw ourselves on the mercy of whomever.

"Hello?" Scott calls.

"Anybody home?" I say.

I try to shout. The words don't come out as loudly as I'd intended. But I don't care how my voice sounds. We're in the middle of the road and there's no way we can avoid being in a crossfire, if a crossfire is what we are about to receive. May it not come to that, Lord, but if it does, it's Your will, so please guide the bullets straight and true, and bless this bountiful crossfire to our bodies.

The Bucket 'o Blood Saloon has seen better days. White paint is flaking onto the graywood boardwalk. There's a boarded-up fudge shop behind us. A knickknack shop and a camera shop and a coffee shop and the Ye Olde Café. Both sides of the street are lined with sagging boardwalks and the old, wooden store signs are swinging and banging around on their rusted chains, but there aren't any tourists to tempt. And the signs seem to have taken on a new meaning. They're saying, We regret...We regret to...We regret to inform you that we're sorry, they say. Our deepest sympathies are with you. Maybe someday you'll come again with money in your wallets and purses, and your smiling kiddies in tow, and you'll eat and drink under sunny skies, your vacation budgets the only limitation to your pleasure, but don't worry about that now, poor dears.

The front door of the saloon bangs open. A man steps onto the boardwalk. He's not young, but he's tall and strong-looking.

He has a salt-and-pepper ponytail and a gray beard. He wears a holstered pistol at his side, but he doesn't make any threatening movements. Scott looks up at the second-story windows. I follow his line of sight and see the muzzles of rifles and shotguns pointed at us.

"Come on over. Let's see what we've got."

The man's voice is reasonable-sounding, with the depth of authority. It's the voice of a broadcaster or a trial lawyer or a politician. Maybe it's the voice of a good man, but there's no way to tell, and no reason to assume it.

He gestures us forward. We walk shoulder to shoulder. The man is above us on the boardwalk and we look up into his face. His eyes are wide but unreadable, and he could be a saint or a he could be a lunatic. He's older than I am. He's an aging Baby Boomer but first impressions are what keep us alive, the less favorable the better, so I don't trust him, not at all. I push a small giggle back down into my throat, and maybe it isn't appropriate but I can no longer find the line between humor and hysteria.

"Mother and son, I take it?"

We nod. I'm trying not to smile like an idiot. Like a killer about to die.

"Yes, praise God. I see the family resemblance. I'm James Johnson, but people call me Pastor Jim." He turns to the saloon and puts his hand on the doorknob. "We'll get you warmed up and fed, just as soon as you put your weapon on the ground and let us search you."

A man and a woman come out of the saloon. They're the same general age as the ponytail man—Baby Boomers with wrinkles and gray hair and they're no doubt packing varicose veins and cellulite and hemorrhoids and all of it. Not so long ago, it seemed like the whole U.S. economy was organized to treat the nasty little personal problems of aging Baby Boomers, but not anymore. Now they're growing old with all the simple harshness that nature intended. The woman looks very tired and otherwise unwell. Her face is long and loose and it hangs from the front of her skull like a coating of wax.

The woman comes at me, holding her hands out for the shotgun. She puts her hands on it, like a blind woman trying to see what it is. I let go and she takes it. The wind steadily blows away what's left of our warmth. The world smells like dried mud and dead grass and a coming snow. The barrels of the long guns above us don't waver. Scotty's arm is pressed against mine and he tenses it hard. I step in front of my son and let the over-looking muzzles track me. Scott sighs in my ear. "No, Mom," he says, and he steps out beside me again.

The woman props my shotgun against the boardwalk, and she and the man search us. They unzip our coats and reach into our shirts and run their hands down our legs. They turn our pockets out, and the man clucks his tongue and takes Scott's folding knife.

All hints of humor leave my hysteria, and I want to giggle like a madwoman. Pastor Jim opens his arms wide, as if he's about to take flight. He smiles and his teeth are capped a hard, neon white, but his gums have a grayish tinge. The mountain wind blows harder and the clouds look serious, threatening, and I'm sure they carry snow. Pastor Jim stops smiling and shakes his head.

He turns his back and has a conversation with God. Apparently God has a lot on His mind, because it takes a while. Pastor Jim finally nods and turns back to face us.

"Look here, it's lack of faith that got us into this predicament."

He looks into the sky and narrows his eyes. He waves at the men looking down on us, and they pull their weapons inside and close the window. "This time there's room at the inn for everyone. Come inside and meet us, will you?"

Scott steps up on the boardwalk and approaches Pastor Jim. He holds out his hand and they shake. Scott makes the introductions. I don't know why he pretends to trust this man. He's always had a very good BS detector, and I feel like I felt when he was a little boy, running up and starting conversations with strangers. I'd thought then that it was simple animal behavior, the naïve exuberance of the puppy, but now I see that it's become a calculated thing, fully part of him, and also it's a ploy. Only his mother can see the seams in the veneer of his friendly sincerity. My son can no longer bring himself to trust anyone. My sweet boy has become a cunning man, and he's measuring Pastor Jim for a coffin, or a pat on the back, and I don't know which.

We thump across the boardwalk and enter the saloon. It's warm inside, but at first I can't feel it. A fire roars in a cast-iron cookstove and a pot of stew is bubbling its rich promise into the world. The pain of thawing starts and I'm unsteady. My skin starts to itch from my top to my bottom. I sway on my feet for a while before I realize that we're in a room crowded with people. They're ordinary-seeming people gathered together in the saloon. Men and women of various ages and races sitting at tables and drinking glasses of wine and pints of beer. They stand from their tables and the people at the bar turn to greet us. Nods and lifted hands and tight little grins—the rituals of the all-important first impression.

Children peer from behind the adults and I try to smile at them. My face is frozen into what I hope is a pleasant grin, but what I fear is a grimace. So many people meeting us for the first time, and we're among them and we're not shooting at each other. The saloon is close with heat and breath, and people have been living without basic services for so long that I expect them to put out a powerful stench, but I catch whiffs of floral scents, perfume and deodorant and aftershave lotion. My own body smells like fear and grime and anger, and for the first time since the bombs fell, I feel unclean in comparison to others.

The drinkers clear two barstools at the shiny mahogany bar, but we remain standing. A young woman looks into my eyes and she seems to understand our lack of trust. She raises her eyebrows as if to say that everything will be okay. She looks at Scott in a different way entirely, and I feel both protective and relieved.

Pastor Jim makes a great show of putting on a white apron before he steps behind the bar.

"What'll it be, folks?"

I want to be polite, but it's been so long since I've been served that I don't know what to say. We stand dumbly at the bar.

"Okay, then," says Pastor Jim. "A shot of brandy for the lady and a whiskey for the young man."

"No," I say. My voice is rough. I sound like an old, heavy-smoking barfly. "Something nonalcoholic for me."

He smiles and nods.

"The fruit of the vine and spirit of the still isn't for everyone, and wise is the person who knows it."

He points to the cookstove. A young woman in a long dress takes up a heating pad and wraps it around the handle of a tea kettle. She lifts it from the stove and brings it to Pastor Jim. He reaches for it and she's careful to make sure his hand is protected by the heating pad. Their hands touch when they make the transfer and she's very gentle and Pastor Jim smiles down at her and she blushes.

Pastor Jim pours a clean, hot stream into two mugs and rips open packages of instant hot chocolate and uses a silver spoon to mix it. He lifts a bottle of whiskey and looks at Scott and Scott grins and nods and he pours a generous shot into Scott's mug. He mixes the drinks again with his spoon and slides the mugs in front of us.

I pick up the mug with no whiskey in it and hold it in my raw and itching hands. I breathe in the smell and the steam. I take a sip. It burns the roof of my mouth, but I immediately take another sip. It's good and sweet and hot. My mouth tightens from the sudden blessing of sugar, and then I'm in heaven, sipping hot chocolate in the company of friendly seeming people.

Scott takes his mug and lifts it to Pastor Jim. He holds it like it's the most precious thing he's held in years. He takes a sip and he can't help but sigh. It's a loud sigh and he smacks his lips beneath a thick hot chocolate mustache. The people laugh and raise their glasses and we raise ours in return and we drink deeply, not fully trusting our new closeness to others, but not pushing away from them, either.

Melanie

Dad talks tough but his face is a mess of half-dried blood. His wounds are rubbery like old ketchup and I watch him spitting dark blotches into his canteen cup.

"How are you, really?"

He stands up straight, but it takes a sad, long time for him to do it. He bends his destroyed face into a look of fake seriousness. It's like he's pretending to be a president or a king or something.

"If I were any better, I'd have a serious paparazzi problem."

I laugh before I can catch myself.

"I'll have you know that minstrels will yet write songs about us," he says.

His voice is muffled by the swelling in his face. He sounds like Marlon Brando in *The Godfather*. I think he's *trying* to sound like Brando, but I can guess how desperate he is, and how he's trying to make me feel better. I want to cry. I want to give him a hug that might make us both feel better, but I'm afraid he'll fall down if I try it.

"Sit down," I say.

He's swaying like a drunk.

"Please," I say.

I reach for him but he puts his hands at the small of his back and staggers in front of me like a stoned general inspecting his command. He's trying to smile but he has to be in pain.

Something hurts inside him and I can see the pain-waves pass through his expression. For a second, his eyes get so far away that I almost move close to catch him, but then it passes.

"I'm okay. I'm still here, baby. Don't give up. Don't you ever give up," he says.

"Not me. And not you, either."

"Not ever."

"It's just not going to happen."

"No way, no how."

Part of me is broken, too, but I can't let him see it. Not now. Not ever. I give him a hard look instead, the one that means I'm in a fighting mood. He's seen it plenty of times before, and when he sees it now, he lets that thing into his eyes—the flash of light that shows pride and love and the opening of his competitive streak, all at once. It's a classic Dad look. I don't know how much it hurts him to beam those waves at me, but I'm happy to see them.

"Do you see me standing here?" I say. "Do you know who I am?"

"You're Melanie the Strong, high priestess of peace and the vegetarian way."

"You bet I am."

"Defender of all shadow-casting life, wielder of the supernatural powers bestowed upon those who eat meatless chickens."

He can still piss me off and crack me up at the same time. I smile with my eyes. It's been a long time since I've been able to do that. Dad must've let all the air out of his lungs, because he takes a deep breath. He winces and mouths the word "Dammit." It doesn't take a doctor to see that he has at least one broken rib.

We stand close. The door of the shack is open and one of the boys is watching us, so Dad doesn't stoop to a public display of affection. But he nods, and it's the same Dad nod I've seen all my life.

I give him sips of water and he sleeps most of the day. The boys give us a can of Dinty Moore stew and I save it for as long as I can. I let it sit untouched until the thought of it drives me crazy. I use a little military can opener to get the top off and I let the food warm next to the propane heater, taking my time to heighten the anticipation. It smells rich and salty, and I can't wait too long, for fear that one of the boys will come and take it.

The food bubbles and I hold the can in a filthy gray rag that might've been a bright red color when it was new. I stir, then I use a plastic spoon to pick out a selection of the veggies, steaming from the can, into a plastic thermos cup. I slurp them down as Dad sleeps, or pretends to sleep, I can never tell with Dad. I eat celery and carrots and pieces of potatoes and the tender shreds of beef that I accidentally-on-purpose allow to stick to the vegetables. It's a warm slice of heaven, and I can't help but enjoy myself, no matter how stupid and pathetic it seems under the circumstances.

I eat a third of the stew, then I lift the can with the dirty rag and tap it on the floor near Dad. He opens his eyes. He groans before he can stop himself, and then he struggles into a sitting position. I hold out the can. He takes my spoon and reaches in and takes a piece of the meat and puts it in his mouth. He tries to chew but he grimaces and it takes him a long time to get it down. He dips out some of the gravy, but that's about all he can get down. He pretends to belch, thanks me, asks me if I'm okay, then he sleeps the sun into the ground.

* * *

When he wakes up in the morning he starts a slow stretching routine that makes him look like a giant sloth. His face is blank, but he's not fooling me about the pain. He staggers for a while at quarter speed, trying to pace. He's stiff but then he either limbers up or he simply puts the pain out of his mind. I think it's probably only by force of will that he manages to walk in slow motion up a row of Fords and around the Chevy and back. He has a lousy walking form. It's very early and most of the boys are still asleep, except the two who are standing guard. The guards watch him. One of them giggles and points, and the other one doesn't laugh in return.

Most of the boys sleep late, but eventually Bill Junior takes Dad away. He's gone for three hours. I have no idea what Dad is telling them, but it has to be bullshit. I hope he talks them into doing something that will get them caught or killed, and I don't feel very bad about hoping it.

While Dad is away, I take some clothes from a pile of looted stuff. A kid named Benwah is guarding me, but he doesn't say anything. I can tell he wants to do something to me, but he doesn't dare. So I have a flannel shirt and a pair of pants for Dad, and a pair of overalls for me. The overalls have about twenty buttons, and I like them because they won't be easy to take off.

Dad comes back at about 4 p.m. It's getting really cold, and a wind is blowing. The boys don't give us anything to eat. I lead Dad toward the shack, but some of the boys are in there, warming themselves. Benwah is their spokesman. He tells me that since I'm not putting out anymore, we can't stay in the shack anymore.

We sit on a stack of old tires outside. It's a cold night and the clouds are boiling. They look like they're about to drop snow. They're still a weird color, and I know they're up to something, but I'm not a weather expert, so I could be wrong.

When it starts to get dark, Bill Junior walks past us, strolling across the dirty junkyard gravel like it's the deck of a ship. I ask him if we can sleep in one of the wrecked cars. He says, "Knock yourself out." He's standing with his chest out, trying to be all studly, but he must know I'm not buying it.

"Take care of your old man," he says. He says it in a soft way, and he could be showing me that he's a normal human being, or he could be trying to trick me into thinking he cares. I wonder if he has a living father. I'm sure that if he does, they don't talk much. I try to care about him, but I'm not Jesus Christ or anything.

The car I choose for us is an old yellow Ford taxi with wide bench seats. It was rear-ended, but the passenger compartment is in pretty good shape. We get in and cover ourselves with the clothes I took. They're still damp, but the car warms with our body heat, and it's not too uncomfortable. Dad tries to sleep in the front seat and I try to sleep in the back. The vinyl upholstery smells like all the butts that sat in the taxi and it's cold, but then the night goes all soft and quiet and warm, and I sleep hard.

I'm having one of those dreams that let me have full control. We're in Hawaii, all of us on the beach. I know it's a dream, right at the beginning, but I manage to hold on to it until it becomes more real. We're laughing. We're stretched out on lounge chairs, letting the sun warm our skin. I think we might be drunk, but it's warm and the sea rolls in and out and smoke from a Hawaiian barbecue is wafting over to us. Then we're sitting at a table and half-naked men are bringing the food.

Barbecued pork with pineapple sauce for the omnivores. Grilled veggie kabobs for me, with caramelized onions and zucchini and cherry tomatoes and papaya, all glazed with a sweet Polynesian sauce.

I lift my hands to the food, then I lift a kabob out to Mom and Dad and Scotty, like I'm giving a toast, and then I'm holding a mai tai glass. We lift our glasses to each other. I get the drinking straw into my lips, but it's not like most of my dreams because I actually get to take a big pull. It's pure heaven, the sweet punch flowing into me like love, confidence, peace. I get goose bumps and I'm laughing, but then there's an earthquake. The island is heaving and rolling like it's on springs and Dad puts his hand on my shoulder and gives me a shake. It's dark; we're in a smashed-up taxi and he's telling me to be quiet.

It smells like something's burning. The car windows are covered with snow. Dad must've been outside in it, because his hair is full of snowflakes. I can't see anything outside but blankness. The snow has us insulated and I'm warmer than I've been in weeks. I remember how Dad used to wake us up when we were visiting Portland at Christmastime and we had a rare snowfall. He and Mom would wake Scotty and me and make us hot chocolate and we'd watch the snow fall, the four of us watching as the clean blanket put itself together over the mud and the gray stalks of Gramma's flowerbed, and flocked the dark stands of Douglas firs. We'd watch the magic of it, the way it added the light of excitement to the night, then we'd go back to bed happy and warm.

But we're in a stinking taxi now and I'm not into the magic of snow. Something smells burned, and I don't know what it is. I try to huddle again beneath my covers, but Dad keeps shaking my shoulder until I have no choice but to sit up.

"Get bundled. Let's go."

He opens the driver's side door. Giant flakes wobble from the dark sky. The smell of burning gets stronger. I think there's something wrong with the snow. There's no wind and it's falling like frozen volcanic ash. I roll down a window but there isn't any sign of the boys. They're huddled in their motel rooms, no doubt. I don't feel their eyes watching me and it crosses my mind that maybe a snowstorm makes guys less sure of themselves, at least at first. Maybe a big change in the weather distracts them from their confidence, because it shows them that they're not in complete control of the universe.

My lungs go tight. The outside air swirls into the car, and it's colder than any air I've ever breathed. I don't have to mention that we'll probably die if we go out in this. Dad has to know it, but he tosses clothes into the backseat and I put them on in layers, pantyhose and sweatpants and a sweatshirt and then the overalls with twenty buttons. He throws me another sweatshirt, and it has a green marijuana leaf on the front, and then he hands me a big coat. We have enough layers to maybe give us a chance. Dad must've stolen the stuff from the boys. With the stuff I took earlier, it just might be enough to keep me from freezing.

I put the clothes on in the order Dad throws them. It's no accident that everything fits me just fine. Dad always seems to be able to solve problems, just when everyone else is giving up. Sometimes I wonder if he waits on purpose for people to start giving up before he steps in to solve problems.

Anyhow, I'm bundled like a mummy in clothes that smell like other people, bad living people and good dead people, but I feel almost safe. Dad gets dressed and the taxi shakes on its springs when he moves. The boys didn't take our boots, so we put them on over two layers of filthy socks. I have no idea where

Dad found the socks. I've been looking for a decent pair ever since I got here. Gloves are even more rare, but Dad gives me a pair of those fancy women's gloves they sell at Christmastime. He pulls a pair of wool socks over his hands and we get out and make for the freeway.

Dad holds my hand as we stumble through the junkyard. It's a maze of wrecks, and it's full of sleeping monsters, but somehow we manage to pass through the front gate. We take the cold alley to a road that leads to the highway. I can't see the alley, but only remember it, and I paste that memory on top of the snowblind nothingness around us, so I can at least pretend to know where we're going. The snow covers the land, and we're covered with it, too. It smells like barbecued crap, but it softens our footsteps and makes us invisible. Dad is walking all hunched over, but he's setting a good pace, and we're free and invisible and blind on the open plain.

Scott

It feels weird to be warm and surrounded by people who aren't trying to kill us. But they also aren't trying very hard to convince us that they're happy to see us, either. They watch us drink our drinks. They smile, but nobody talks to us. A really hot girl lowers her head and looks at me through the tops of her eyes. Her eyes aren't green or brown or green-blue or gray-blue. They're deep blue-blue, the color of Crater Lake in wintertime. It's my favorite color. She's wearing a hippie sundress kind of thing with no bra. She's long-legged and barefoot and her calves are curved in a way that has my complete attention. She's tapping her foot against the floor and the beat she's keeping causes her goodies to jiggle under the sundress. I could look at her all day long, but I look at her face and there's something in her expression, a warning maybe. The people go back to talking about whatever they were talking about before, but it seems kind of fake. I'm trying not to look at the hippie girl when Pastor Jim takes my mug and adds another shot of whiskey and leans forward.

"You and your mother look pretty used up. It's no picnic out there, is it?"

"It's pretty bad."

"Glad you found us?"

"Sure."

Pastor Jim leans even closer and talks in a low voice.

"Any sign of the government?"

"Only the bombers that fly over."

He nods and moves out of my personal space. Mom is shivering even though the stove is putting out some serious BTUs. She drains her mug.

"We're from Sacramento," she says. "Originally."

"I'm sorry," Pastor Jim says. He picks up a bar towel and wipes a drink puddle from the bar. "Sacramento was a great town and, being a religious man, I've always been partial to its name."

Mom sputters or coughs and Pastor Jim holds out his hand to her. She looks confused for a second but then she pushes her mug at him and he fills it with coffee and hands it back.

Five guys come downstairs. They're carrying long guns. One by one they hand their weapons to Pastor Jim. He stacks them behind the bar. One of the guys is my age. His hair is short, like the jarhead haircut Dad wore in the Marines. He sees the whiskey bottle on the bar. He motions to Pastor Jim for a shot, and Pastor Jim pours him one.

"Life's a bitch, huh?" the young guy says to me.

"It's not so bad right now."

"Yeah? Is that your mother beside you?"

I nod. He chugs down his beer.

"Nice-looking lady. My mom's over there."

He turns his back to the bar. He waves a hand at one of the tables across the room, but I can't tell which lady is his mother.

"It's kinda funny. She used to run her own business. That café across the street? She made the best chili in Nevada. Nobody hardly ever ate the crap they serve in here."

The guy gets a weird smile, like he's crazy or he's about to get into a fight. He leans in close. "But that's all over and done with. Right now, my old lady is one of Pastor Jim's whores, and she's not his favorite whore, either, if you know what I mean."

The other guys who came downstairs close around the young guy like magnets to steel. The young guy smiles really big and turns to face the bar. Pastor Jim reaches out and snatches the shot glass from his hand.

"Why not try to be friendly, Sam?"

"Oops. I guess you didn't tell 'em what's goin' on here."

I put my mug on the bar and move closer to Mom. Pastor Jim's face goes blank, but it's a lousy poker face. He's killing mad. He nods and three of the upstairs guys grab the Sam guy, one on each arm, and a huge dude grabs Sam by the shirt and twists it until the buttons start to pop. Sam is yelling something about "You're no more God's prophet than I am." He says, "Phony, phony bastard," and Pastor Jim's hand flicks over the bar and backhands Sam in the mouth.

The other people stay at their tables. They look down and

around and anywhere but at the action that's happening. Some of them look at each other and some of them shrug.

Sam takes the pastor's knuckles hard across the mouth. A line of blood runs down from his lips to the tip of his chin and drips onto the floor, but Sam smiles and asks for another whiskey. I like the guy, then. Pastor Jim smiles back at him and pours another shot, but I get the impression he's granting Sam a last wish. He pours shots for all the upstairs guys and they belly up to the bar, all but the big guy, who stays close behind Sam. Pastor Jim nods and the big guy puts a meaty hand on his belt knife and clicks open the retaining snap.

I bump my shoulder against Mom and she takes the hint and we slide toward the door. We try to move without seeming to move, but it feels like we're standing on a stage with a spotlight on us. The people at the tables see what we're doing, and they look like they're desperate to tell Pastor Jim, but they don't say anything. They make weird expressions and point their faces at us and a fat man in coveralls goes into a fake coughing fit that turns his big cheeks red, but Pastor Jim's attention isn't on us.

We back away until I can put my hand on the doorknob. It's cold. It's kind of dark in the saloon and kind of light outside, and I hesitate to open the door, but then Mom wraps her hand around mine and we turn the doorknob together. We shoulder the door open and fall outside and it's like we got pulled into a big snow globe, because the stuff is falling like crazy all over us. It's the weirdest snow I've ever seen, because it's gray, mostly, with something like charcoal in it, and it smells like a crack-house fire.

We run up the street and turn into an alley. We take a side street for a while and then we get ourselves completely lost in the gray blizzard. We hear shouts and swearing and a few wild shots, but we're gone, baby, gone. The gray snow is blowing and we can't see anything, but we manage to jog onto the highway and north out of town. I'm scared shitless, and it sucks to be unarmed. We can't see more than ten feet in front of us. The road has ditches on both sides and that's how we manage to stay on it. We slow to a fast walk, then a slower one. I've never been this cold before. I don't know how many degrees below zero it is, but it's a lot. We seem to walk forever, and maybe it's only all in my head, but the snow all of a sudden is up to our ankles and then it's up to our shins and then I don't know how deep it is. We push our feet into it and through it, walking until walking in the open would be a death sentence, even if there wasn't any radiation in the snow.

Mom is praying. She's praying straight into the storm and we stumble onto something man-made. It's a hollow thing sticking up like a yellow shoebox in the middle of the road. We stop and kick our boots against it. I lean down and clear away some snow and pound my frozen hand against it. It makes a hollow sheet-metal sound. I brush away more of the dirty snow, and my hand is smeared black, but I start to dig.

It's an overturned school bus. Mom yells a prayer of thanks into the wind. The snow is drifted against everything that hasn't blown away, and it's a miracle we found the bus instead of walking straight past it into frozen hell. The bus is lying on its driver's side, so we dig until we find the passenger door. I push against the door's long hinges but my frozen hands can't make anything happen. I pull and push and Mom pulls with me, but the door won't open and I'm starting to feel warm all over. I know it's not a good thing to be warm now, but it feels pretty good. I tell Mom I want to lie down, but she doesn't hear my voice in the wind.

So I do lie down. I curl up on the door and wipe away the crappy snow and I look through a window into the interior. Mom lies down, too, and wraps herself around me. The snow is burying us and we're kind of warm but then I get an adrenaline rush that makes me stand up. I'm about to pound my head against the glass when our combined weight causes the door to move. The door opens a crack and I put my hand in the crack and Mom helps me and we use our weight and the leverage of our forearms and the last of our energy to make the crack big enough, then we fall into the bus. We're maybe only prolonging the inevitable by falling out of cold death and into dark purgatory, but it feels good to be out of the wind.

Bill Junior

The man on duty that night is one of the boozers. He's about fifteen and I call him Dog, because he gets a really funny hang-dog look on his face when he realizes that he's chugged down all the booze in sight. When he knocks on the door of my motel room, he's only slightly buzzed. It's the armpit of the night, and I answer the door with the Ruger .44 held behind me.

Dog tries to stand up straight, like a fake soldier standing at attention in a movie, but he's swaying back and forth.

"They took off," he says.

"Who did?"

"The girl and her old man."

I let the Ruger hang down beside my leg. Dog tries to keep a straight face, but he's practically pissing himself. He stands at attention and I think he'd sell his mother for a bottle of Jim Beam, but I'm cool with him. I don't tax him or have him whipped, and he's grateful as hell. He says it was on account of the snow. He says he's sorry. He says that if there's anything he can do for me, he'll do it, and I tell him I know he will.

It's snowing outside. The bonfire is smoking, or something, because I'm about to puke from the smell of it. I'm not in any hurry. I get back into my warm bed and it feels good to think about what I'll do next. I'm pissed, yeah, but part of me is happy to have something fun to do. Dog is still hanging around my room and I tell him that we'll give the rabbits a good head start before we do our thing. I tell him we'll be like tigers playing with rabbits, and we'll have more fun if we give them a little more time to run. He says okay, and he looks relieved, but when I tell him not to talk about it to anyone, he looks scared again, and that's okay with me.

I get up early in the morning. Everything is covered with something nasty. It's the snow. It stinks and it looks like it came out of the sky's asshole. I get the men up, walking through the stinking snow and whooping it up to get the show going. I put together a crew to shovel walkways to the firepit.

The morning crew uses gasoline to get a fire going. I tell them to make something special for breakfast. Lots of kids who end up in juvie have experience in the food industry and it comes in handy sometimes. The men on breakfast crew do a kick-ass job of it. They get eggs from the chicken coop and some milk from our new cows and they use some of the hippie cheese to make us omelets.

The snow smells like shit, but we eat our hot omelets and drink our strong coffee to get ourselves going. When I finish my breakfast, I light a cigar, and the men who have smokes light up with me. I feel like a rich man. My stomach doesn't feel so good, but then it mellows out. Some of the men barf up their breakfasts. I don't say anything, because either it's their own damned fault for drinking too much last night or the snow has radiation in it—and there's shit-all I can do about that. Anyhow, if we've only got a few days left to live, we might as well do what makes us happy.

My stomach cramps up and some of the men run back to their motel rooms. I spit for a while, but then the sick time passes. We get mostly better, and the men pretend to be all worked up about the hunt. Before they can start bitching about their little tummyaches, I give a direct order. I tell them to make snowshoes out of whatever they can find. Luscious divides them into teams, one team to get stuff and another team to make the snowshoes. They use hacksaws to cut metal from cars. They use hand drills to bolt together frames from the seat brackets of SUVs, then they tie on laced strips of upholstery, then they tie their creations to their boots.

By the middle of the morning, the sun shines strong enough through the overcast that we can almost see our shadows. There's too much snow for our trucks, so we'll be carrying everything on our backs, our food and shelter and weapons and ammo. Four of the men are too sick to go with us. I tell them to stay, and to post a guard while we're gone.

The others load themselves up like pack mules. They walk all hunched over, like they're trying not to shit themselves, but they don't bitch about anything. They're like dogs before a hunt. It's like they changed from apes into human beings, over thousands and thousands of years, to do just exactly *this*.

Jerry

She hasn't let me hold her hand since she was four years old. We walk carefully into a blizzard that smells like fire. We have a new enemy now, and we shouldn't be breathing it into our bodies. I unzip my coat and tear off a strip of the lining and wrap it around Melanie's nose and mouth. It's thin protection, but it's all I can give. She lets me do it, and she waits while I cover my own face. Then we walk hand in hand, as if I'm a new father again, and she's still learning the trick of walking in wide-open places. It's like we're crossing a huge parking lot together, exposed to the threats of the world, and trusting only each other.

There's not enough wind to make a Hollywood-style blizzard, but visibility is less than ten feet. It's a weird dreamscape and it causes me to doubt that we're really here, and free. I listen for shouts or gunfire, but I only hear the sound of the wind and our breathing and our feet shushing through the snow. I'm full to the brim with adrenaline, and I feel sick to my stomach, and the pain in my head is throbbing at different beats than the pain in my ribs.

I pray for wisdom and luck and protection from alpha, beta, and gamma radiation. But I've done too much praying lately and I don't want to wear out my welcome on high, so I give it a rest. There's no telling which way we're traveling. Our only chance is to find the road and try to figure out our north from our south. But no. This isn't about escaping anymore. We need to find shelter, no matter how close we are to our enemies. I'm tired and I let my mind drift into smartass territory. I pray for Him to guide us to a hotel that has a roaring fireplace and an open bar with hot coffee drinks and a buffet table piled high with hot chow. I pray for a bubbling hot tub and maybe a jazz quartet with a stand-up bass and a vibraphone and a clean hollow-body guitar and a wicked technician on the skins. I try to smile and I hope God is laughing with me, rather than at me, but there's no way to tell.

My skull feels like the shell of a dropped hard-boiled egg. I walk for minutes at a time without knowing which way we're going. My stomach cramps with nausea, but I hold my gorge back with the undependable power of my mind. Melanie seems to be okay. She stumbles sometimes, and it's not her normal way of walking, but the girl has been through things I don't want to think about.

I feel bad for her, because she must think I have a plan. She's trusting me to lead us to safety and I can't let myself stagger, and mostly I don't. The snow makes the air feel warmer, but that can't be true. I don't let myself trust the warmth that seeps up my arms and legs, closer to the core of me.

After a long, unreal time, I walk into a mile marker. I brush the snow away to get a better look. It's a white sign against gray snow and it has a black "5" on it. I have no idea what the number represents, but I know we're standing next to the highway. I pull Melanie along faster, her frozen hand in mine. She follows me without comment or complaint, and that starts to worry me, and then I walk straight into an invisible wall. But it's not really a wall. It's the aluminum skin of an RV. I feel along the flank of the great metallic beast until I find the door. It's not locked. I pull it open but then I close it again. I try to brush the snow from Melanie's clothes, but it feels like I'm smearing mud into them. We're contaminated, but it's too damned cold to do without clothes, so the best I can do is pray.

The RV creaks on its springs when we climb aboard. It's dark and cold inside, but we're sealed from the weather. I pull the flowered curtains and rummage around for something heavier to hang over the windows, but the interior of the place has been looted, and it's no mystery who looted it.

I grope my way to the galley. I pull the wool socks from my hands, and it's like my fingers are made of wood. I turn on one of the burners and I hear a propane hiss, but the igniter doesn't work and I don't have any matches. I turn off the gas and feel into every nook and cranny of the cupboards with my frozen hands. I can't find any matches. I go to the cab and check the glove box and storage bins. I'm beat to hell and freezing and tired and sick to my stomach and I haven't cried since forever but tears start to come. It's very strange because I don't feel much of anything inside. The pressure releases itself from my tear ducts and I'm about to curl up and pick the place where we'll freeze to death, when Melanie taps me on the shoulder. She hands me a smooth plastic shape that turns out to be a Bic lighter.

It takes me almost a full minute to get the propane burners lit, but I finally manage to do it. The despair is gone for the time being as we warm our hands over sweet blue flames. The pain of thawing sets in and it crosses my mind that our shadows must be huge on the wall behind us, but I don't turn to look. I get my hands to work again and then I open the oven and I light it, too. I put my arm around Melanie's shoulder and she doesn't rebuff me.

"You don't have any marshmallows on you, do you?" I say.

I look into her half-lit face. She tries to smile but she

doesn't quite pull it off. I'm trying to think of something to say, something light and confident, but then something goes wrong inside me. My stomach clenches up, and there's no will-power on earth strong enough to stop what's coming. I open the door just in time, puking so hard that the plates of my skull move.

The sickness doesn't pass, but my stomach is empty, so I go back inside. I try to keep my dry heaves to myself, but it isn't an easy thing to do. The heaves make me feel as if I'm pass-ing my soul from my body. I'm about to pass out on my feet, so I lie down on the RV's couch and curl up. I hear Melanie getting sick in the RV's little bathroom, and my tears start to come again, but then God has mercy, and He takes my pain away.

When I wake up, the pain and nausea make me want to pass out again, so that's just what I do. I get a series of little flashes between the time my eyes open and my circuit breaker pops. I don't know how many times I try to swim back to the surface, but after a while I manage to climb back into the world.

I'm in a warm place. The wind has picked up and the RV rocks on its springs. Melanie is on the floor beside me. I reach out to check her vitals. The pain of moving takes my breath away, but I put my hand to her throat. She's warm and her heartbeat is strong. I thank God.

It's warm enough inside that our breath isn't condensing the air, and then it gets warm enough for us to start to sweat. I take off my coat. I wake Melanie and tell her to take off her coat. If we get soaked with sweat, we won't live long if we have to go outside. I hang our coats over the windows that face the camp of our enemies.

"Are we dying?" Melanie asks. "Because if we're dying,

shouldn't we be saying stuff like 'I'm sorry' and 'I love you' and things like that?"

"I'm sorry. I love you. But I don't think we're dying."

"How do you know?"

"We'd be sicker if we were."

"Tell me the truth. You learned about radiation by watching movies, didn't you?"

"No. I was trained to fight in an NBC environment. NBC stands for nuclear, biological, and chemical."

"Great. Good for you. What about cancer?"

"Let's not worry about that now, okay?"

"Remember when I went through my hypochondriac phase?"

"Yeah."

"Well, I think it's coming back."

It's getting a bit too warm. I turn down the burners and the stove, and then I give the RV a more careful search. Hand-sewn curtains and cabinetry refinished by clumsy hands and a puked-in crapper and a mattress with two sunken ovals where its owners once slept. The vehicle is registered in the state of Arizona to a Mr. and Mrs. Weiner. I tell Melanie, pronouncing it "Weener," and she says their family name makes perfect sense, and that maybe it sums up the whole human race.

It makes me happy to hear her old tone of voice. She riffs on it, talking about weener-mobiles and weener-controlled houses of government and little weeners who like to blow things up. When she decides to give the Weiner thing a break, I go back to searching the RV. I imagine the RV people were a retired couple, taking a trip to see what they could of the world before their time was up. Maybe they were driving their house on wheels over the river and through the woods to visit their grandkids.

The vinyl of the driver's seat is cracked. It smells like old people who believed in saving water, and I almost get sick again. When I regain some control of my gullet, I reach beneath the driver's seat, afraid that I'll find the leavings of a picked nose or the last gray hairs from a bald head, but what I find is a homemade compartment. It's open and empty. I guess Mr. Weiner might've had a gun in there. I check beneath the passenger seat and find that Mrs. Weiner also had a compartment. Equal-opportunity kind of people, they were. What's good for him is good for her, share and share alike.

Mrs. Weiner's compartment is smaller and I almost don't find it, but it's there and it's still closed. Its plywood door isn't locked. I pull it open and put my hand on a snub-nosed Chief's Special Airweight revolver. I open the cylinder and I thank God that it's carrying a full load of five hollowpoints. I reach in again and find a box of Hydra-Shoks, twenty rounds of extra determination and wherewithal and individuality, and I think Mr. Weiner was a good and caring person who wanted the best of everything for his wife. I think he must've been a serious, loving man to give his wife such a fine gift, and I say a prayer for both of them.

The boys were sloppy in their looting, and I have no idea why the Weiners left the gun, but I take it as a sign. I'd been thinking about staying in the RV until the boys found us. They live to hunt, but by staying, I'd take the thrill of the hunt away from them. I wouldn't have to hear their bullets snapping at my daughter's life force and I wouldn't have to lead them away from her and I wouldn't have to die this soon in life's journey. But the small revolver gives me enough hope to dare, and enough courage to believe, so I put all thoughts of surrender out of my head.

I show the revolver to Melanie and she shakes her head.

"What good is that? I'd trade it for Dramamine or some Pepto-Bismol right now."

"Me, too," I say, but we both know it's a lie.

Susan

We fall into the bus and I give a prayer of thanks. We try to push the door closed but we bent something in the folding mechanism. We're dead if we can't close it. Scott pushes with all his strength but it's not enough, so he takes off his coat and jams it into the gap. The wind blasts above us and snow drifts over the coat until only a gray light falls into our shelter, then snow drifts over the glass of the door until there's barely enough light to see. Scotty peels the wrapper from a chemical snaplight and cracks it and shakes it until we're swimming in its green glow. I don't know where he got it. He's like his father that way, always coming up with something unlikely and unexpected, but completely necessary.

We search the interior of the bus. We were in a car and an airplane and now we're in a school bus that's made its last stop. It's not a full-size school bus. It's one of the short buses used to transport special kids, and one of them is still here, dead in her wheelchair, frozen solid in her wrecked yellow tomb. Scott holds the light close to her face. She's maybe ten years old, with long black hair and a white shirt and a plaid skirt.

She was a quadriplegic. Her body is still strapped to its chair, but her spirit is running free through grassy fields. I'd like to say that her mortal remains look composed and peaceful, but I can't. She must've been killed when the bus crashed onto its side, but I can't tell what killed her and it doesn't matter now.

If I were Catholic I'd have something to say. I'd have the comfort of a memorized prayer to guide her to heaven, but my people didn't believe in a God who could be satisfied with memorized prayers. At least that's what they believed when they were alive. But maybe the Catholics have it right, so I start to say a little prayer over the dead girl, but I don't know the proper ritualistic words, and my free-verse praying doesn't sound very convincing. It sounds pathetic and insufficient, so I stop.

Scott turns away and makes himself busy. He has a pocket-knife out and he's cutting sheets of vinyl from the seats. He gets quite a bushel and he makes a sour nest for us on the floor. It's a rat's nest, but maybe it will be enough. I take off my coat and drape it over the nest. Our breath condenses and makes a fog that causes the glow of the chemical light to look as if it's coming from another dimension. We get down into the nest and pull the vinyl and the coat over us. It's sticky and sour with the smell of hard-luck kids, and it's very cold at first, but then our small heat rises beneath it, and I'm grateful for even so much as this.

"It might be warm enough to save us."

"Yeah."

"Can't light a fire in here."

"Nope."

"Lucky to have found this place."

"We'll see."

I'm not sure who said what—who was the optimist and who

was the pessimist. I squeeze Scott's shoulder and he half turns and nods. He doesn't have much meat on his bones. He's shivering, but gradually our nest does its job and I start to drift off into sleep. I wake up, wanting to tell Jerry something, but he's not here and I don't remember what I wanted to say. God knows I miss that man. I don't know if I would've stayed with him through his retirement and into the valley of the shadow of old farthood, with all its indignities and bodily assaults and demands and regrets. I'm still not sure I won't make a final decision about us, someday. I can't quite bring myself to admit that my last big decision is behind me, and all that's left for me is to ride out the choices I've already made.

But I don't want to end things like this, disappearing without so much as a nod goodbye. I can't let go of Scott. And I can't let our Melanie go. Not like this. Not any other way, either. I miss her so badly that I can't help but cry.

I send every mote and beam of energy I can spare to Jerry and Melanie. I try to send them hugs, real hugs, and I'm not sure if it's prayer or an attempt at telekinesis. I can't stop shivering. I hover above real sleep, remembering the final slumber that tempted me outside in the storm, but this new sleep is probably the ordinary kind, and I let myself fall back down into it. I sleep as if it's my duty to set an example for Scott. I'm not sure that I'll wake up, but I'll admit that it feels fine to drift away to a better place.

When I get deep enough to have some control over things, I visit Portland. The wind is howling and it's an east wind coming straight and cold down the Columbia River Gorge. I'm a little girl wearing red rubber boots and jumping in mud puddles, but the puddles are frozen hard as stone. I'm wearing a thrift-store coat that's made of fake fur that turned into dingle-balls after too many cycles in a hot clothes dryer. My cheeks are hot but my hands are cold, so I go home.

Mom is listening to KPDQ-FM on her old Grundig radio. The show she's listening to is *Through the Bible, with J. Vernon McGee*. He's a Southern preacher, and he sounds more sure of himself than anyone I've ever met in real life. He's going on about how we should set good examples for others. He says we can never be as good as Jesus was, but we should never stop trying. Mom is listening to a man she never met tell her that she'll certainly fail, but it doesn't seem to bother her. She's dreamy-looking and she takes a sheet of Toll House cookies from the oven.

The kitchen fills itself with the perfect smells of butter and flour and sugar and chocolate. The windows are steamed against the cold. Mom gives me a peck on the cheek and pours me a glass of milk. I want to grab a cookie, but I know the chocolate chips are hot enough to burn my tongue silly, so I wait. I'm not really hungry, but you don't have to be hungry to long for a fresh cookie. Anyway, it feels fine to wait in that warm kitchen. Mom asks me how my day went, and I say it was okay. I say it was a hard day, with long division and a spelling test, but I knew most of the answers.

Mom says, Good for you. Good for you, my smart girl. Hard days are the ones we remember, because of the way we have to fight to get through them, and I say, Yeah, I guess so.

J. Vernon McGee finishes his sermon and a choir starts in on a sad hymn about how things will be better when we're dead and in heaven. I like the idea of heaven but I don't want to think about how people get there. I reach for a Toll House cookie, but when I touch it, when I pick it up and feel its warmth in my hand, it turns into an ear, a burned human ear.

Scott shakes me awake and my entire body flinches.

"You okay?"

"Yes."

In truth, my stomach is so upset that I can barely talk.

"You were thrashing around," he says.

"It wasn't a nightmare. It was a good dream. I was in your grandmother's kitchen."

"Okay. Sorry."

I'm fully awake and too nauseated to fall back into dreams, so I pull out our last MRE entree. It's Tuna in Pouch.

"You should eat," I say.

"I can't. I'm sick. It's why I woke you up."

"Oh no."

Scott flinches when I say that, but then he leans over and holds the chemical light to my face.

"You're sick, too, aren't you?" he says.

I turn away from the light. My gums are tender. My head itches and hurts at the same time. The skin on my face itches like I've been in the sun too long.

"Oh, God," he says.

I know I should pray. I should say a prayer and then tell a mother's lie to reduce my son's worries, but the horrible unfairness of everything overwhelms me. I don't want to communicate with the one who allowed this to happen. If I prayed, it would be like paying homage to a murderer. But I'm still a mother, and I'm still alive.

"You should eat," I say.

I don't have any heat tabs, but I push the MRE entree at Scott. I wish I could find a way to make it special for him, set a table and light candles, but I don't have a way to do that.

Scott takes the meal, but he drops it. The dirty snow has drifted over us and I can't tell if the wind is still blowing. We're wrapped in our stinking vinyl nest that might end up being our shroud, and there's a dead little girl behind us, and the green glow of the snaplight makes everything thick and slow. If radiation was visible to the naked eye, I'm sure it would look like the hazy green syrup of a chemical light.

I pick up the meal again. I remember the prayer my father used to say at dinnertime, "Dear Lord, please bless this food to our bodies." I always thought it was a strange thing to ask for. Why *wouldn't* God allow our bodies to digest the perfect meals my mother cooked? Wasn't my father insulting my mother's cooking when he said that prayer? I never really understood it until now.

I give the meal package back to Scott. He takes it this time. He opens it and dips his finger into the tuna and puts it in his mouth and immediately retches. When he's finished, I stretch my coat over us and reposition our nest. We're back to back, and there's enough heat to allow us to sleep. The bus is our submarine, our snow cave, our irradiated time capsule, and I hope there's enough oxygen to keep us alive until the storm passes. *Lord bless this oxygen to our bodies.* I hope He will, because the sleep is on us now. Scott falls asleep. I listen to him breathe in and out. He's had something to eat and he's warm and safe and sleeping, so I close my eyes and go in search of my dead mother's kitchen.

Melanie

It gets warm in the RV. We smell bad, but for a while the warmth outweighs the bad things in the world. We dry our clothes. We're sick for most of the night, but the nausea finally passes. I'm very weak now. Dad looks like hell. We don't want to leave the RV, but the boys will be after us soon, and the crazy idea of leaving is our only sane choice.

We go back outside just as it's starting to get light. The snow is only dribbling from the clouds, and the new snow doesn't smell so bad. When my eyes adjust to the light, I can see that most of the new flakes are white, and the new stuff is burying the dirty stuff. I can finally admit to myself that the dirty snow is *fallout*. I might as well call it by its true name.

The wind is dying down, but it still cuts right through my coat and into the core of me. Dad says we have to walk a few miles while it's still snowing, so we won't be as easy to track. He's carrying the silly little gun he found, but he's wearing socks on his hands instead of gloves, and I don't think he can pull a trigger that way. Anyhow, it won't be long until his fingers are frozen again, and then he won't be able to shoot anyone, even if it's the thing he wants most to do in all the world. Maybe when the boys find us, their hands will be frozen, too, and nobody will be able to shoot their guns. And if that happened we'd have a footrace, maybe. I would pull ahead, and Dad would fall behind, and the boys would get him. Yeah, that's exactly what would happen, so never mind.

He's in bad shape. He's running on the invisible energy of love and hate. I walk behind him and I catch whiffs of sweat and smoke and puke and blood. His scalp wound opened up again. When the morning sun makes the overcast glow, I see that his coat is spattered with blood. His head is leaking again and it's leaving pinkish marks in the snow. We're leaving a trail that even a blind person could follow. We have to stop to rest every few minutes. The boys will be on us soon, but I won't run away from my dad.

It isn't long before I feel their eyes on us. I can't see them yet, but I know they're coming. Dad must feel it, too, because he picks up the pace. We're not moving very fast, and we're out on the open plain. I feel naked. We're fighting through snow that's up past our thighs. It's like one of those nightmares where your legs and feet don't work very well, and there's something big and fast coming after you. It's like we're about to be lynched, which probably isn't far from the truth. But there's an upside to all this snow, too. It's too deep for the boys to use their trucks to run us down.

I'm starting to freak out, so I push my thoughts somewhere else. If it hadn't snowed, we probably couldn't have gotten away. But if we had escaped on a clear night, we'd either be in the woods, where Dad could maybe lose the boys, or we'd be shot dead. Dad might say that the snow was a gift from heaven, but he'd only say it to get my mind away from the fear of what it contains.

Mom would most definitely say that God sent the snow, radiation and all, and that it's His will, so there isn't anything to be afraid of, because no matter what our fears might be, God's *will* is the thing that matters. It used to drive me crazy to see the way she gives her life and her freedom over to her imaginary friend. But now I'm almost jealous of the way she can stay so calm when shitty things happen. I know she's not naturally a brave woman, and sometimes I'm jealous of her ability to accept whatever happens, the good with the bad, because she thinks it's part of some great and mysterious plan, so there's no point in being afraid of what is Meant To Be.

We hear the boys behind us. They give a little whoop when they come out onto the plain. There's a house in the distance. It's a white house with green trim. We're breathing hard. Dad's eyes look kind of wild. He glances at the abandoned cars and trucks all snow-covered in the freeway, and I think he's trying to figure out a way to use them to keep us alive, but he shakes his head and keeps up the pace. We walk toward the house. It doesn't seem to be too far away, but it takes us half an hour to get there.

When we get close, Dad is breathing like a woman in labor. His face is bright red and he's not sweating as much as he should be. I'm getting pretty close to the first level of exhaustion I used to reach during a gymnastics workout. There's a tickle in my lungs from the cold and I'm not getting quite enough air, but I know I can get past this first level and push hard for a good while more.

We make it to the house. There aren't any trees or shrubs around it. Dead birds are scattered on the snow in the front yard. Most of them are crows. The breeze lifts their blue-black feathers up and then puts them down again. The windows of the house are dark and they have a layer of dust that's turned to grime. The house looks like someone wants it to

216

look abandoned. There's a picket fence, but the snow is deep enough to allow us to step right over it. We stagger to the front door. We don't have time to knock. The boys are running now. They're only about a quarter mile back, and they're howling like wolves, but they aren't shooting yet. They're running on top of the snow, so they must be wearing snowshoes. The farmhouse is dark and there's no smoke coming from the chimney and none of the snow at the door has been shoveled.

The door is half buried. Dad digs down to the doorknob. He tries to turn it, but it's locked. He puts his shoulder into it, but it's a strong door and he's too weak to break it down. He goes to a window. It's the front window of a breakfast nook. I get a flashy kind of fantasy of us sitting in the breakfast nook on a sunny morning. We're all there, Mom and Scotty, too, and we're eating scrambled eggs and drinking coffee and sharing sections of the newspaper, but the vision pops, and I'm looking at the sorry reflection of us in the window.

The snow is so deep that Dad has to bend down to look inside. He reaches out with his stupid little gun and he's about to break the glass when a man appears in the window. Dad takes a shooting grip on the gun. He points it at the man and looks into his eyes. I can't see Dad's expression, but there's probably enough desperation in it to tell our story. The other man's face is pale, but his eyes are steady. His hands are empty and he keeps them in plain sight. He shakes his head at Dad. He says, "Go around to the back," and his voice is muffled. I get the idea that he's more offended that Dad was about to break one of his windows than he is from having a gun pointed at his face. It's more like an annoyance. He motions and says it again, "Go around to the back," and his voice is strong, and it doesn't sound like the voice of an enemy.

He could be a serial killer and it wouldn't matter; we'd still do what he said. We push through the snow. The patio at the back of the house is shoveled and sprinkled with rock salt. The man opens the door for us. He's fifty or sixty, a big man, more muscular than Dad, but he's clean-shaven and dressed in clean Levi's and a tucked-in button-down shirt, and his dark hair is slicked back.

He holds up his right hand, and we stop. His left hand comes up. It's holding something long and thin, and Dad almost shoots him, but he's only holding a broom.

"Gotta get that contaminated snow off you before you come inside."

Dad puts the revolver in his waistband, grabs the broom, and brushes me down. He's coughing and bleeding and weaving on his feet, and the boys are coming fast, but he does his usual thorough work. My brain is screaming for him to hurry, to not be such a perfectionist for just once in his life.

When I can't stand it anymore, I grab the broom and give Dad a quick cleaning. I move toward the door, but the man shakes his head. I brush more snow from Dad, but apparently I don't do a good enough job, because the man comes outside and grabs the broom and finishes up.

When we go inside I have to pass very close to him. He smells like old-time grooming products. He smells like my maternal grandfather used to smell, like Brylcreem and Old Spice, and I hope he's half the man my grandfather was. I hope he's half as wholesome and kind and generous and regretful as my Vietnam War–surviving granddad.

The man leads us through a laundry room and into the living room. Sandbags are stacked against the walls and around the living room windows. There's a pile of sandbags in the middle of the living room floor. The man lights a kerosene lantern, and lifts it like a ghost who wants us to follow it. He leads us through a door and down a narrow staircase and into the cellar. He holds the lantern close so it lights our faces. I remember the exaggerated way my grandfather used to talk. You look a *sight*, he would've said.

"Name's Bob Wickersham," says the man.

Dad's still whooping in big breaths of air, but he manages to say our names. Wickersham nods at us.

"Your radiation sickness, how bad is it?"

Dad doesn't have the breath to answer.

"We were sick last night, but I think we're getting better," I say.

Wickersham opens his mouth to say something more, but the boys start shooting. They shoot out some of the upstairs windows. Mr. Wickersham winces, then calms his face.

"Well, it was bound to happen sooner or later," he says. "Don't feel guilty about gettin' me involved. Those boys knew I was in here, sure enough. This fight's been comin' for a long time now."

Mr. Wickersham's voice is kind of high for such a big man. He has the local country accent I recognize from the other times we passed through Weed and Yreka.

"To tell the truth, I'm glad it's finally comin' to a head."

He pulls back a black curtain that stretches across one wall of the cellar. He does it like he's on the stage of an old game show, showing us what we've just won. He reveals a big gun safe. He works the combination and opens it. He takes out something heavy. It's a machine gun, I think. Dad gives a low whistle and it surprises me because I don't have any control over my lips, so how could he?

Mr. Wickersham asks Dad if he knows anything about M-60s, and Dad tells him he was a Marine and he knows plenty about M-60s. Mr. Wickersham smiles in a mean way that probably doesn't look like his usual smile. He pulls another machine gun from the safe.

"I had me a gun shop, once. Got me a Class Three license from the Feds, and all. When it seemed like the world was goin' to hell, I collected a few things I thought might come in handy."

He pops open a green metal can and pulls out belts of ammunition. He gives a belt to Dad, and Dad wraps it around himself. Mr. Wickersham takes a belt for himself and they stand all clattering and clinking in their new bullet shirts. Dad's still weaving back and forth. Mr. Wickersham says, "Let's get this show on the road, huh?" His voice sounds almost happy. He's either a psychopath or he's scared shitless and tired of waiting for the boys to attack, and so he's showing off his manly, dark humor.

"I'll take the front; you take the back."

"Sure thing," Dad says. His voice is rough, and it tells me that he's holding back a ton of pain.

"They'll surely try to burn us out," says Wickersham.

He lifts a big fire extinguisher and puts it down at my feet. He pulls out the safety pin.

"Can you handle this, sweetheart?"

I'm about to tell him to stick that "sweetheart" crap up his ass, but the boys shoot at the house again and their bullets break lots of stuff upstairs. We wait until they stop shooting and Dad tells Mr. Wickersham that the boys probably have dynamite, too.

I don't want to, but I follow them up the stairs. I take the fire extinguisher with me. The living room windows are shot out. The sandbags are piled two deep in front of the windows. Mr. Wickersham grabs some sandbags and tosses them over the glass near the breakfast nook windows. He kneels down behind the window, and it's a bunker, a pillbox, a machine-gun nest. Dad puts down his gun and sets up a sandbag semicircle in front of the brick fireplace. He tells me to get behind it. I don't want to, but I do. He kind of grimaces and blinks, and I think he was trying to smile and wink. He pulls out the stupid little gun he found in the RV and puts it on a sandbag beside me. I shake my head and he manages to really smile, but he leaves the gun on the sandbag. He stacks more bags near the base of the back window and opens the top of his machine gun and feeds it with a belt of ammunition.

There are two other windows, but they have shutters and the shutters are closed. I hear running footsteps and orders and shouts. I recognize the voices of Bill Junior and Luscious and a few of the others. They're not talking to us. They're getting themselves set up for their attack. I know it must burn Bill Junior's ass that we were able to just walk away from him. He won't want to let it happen again.

And then all in one motion, Mr. Wickersham pushes the barrel of his gun up onto the sandbags and into the light of day and pulls the trigger. It's the loudest thing I've ever heard. The sound of killing rips into my ears. Lines of red reach for the boys and hot brass streams against the wall and bounces across the floor and hits my legs. Dad starts shooting from the back window. It's loud enough to make me start to lose my mind.

I put my hands over my ears while they try to sweep the boys away. They start to shoot shorter bursts and I hear a boy screaming and then I can only hear our fire. Yes, it's *our* fire, and I have to claim it, too. My brain runs around and I can't control my thoughts and they bounce like hot brass against the walls of my skull. I hope the scream I heard wasn't from Donnie Darko. I hope it was one of the mean ones, even though no one deserves to be machine-gunned in the snow. Maybe even Hitler wouldn't deserve that. But I can still feel their dirty hands on my skin and their stinking bodies pushing into me. I know I should feel terrible about all the shooting, but my lips are trying to smile, and I feel guilty and helpless and powerful. I stay down in my sandbagged place. I push my lips flat and straight so I'm not grinning like a cold-blooded killer. I do my thing; I curl into a ball.

It doesn't take long for the boys to regroup. They manage to shoot more holes in our sandbags, and then I'm cursing. It seems to be the only thing I know how to do. I wish I could just accept things and do what comes naturally to other people in times like these, run or fight. I wish I could believe that I'm part of some god's special plan, but all I can do is bang my head against the floor and curse the world of people and the shitty choices we have to make.

Dad and Mr. Wickersham go after the boys' fire. They're not shy about shooting dozens of rounds in response to a single shot. They're trying as hard as they can to kill.

Dad says something to me, but I can't hear him. He's shouting and it takes me a while to understand that he's telling me to go to the cellar for more ammunition. I don't move fast enough, so he goes himself. It's quieter with only one gun firing. I think it's a good thing that it's quieter, but the boys will think so, too.

Dad comes back upstairs with two green cans. He falls at the top of the stairs, and he doesn't get up. He's coughing on the hardwood floor. Wickersham tells me to bring him a box of ammunition, but I don't want to. I go to my Goggy and try to make him better. I take off my coat and wrap him in it, but he pushes me away and manages to stand up. He drags a can of ammunition to Wickersham, then he gets his own gun firing again. I bring him my canteen, but he's too busy shooting to see me behind him. He's still coughing. I want to pat him on the back or something, but I go back to my little sandbag nest.

They keep shooting and I can't hear anything except a single loud ringing. The boys were on us like dogs on rabbits, but now they aren't so sure of themselves. Now they're targets, too, and they'll have to be smart if they want to live. But they *are* smart.

The boys stop shooting, and so do Dad and Wickersham. I bring Dad my canteen. As soon as he can, Dad turns to find me. He looks surprised to see me standing behind him, then he smiles and takes a drink.

"You okay?"

"Yeah. You?"

"Never better. You know how it is with we Sharpes."

He has blood on his lips. I kneel beside him. I want to tell him I don't hate him for shooting people, but I can't shape the words. He tries to ruffle my hair, but I step back. It's like we're only camping or something, but then we hear something, and he turns back to his gun.

Right now the boys are hiding and thinking. But they'll come again soon. They'll get their shit together and come from all directions. And that's just what they do. They wait until twilight. They're very quiet and I don't trust them when they're quiet, so I look out from behind Dad's sandbags. It takes me a while to figure out what's happening, but then I see them coming. At first I think I'm getting dizzy, and I start to feel sick to my stomach, because the snow is moving. Dad and Mr. Wickersham can't see it. The boys are camouflaged with dirty sheets that make them almost invisible in the snow, and they're almost right on top of us.

Scott

The air in the bus is ripe. I don't know how long we slept but the air doesn't seem to have enough oxygen to allow a fart to burn. I'm warm clear through, and the snaplight is almost used up. We're soaked with sweat under our vinyl nest. The dead girl is getting rotten enough to gag a cockroach, but Mom is okay and we're together.

Mom might've been lying about dreaming she was in Gramma's kitchen, but maybe she wasn't. She doesn't tell lies very often, now that she's off the booze. But there's no telling what she'll do to try to put my mind at ease, and I want her to know that I'm okay. I know there's a plan for me, and so whatever happens is cool with me, one way or the other, because either I'll be God's terrible vengeance on earth, or I'll be sitting at His table in paradise. There's no downside that I can see.

I start to tell her, but she starts talking about her dream.

"It was raining outside, at your grandmother's house."

"It rains in Portland?"

"Yes it does, Mr. Wiseacre. But there are different kinds of rain. You know how Eskimos have lots of words for snow? Well, for any person with eyes and a brain, there are different kinds of rain in Portland. This rain I'm talking about was a *sharp* rain, the kind that makes a person stubborn, holing up and looking for something good and wholesome, finding comfort in any way possible. It was somewhere between drizzle and shower, with drops so cold they felt like needles. It was the kind of sharp rain that makes you appreciate things, and it was warm in the kitchen. The windows were all steamed up because your grandmother had just baked a sheet of Toll House cookies. She was listening to KPDQ on the radio, and there was a sermon on, a sad one that made me want to hug her, and we were safe from the sharp rain."

Mom mists up and then she gets pissed off at herself, because she was trying to make me feel better and failed.

"It's okay," I say. "I know what you mean."

I put my arm around her shoulders and give her a squeeze. She pats my arm and smiles and laughs as if it's silly for her to cry. I don't tell her that we all need to get harder about things. I was weak before, but I have a purpose now. I need to focus on my mission and let go of all the other stuff, even if it comes down to losing part or all of my family, here on earth. The thought of it makes me cry, but I need to be able to take whatever's coming, so I can become God's sure and swift right hand, God's wrath unleashed on the monsters of the world, starting with the little fuckers who are probably raping my sister.

We need air, so I break free of our nest and go to find some. I'm weaker than I can ever remember being. I get the dry heaves again, and it seems to take away all my reserves of energy. I crawl to the front of the bus. I pull myself into a standing position. I push up on the door. I push it open enough to grab my coat and I pull and pry until the coat falls into the bus. It's frozen solid and heavy. It lands on my left foot. I hear it hit me, but it takes a while for the pain to register. When it does, it's the last straw. I don't have the energy to curse, so I fall down and pass out.

A small avalanche of powder snow wakes me up. It keeps streaming in until I'm about to stuff my coat back into the hole, but then the little avalanche stops. Daylight and sweet, fresh air are pouring in. I take three or four deep breaths and it's beautiful air, but then the cold cuts into me again. We're soaking wet, and the cold will kill us very fast. It's a shitty deal: suffocate or freeze or live long enough to die from gunshot wounds or from the radiation.

I try to shake out my coat, but it's so frozen that it's like a lump of metal. I bang it against the stainless-steel handrail that the special kids used to board their bus, and the ice cracks in enough places that the coat is almost flexible again. I take off my gloves and I manage to cram my arms into my coat sleeves. It's like wearing a rusted suit of armor. Somehow I get it zipped up before my hands stop working. I put my gloves back on and wait to see if I'll be able to move my fingers. The air coming into the bus is so cold that it refreezes the outside layer of everything, our clothes and the vinyl nest and the face of the dead girl. I can almost see the crystals growing. The cold hits the humid air inside the bus and it makes a fog, like when you open a super-cold freezer on a hot summer day.

But the cold doesn't stop at the first layer of things. Mom and I are wet clear through, and our layers of clothes freeze up, and we're dying. I go kind of crazy, because I know that if I don't do something fast, I won't get another chance. I get Mom up, and she's full of adrenaline, too, and we walk back and forth and we yell and clap our hands and bounce off the walls of that damned bus, but it's not helping. It's not enough, so I tell Mom to keep moving, and she starts to sing a crappy Christian song from the seventies, something about God telling Noah to build him an arky-arky, and I'm laughing like a maniac and trying to push away the pile of snow at the door so I can light a fire there.

I get the snow pushed back into the bus and I'm grabbing scraps of vinyl and stacking them under the open door, wondering how the hell I'll be able to light them, knowing all the time that the smoke will probably kill us. I can't feel my hands, but I bang away on the wheel of my Bic lighter until I get it lit. I hold the flame under a scrap of vinyl and it lights and burns slowly at first, and then it builds into a hissing, smoking chemical fire. It puts out good heat, but it won't last long, so we get right up to the flames. Most of the smoke is pulled up through the door, so we're okay for a while.

But it doesn't last long. The fire dies out and there isn't anything else to burn. I tell Mom that I'll try to get some diesel from the tanks and we can burn it in our canteen cups. The wild edge of desperation is wearing off, and I'm getting very tired. I start to pull myself up through the door, but I hear voices outside.

"Over here," one of them says, and then I'm backing away from the door and reaching for my rifle, but then I remember that I don't have one, and my hands are gone, baby, gone, and there's no way I'll be able to shoot off anything except my mouth. Mom's face looks like she was just betrayed by someone she loved and trusted, but then she smiles at me. I know she's accepting whatever's coming, the next installment of His mysterious plan, and I smile back at her, and we're okay then, the two of us freezing but at peace, because we have each other and a mustard seed of faith between us.

Bill Junior

We're close enough to throw dynamite into the house, but I don't want to kill the girl. That big bastard Wickersham isn't anyone to fool around with. My pops told me to steer clear of this place, back when my pops was still talking to me. We knew right at the beginning that Wickersham would put up a good fight, and we kind of saved him as a problem we'd take care of later, when we got super-bored or super-hungry.

I've lost four men today, and three more are wounded, but we're in the middle of a battle, and I'll leave the wounded to take care of themselves. Only pussies spend a lot of time taking care of their wounded while the fight is still on. It's timing and momentum that wins fights, and it doesn't make sense to waste time on men who might die anyway, if you ask me. My stomach isn't so bad now, and maybe we're getting better, but this could be our last battle, and I intend to win it.

There. I get close enough to see Wickersham peeking at us every now and then. It's either him or that prick Sharpe. They have machine guns and good cover behind those damn sandbags, but I have a plan. I dig under my coat to find the sports whistle I'm wearing on a cord around my neck. I wish I had a bugle, but there's nowhere to get one. A bugle would really make our enemies piss themselves, but all I have is the whistle, and I give it a short blast to send them forward.

Luscious and Stumpie move under their white sheets until they're right up next to the walls. Luscious takes the front of the house and Stumpie takes the back. They each put two wrapped sticks of dynamite right up against the walls and then they back away. I can't actually see them do it, but that's what I told them to do. They know how to follow my orders, so I don't let myself worry about it.

They don't take any fire, going in. I give them what I think is enough time to get back, then I give a longer blast on the whistle. Seconds pass, and it feels like a whole minute goes by before they set off their charges. The explosions don't happen at the same time, like I'd hoped, but that was only me being a perfectionist. There's almost a whole second between the blasts, but they blast open the walls, front and back, and the sandbags are blown away. We can see clear through the house, from the breakfast nook to the back patio. I hit the whistle again, and Darko and Biggus light highway flares and throw them into the house, and we have us a nice, bright shooting gallery.

The trouble is, there isn't anyone to shoot. We run into the house, ready to kill the old farts and take the girl, but nobody's home. We clear the first floor. I send men upstairs and down into the cellar, but we don't find them. It's a plain mystery, but I'm not the kind to sit and scratch my head. I send Luscious and Stumpie and the two wounded men that can still walk outside. I throw them highway flares.

"Check all around. There's no need to spare anyone. You see them, you shoot them. The girl, too."

"Damn waste," says Luscious, "but okay, we'll do her."

And off they go, the light of their flares making them look like rescue workers searching a crash site. In the dark with their flares, they look big and professional and important, and I'm proud that they're my men, following my orders.

Inside the house, we rip apart the cellar. We look for a tunnel, but we don't find one. We cut open the furniture and empty the cabinets and bash holes in the sheetrock of the walls and ceiling, but there aren't any hidden compartments or passages. Somehow, the fuckers just plain disappeared.

I send men onto the roof and we check the chimney, but it's like someone reached down and pulled them up into the sky. The old buzzards are gone. They left their machine guns behind, but there's no more ammo for them. They shot us up pretty bad, but the thing they shouldn't have done was to take my girl with them. That was going too far and, too bad for them, they've gone and got me mad, and there's not so much as a fly turd of mercy in my heart.

Jerry

There's no doubt that Wickersham is an actual paranoid survivalist, because he takes us to a passageway that's hidden behind his dishwasher. He kneels in front of the machine and I think he's gone crazy, but then he unlatches some kind of mechanism and rolls the entire sealed box of the old Maytag out onto the kitchen floor. He points to a tunnel. Our mouths open and Melanie giggles. I haven't heard that sound in a long time, and it makes me happy. It makes me greedy, too, because I want to hear my wife's laughter, too, and Scotty's nervous bray, and it's all my fault that they aren't with me, but I let up on myself and push Melanie toward the tunnel.

Melanie disappears into the dishwasher feet-first. She whispers something that sounds like, "Sleep, spiders, sleep." I'm next. Maybe the dishwasher leaks, because it smells very bad in the hole. It's like being born again via the wrong orifice, but we descend beneath the snow and volcanic rock. I feel safe for the first time in a long while.

Wickersham lets himself into the tunnel above us. He stands on a ledge and rolls the dishwasher back into place. He comes down with a chemical light, and its weird glow casts our shadows like green smoke on the tunnel walls.

When we near the tunnel exit, Wickersham drops the chemical light and we crawl the last ten yards in near-darkness. A ladder is buried at an incline. We climb it, Melanie first, and we come up into the snow-muffled night. Wickersham comes up and I look at the tunnel exit.

We've come up from the earth through a hinged stump. It's exactly like the escape tunnel exit from the TV show *Hogan's Heroes*. I can't help but laugh, and my laughing comes up into the world quietly. I start coughing again, but no more blood comes up.

The craftsmanship of the escape tunnel is amazing. It's a hell of a design, and there's some humor mixed with the paranoia of it, so I slap Wickersham on the back and thank God for the crazy, TV-rerun-addicted survivalist loners of this world.

We wipe the tunnel dirt from our hands and knees and crouch near the exit. Wickersham turns and asks me if I've ever watched *Hogan's Heroes* on TV. I'm about to answer when the boys run out of the blasted house and start shooting at anything and everything.

Wickersham isn't lucky or blessed. He takes a round in the chest, and he isn't shy about taking his leave from the world. We leave him mouth-open in the snow and run away. The boys aren't on our trail, but we're leaving tracks and it's only a matter of time. We need to get some distance between us before first light. My knees are clicking and my quadriceps won't last long at this pace and my head weighs a hundred pounds and my head is bleeding again. We finally get to a place where the snow can better support our weight. We make better time, and my legs hold off their impending mutiny, but we're still leaving tracks. The clouds are low and thick and roiling above us. I pray for just enough snow to cover our tracks, but the sky holds on to its moisture.

We slow to a fast march. I'm about to puke, but then my mind wanders again from the pain and I'm okay. Melanie pulls up beside me, breathing cleanly and moving with good form. Maybe we'll survive after all.

Sometimes we're walking almost directly back toward the junkyard. It's dark, and we need to make best possible speed, so we walk a snow-buried country road. The road is lined with ditches. An occasional lonely-looking mailbox rises out of the gloom as we pass by. Power lines droop unpowered between their creosote-soaked poles, and it's very quiet. There aren't any animals, no dogs or birds or squirrels. I start to worry about radiation again, the *cumulative* effects, and the worry keeps me warm for a few miles, but that's about all it's good for.

We walk single file. Every half hour or so, I trade places with Melanie at point, breaking trail through the snow, but it doesn't take long before I'm used up. Melanie powers ahead of me, and I have no choice but to follow.

*　　*　　*

We walk into the foothills of Mount Shasta. I think we're headed in the direction of Mount Shasta City. The road twists through the hills, and we walk its snowy switchbacks. We take a small single-lane track off the road, and it seems to dead-end at a growth of blackberries, but it doesn't. There's a walk-around through the brambles. The trail snakes through underbrush that seems like it's from somewhere else, blackberry and vine maple and fern. We follow and it leads us to a cabin.

It's a true log cabin, a big two-story job. The small first-floor windows are covered by rough-cut shutters. The exterior is smeared with mud and furry with patches of moss and lichen. The place is surrounded by blackberry vines that look as if they're trying to swallow the place whole, and just might manage it. The logs of the structure look old and maybe past their prime, but I pound on a few of them, and they're solid and perfectly seasoned and they seem to be well-sealed against the elements.

As a born-and-bred product of the suburbs, I can't help but wonder what the place would look like all cleaned up, with a clear coat of varnish and a covered porch and a tasteful chandelier in the dining room and maybe some low-wattage lights out front. But then I realize why the place won't ever appear on the cover of an architectural magazine. It looks like a crap-smeared old wreck because that's the way it's supposed to look. I knock on the door, but there's no answer. I wait and listen to the sound of wind in trees, but we're tired and cold, so I kick the door. I'm running on nothing but adrenaline. The impact of the kick reverberates in my head and ribs and in my irradiated guts, but I kick until wood splinters and the door swings open.

"Welcome to *mi hacienda*, et cetera," I say.

"Thanks for having me over," Melanie says.

"*De nada*, and so on and so forth. *Mi casa es su casa*, but let's speak English, shall we?"

We go inside and I find a wooden chair and I jam it against the door to keep it closed. There's a staircase to the left of the front door. I light a kitchen match and circle the ground floor, checking to see that we're alone, and that the curtains are pulled. I stumble into a low table, and there's a sand candle on it, and I light it.

Melanie gives me a smile. It's a "what the hell are you gonna do?" kind of smile. She looks down. Her pants are filthy, and I'm a mess, too. Now that I've caught my breath, I can smell it on us, the smell of wet soot from burned cities and burned people.

Melanie goes upstairs and returns with an armload of blankets. She strips off her sopping, contaminated clothes and wraps herself in blankets decorated with scenes of elk and bear and salmon and eagles. I manage to throw the clothes outside. I strip out of my own nasty clothes and throw them into what's left of God's nature, and wrap myself in a blanket advertising Remington Arms.

I stand at a window high in the logs and peer through thick curtains. It would make a fine firing position, but all I have is the little belly gun. Melanie finds a lantern and I light it. The great room is clean and appears to have been furnished from a Cabela's catalog. The hardwood floors are polished and everything is squared away. There's an old-fashioned hutch to display the china, and the kitchen is spotless. A selection of books are fanned out on the handcrafted coffee table: a 9/11 conspiracy book, a pictorial history of failed United Nations military actions, *The Anarchist Cookbook*, and a do-it-yourself book about distilling alcohol.

There aren't any subwalls or finish carpentry extras inside the cabin. The walls are unpolished rough-cut logs. They're more than two feet in diameter—thick enough to stop the 5.56 rounds that the boys are so fond of. There's a fireplace made of stone. A good compound bow hangs above the fireplace with a quiver of hunting arrows.

I put out the lantern. It's dark outside, and the dirty snow doesn't have much of a night glow to it. I peer through blackout curtains and look for whatever's coming next. I weigh my options. I could use the bow, ambush the boys and pick some of them off. Maybe I could take one of their rifles and lead them away from the cabin.

I'm sick and battered and naked beneath my blankets, but I'm getting myself worked up to do it when a big gust of wind hits the cabin. It blows the sooty flocking from the trees, and the world goes gray. It makes the shutters bang against their latches, and it blows under the door and flutters the pages of the coffee-table books. I pray for more, and a storm blows in with high wind and more snow than I've ever seen. It's a certifiable blizzard. It's clean snow, too, and I'm not ashamed to give a prayer of thanks, right out loud. I use the conversational voice I used back when I stood a chance of making my family feel safe and loved and special. I talk to God as if He's my beer buddy, and it makes me feel fine to do it. I pray without thinking and I don't remember the words after I've said them.

When I'm finished, Melanie rolls her eyes, then smiles. We've almost certainly received a stay of execution, no matter its source. We won't have to kill or die tonight, and I give a cheer, howling like a wolf while the storm wipes our tracks away. I dance a painful jig, circling and kicking up my feet, and I haven't ever danced a jig in my life, until today.

Susan

I'm not sure where I am. I can't remember in my normal way of remembering. The light of the world changes when a person is dying, and I remember the darnedest things.

They must've pulled the bus door open at some point. Powder snow floated down when they laid on their bellies and looked inside. There were pieces of ash in the snow like bits of vanilla bean in good ice cream. The light above was thick and yellow and it looked like it should taste of lemons. The last of the smoke from Scott's little fire was whisked away by the wind, and I remember watching it go, thinking that our souls would soon be chasing it up over the mountains.

A young man stuck his head and shoulders down into the bus. He said, "We saw your smoke." He didn't point a gun at us, and we didn't have any guns to point at him. We only stood and watched to see what he would do. He was backlit by the lemon-colored light, and he had wings on his back. He was a very handsome man, with the bluest eyes I'd ever seen. In my unclear memory of him, they were heart-slaying eyes, and they seemed to carry knowledge of things that other people could never know—knowledge about the whys and wherefores of cities and kingdoms and the truths of man and woman, together.

His presence didn't make any sense to me. Maybe he was one of the gunmen from the saloon, but then why did he have wings? He smiled at me, and his smile seemed to pass through my clothes and lay itself against my skin. It felt very good. My son was there beside me and we were dying of hypothermia and expecting to get shot at any moment. A man with wings was above us in the snow, but my body was preparing itself for lovemaking.

I can't say I'm too proud of it. It's not the kind of thing I'll ever mention to Jerry, but maybe I'll be able to rationalize it later. We were dying after all, and in times like that, instinct takes full control.

When the man with wings grimaced at the stench of the dead girl behind us, I was pulled back into the real world, bad as it ever was. Another man stuck his head into the bus. He was bearded, flat-eyed, and weak-chinned and he was holding a lit highway flare. Scotty tried to put his arm around me, but we were shaking the last of our heat into the sputtering, flare-lit world, and his arm bounced itself from my shoulder.

We were like animals in a bulldozed den. I'd like to say that I was calmed by the power of grace and acceptance, but mostly I was impatient. Our clothes were soaking wet in air that felt like cold fire, and I hoped the men would get to doing whatever it was they planned to do. We shook so violently that it seemed as if we were taking awkward little jumps and flights from the ground. The man with wings shouted to someone we couldn't see.

"They're freezing."

"Well, get them warmed up, why don't you?"

And so they did. They caused us to levitate out of the bus. I didn't believe they were really doing it, or that we'd actually survive, or that the men wouldn't slaughter us right there in the snow. Some of the men had guns, but they kept them slung over their shoulders while other men gave us emergency treatment.

The handsome man pulled the wings from his back and set up a mountain tent in the snow. Another man lit camp heaters in the tent and pushed us inside. Hands reached in and stripped away our wet clothes. Our skin was without feeling and it must've been like disrobing a pair of corpses. They wrapped us in sleeping bags and broke out a thermos and forced hot coffee down our throats. Two of them went back to town to get some dry clothes for us. The ones who stayed had worry in their eyes, and they moved with the speed of rescue workers, although I didn't believe in the concept of rescue anymore.

But in spite of my disbelief, the men treated us with what seemed to be the very best of intentions, and so I wasn't at all sure that we were still alive.

Melanie

In the morning I'm sick again. Outside, the wind settles into a steady gale, and maybe it's the dawn of a new ice age. There's no question of going anywhere. Not today and maybe not ever. I'm so nauseated that I keep myself in a fetal position. The pain is horrible in my guts, and the skin of my face is hot and tight, like I have a sunburn.

I pry myself off the couch and crawl to Dad. He's on the floor, wrapped in Cabela's blankets. He has red blotches on his face. I take his pulse and it seems fine. I take my own pulse and my heart is going like a machine gun. Dad opens his eyes. He parts his cracked lips and moans.

"Hey," I try to say. My voice is a croak. Dad croaks something back at me that sounds like "water."

His canteen is on the floor beside him. I unscrew the cap. Dad tries to sit up, but he can't. I'm afraid for him, and for all of us. The worry rises like an uncontrolled fire. I see things happening, but they don't seem real. We're still taking radiation into our bodies. I read somewhere that radiation is measured by strength and exposure over *time*. Our recovery was only temporary. We're sick anywhere and everywhere again, and then we're curled up and panting.

The hours pass slowly, and the pain in my head doesn't go away. I drag myself across the floor every hour to stoke the fire. We sleep again. When it gets dark, we wake up and light the lantern and candles. Occasionally one of us stands and looks out into the storm. Dad doesn't say a word to me all day and through the night, and he might be playing the Ignoring Game, so I play it, too.

The sickness passes again. I'm grateful when the pain recedes, but good health isn't a thing I can trust anymore. Also, something else is wrong. When I start feeling better, I start feeling guilty. With all the talking and hiding and screaming I've been doing, I haven't done anything that really counts. I didn't kill the animals who took me, but I didn't make my point, either. Maybe it would've been better if I'd killed some of them. At least then I'd be more than a victim. But as it is, I haven't changed anything. Everyone is exactly the same way they'd be if I never existed. I've left it all undone, and I'm pissed off at myself.

To take our minds off of things, we get busy. We try to settle in. We find canned goods and ration them out and we take turns cooking. We take turns doing the dishes, then we prepare a proper list of chores, and we don't try to find ways to avoid the work. In the downtime, Dad dusts and scrubs and whittles, and then cleans up after himself. I find some rusty cast iron skillets in the pantry, and I sand them clean and carbonize them over the fire until they're shiny and black. I tell Dad that I wish I had some yarn and knitting needles, even though I used to believe that knitting was only a way to keep women from ruling the world.

Between storms, Dad goes into the woods on showshoes. He carries the bow and quiver of arrows. He doesn't go very far. He sprinkles MRE cracker crumbs around outside the cabin, and the hungry deer come to him.

Sometimes I watch him from the windows. Maybe he knows I'm watching him, but he doesn't acknowledge it. Even though it's twenty below outside, he moves very slowly. He kind of moves his head like a rudder, and it takes me a while to see that he's pointing himself into the wind so his scent won't give away his presence. He practices his stalking skills until he can get so close to a deer that he can take it with the bow.

The first time I saw him shoot a deer, it made me sick. There wasn't any sound as the arrow disappeared between the ribs of a skinny doe. She got a surprised look on her face, but she didn't fall right away. She turned and I could see the arrow sticking out of her far side. She walked to a pine tree and rubbed herself against it, trying to scratch away the thing that was causing her such pain. Dad put another arrow into her, and it hit her just behind her front leg, and her legs buckled and that was it. I wanted to puke or die, but I did neither.

The venison doesn't make us sick. It's kind of stringy and gamey, but I feel okay after I eat it. I'm not happy that we have to kill to survive. We don't have any other choice, and I think about native peoples, the Indians who lived here, and how they lived in harmony with nature. I try to believe that we're like the Indians now, and that's how I manage to tolerate myself as I watch my dad become one with the trees, moving into the breeze without sound or scent, to turn deer into venison through the nuclear winter.

The spring doesn't come. We hear dripping during the day, but everything freezes up solid again at night. The icy stream creaks and leaks into the dark underbrush, but it doesn't gain its freedom until mid-May, and then it breaks free with nothing more than a sigh. The icicles drip away into the mud and all the world is soft to the touch, but nothing flowers or blossoms, and it's as if all of nature is reflecting the way I feel.

One morning I think I hear a helicopter in the distance, but when I run outside, the sound is gone. I stand with Dad at the window and we pray in our own ways for the world to come alive again. I pray to Gaia and Sophia, and I can almost picture the underbrush beginning to come alive: vine maple and nettles and wild blackberry and strawberry vines filling with life-sap. Tender buds swelling on branches and then pushing their payloads of blossoms into the sky. Animals rising from their sleep and joining the new cycle of seasons, but the sky is still overcast. All of nature is tired and aching for the sun, but Mother Earth is sleeping in.

Scott

The guys got us thawed out and took us back to Virginia City. It's a safe place now. Pastor Jim is gone. He went missing after he chased after us in the storm. Sam, the young guy Pastor Jim backhanded at the bar, he's in charge now.

I think that maybe Pastor Jim's disappearance wasn't an accident. I think maybe the shots we heard when we were running away were what took Pastor Jim out of his leadership role. I don't say anything about it to Sam. Anyhow, I'm not too broken up about Pastor Jim's disappearing act, so there isn't necessarily anything else to say about it, except good riddance.

We're snowbound, but Virginia City isn't short of supplies: shelter, water, food, booze, and guns. Men, women, children, and three or four hot girls that are my age. There are thirty-five people here. Our supplies should last us through to spring, but I'm worried that spring might not come. The sky still doesn't look right, and I think I'm not alone with my worry, but nobody says anything about it.

I meet Sam at the bar every night and we drink whiskey and talk about stuff. There's a mirror behind the bar, and I can see a reflection of my screwed-up face. It looks like a map sewed out of bad meat. Some girls hang out in the bar. The ones that don't look away from me give me looks of pity.

Mom sat with us at first, but then she caught the hint that

I didn't necessarily want her there. She mostly hangs out with ladies her own age, and they drink coffee and talk about their kids, and Mom is starting to sort of relax and I'm happy for her.

At the saloon, we take turns being the bartender, and some of the other young guys in town line up on barstools while we talk. The saloon is the nerve center of the town. Its tables are almost always full of people, and I look around to see if I can find the hippie girl I saw when I first arrived, but she isn't here. There are other girls at the tables and some of them look at me and look away, and some of them are almost as pretty as the hippie girl, but I can't get her out of my mind, so I don't hit on anyone or anything more complicated than a whiskey bottle.

We get drunk and we start to believe that it's up to us to change the world for the better. We drink good whiskey from clean glasses and we make plans. As soon as I thaw out and can sit upright, I tell Sam the facts of life.

"You don't know what it's like out there. There's no way to reason with them. The only thing they understand is killing. The first thing we need to do is fortify the town."

"Yeah," he says. "I'll get right on it."

I think he's only bullshitting me, but the next day he sits at the bar and unrolls a scroll of paper. I pour a round of whiskey for him and the guys while he shows me his drawing of the town.

"We'll set up bunkers. Here and here and here. We'll use plate steel and cast iron and sandbags to make pillboxes. We can borrow stuff from Harry's machine shop." He turns to me. "Whaddya think?"

"Sounds like a good start."

"Do you think we can take them?"

"Maybe. The ones we went up against had dynamite."

Sam scratches his oily blond head. He has ink stains on his fingers and the black fingernails of an old-fashioned newspaperman from the movies. The wind is blowing slower outside, maybe twenty miles an hour, but it's lifting loose powder snow into the air. The snow is white, finally, but the wind uncovers patches of the gray snow. I remember how cold I was in the bus, and I'm not finished being grateful about things like heat and food and booze.

"What we might do," Sam says. He picks up his whiskey glass with his ink-blotched hands and drains it. "What we might do is open up the floor to discussion. Got any other ideas?"

I drain my whiskey glass and pop it down on the bar.

"Maybe. I've been thinking about it."

I step from behind the bar and come around so Sam's drawing of the town isn't upside down.

"How long do you think the snow will last?"

My question raises a few other questions that no one wants to think about, but I have to ask it. Four other guys are at the bar and they don't say a word. They just look at Sam and wait for his opinion. Sam sighs. One of the other guys, Jonathan, goes behind the bar and pours a shot of the good stuff for Sam. Jonathan is a big, flannel-wearing dude who likes to please people, but he doesn't have the shifty eyes of a true kiss-ass, and I wouldn't want to push him too far.

"Yeah, well, that's the question, isn't it?" Sam says. He takes a sip of the good whiskey and smacks his lips. The wind picks up, and a gust blows over the top of the chimney and makes a hooting sound.

"Not long ago, I could spend just about all day sitting in front of a television set. Ask anyone here, they'll say it's true."

He takes another sip, and I'm watching to see exactly how he does it, using hand movements and good timing and his hushed but serious voice, to get us to lean in and really listen to him. A great stage presence is just about the most important thing for a leader to have. There's no doubt that Sam believes he's a leader. He drains his glass.

"I mostly watched the educational channels. I really got off on that shit."

He motions for a refill, and he makes us wait. Jonathan pours again and we watch the golden whiskey gut-gut into Sam's big shot glass. Sam takes a sip and lets his eyes get all distant.

"Remember back when people had their panties in a bunch about global warming, and they made all those horror shows? Yeah? Well, there were also a couple of shows about global *cooling*. One of them was called *The Summer That Never Was*."

It's a good place for him to pause again, and he does. The other guys are eating out of his hand, so he goes on.

"In the year that Krakatoa exploded—maybe you've heard of that volcano, boys—in that year, the winter lasted right through spring, and there wasn't a real summer. The volcano put tons of shit into the atmosphere, and it took more than a year for the sky to clear. There weren't any crops to speak of, that first year. And the animals, people included, didn't have enough to eat."

Big Jonathan pours himself a drink and downs it like he's on autopilot. His eyes are blank.

"So, to answer your question," Sam says, "I think the snow might last for a good long while."

I'm not sure whether to roll my eyes or clap my hands. His words are probably true enough, but his performance is straight out of a reality show. I settle for a nod, hoping it looks like a wise nod, and maybe kind of like a smartass nod, too. It takes a while for Sam to get over himself, but he finally comes around.

"Why do you ask?"

I motion to Jonathan for a refill of my own. The big dude refills my glass but he narrows his eyes at me, saying without words that I haven't earned any favors from him. I don't touch the whiskey. I let it sit there in front of me while I wait a few heartbeats.

"The snow might give us an advantage in a fight," I say. "We could dig tunnels."

Sam gets it, right away. He takes it without hesitation as his own idea, as I was pretty sure he would. He picks up his leaky pen and draws lines that stick out from the town like the spines of an urchin. He inks black circles every few inches on the lines.

"If anyone comes at us, we'll pop up all around them, and behind them, too, here and here and here. Get started digging tunnels in the snow. We'll make them everywhere that make sense, so we can kill the fuckers coming and going. Make wide places in the tunnels, so we can fight the bastards if they get inside. We'll fight like the Viet Cong did, from underground, and we'll win, too."

Bill Junior

We were sick as shit for a while, but we're getting better. Only me and Luscious and Donnie Darko are left. The others are Popsicles in the dirty snow. Most of them were killed during the fights and the ambushes we started and finished, so they died with some honor, the honor of men trying to fill their bellies and maybe get themselves laid. But some of my men were frozen alive in that first big storm, or died from the radiation in it, and that's my fault for not getting us to shelter right away.

The ones that got shot during the fight at Wickersham's place were the first to go. I guess I could blame Wickersham and the girl's old man for that. I'll kill them like dogs if I get another chance, but it's my fault, too, that my men are gone. I really miss some of them, Biggus and the Kelly twins, and Stumpie. It's war, and people die, but I miss having a bunch of guys under my command, a little army to scare the shit out of the people who were happy to lock us up in juvie.

I'm getting pretty bummed out, but then I come around to my natural state of being. I'm the boss and bosses get people to do things. But first they have to get their own head screwed on straight. They have to believe in things with more strength than other people believe.

And so I believe that this is only a little setback. I believe I can get more guys to follow me, because my message is simple:

We take what we want, because that's the only way we're going to get it. The rich assholes of the world make rules and laws to keep themselves rich, but we have as much right to cheat and steal and declare war as anybody else does. I've declared war on them, and on all their kiss-asses and zombies, and my message is an easy thing to sell in this day and age. So I don't think we'll have too much trouble finding more recruits. Yeah, I believe I'll have me a tough little army of scrappers again soon, because I believe that America's biggest crop right now is its crop of screwed-up and pissed-off poor young dudes.

We've got ourselves a nice place. It's some rich asshole's place. It's probably where the owner came to fuck strange pussy. It's the kind of place my old man would laugh about, calling it a *stabbin' cabin*, but it's fancy as hell. The biggest bedroom has slippery sheets and big towels and gold faucets in the bathroom and a shitload of bathrobes in the closets.

We fuck it up, right away. Smears on the mirrors, mud on the rugs, leaving evidence of us everywhere. We treat the place like a rock band would. It's just another place we can use up and leave behind us.

We were lucky to find it in the blizzard, but I've always had pretty good luck with finding good shit. Whoever owned the house was some kind of survivalist, too, because there's a good stockpile of food and water and booze and we have three fireplaces and a big propane generator in one of the sheds out back. I think there must be solar panels on the roof, too, but they don't do us much good, seeing as how they're buried with snow.

The storm blows like a starving whore for five days before it lets up. I start to make plans for us, but another storm comes in and another and another, and we're changing. For one thing, we get sick again. We're sick from both ends, and I'm not sure if we'll make it this time. We're sick and stuck here together, changing back into the way we were in juvie, spending our time on nothing and everything, because time and pain is all we have. We don't clean up after ourselves and we don't stoke the fire or run the generator.

But then we start to get better. We get our energy back, but that's not necessarily a good thing. By the time the storms let up, I'm sleeping upstairs with the Beretta under my pillow and Luscious is downstairs doing sets of a hundred push-ups and Darko is avoiding us both. I'm still the boss, but I think if we're stuck here much longer, there won't be as many of us.

Jerry

The storm is the most brutal weather I've lived through. I alternate between thanking God for it and praying for it to stop. Brief periods of calm rush past, but the clouds are so thick that the trees cast no shadows. The sky upends itself every few hours and there's at least five feet of snow on the ground. Drifts bury the blackberries and rise up over the cabin like frozen sea swells. I'm grateful for it, but I'm also wild to get to Sacramento to see Susan and Scotty. But we have no choice except to hunker down in the cabin and hope that spring will win out over what appears to be a nuclear winter.

We're in stir. Lockup. We're safe, probably, from the goons

of the world, but we need to keep our spirits up. In the purgatory of the stormbound cabin, Melanie becomes an optimist. At least she pretends to be one. She watches the storm rage.

"It's only the earth cleaning up after us," she says. "The bombs put tons of junk into the atmosphere. This is only a mother, cleaning up after her children. It might take a while, but she'll get things straightened up."

"You are very wise, for one so young."

She glowers, then she almost smiles.

There's a combination checkers/chess set in the cabin. Melanie sets it up and we play chess. She's a fine strategist, and we're evenly matched. We win one game apiece, then I lose my concentration and Melanie beats me two games in a row.

Outside, the wind rises into something like a continuous explosion. Trees crack with sounds like high-power gunshots. Heavy timbers fall against the cabin, and I begin to fear that we'll lose the roof.

I stoke up a huge fire. The storm pulls the flames up the chimney like it's drinking heat from a straw. There isn't a lot more we can do. We get into a corny mood, because why the hell not? We sing "Michael Row Your Boat Ashore" and other camp favorites. I hear the parts where Susan and Scott would normally join in, but I sing past them, holding up nothing but my end of the melody. We make hot chocolate and I lace mine with dollops of 190-proof whiskey.

I'm feeling almost fine, but then we get sick again, and my stomach rejects the booze. The place reeks of puke and partially absorbed alcohol. We assume the familiar positions of the irradiated, alternately curling and arching, and I pray it will pass, this time the last, but the roof creaks against the wind and we have no assurances. We hold our shelter over us with nothing but the power of fear, knowing that things could probably be worse, but incapable of feeling gratitude for anything on this earth.

The sickness and the storm pass gradually into history. I'm not sure exactly when it happens. A time comes when the pain is merely horrible, and nature is no longer clawing at our roof. We rise again from our filth, thin and nerve-jangled and weak. I manage to unbolt the door and throw it open. The great wind has blown itself out, and the sky is clear for the first time since the bombs, a curved pate of blue, the most tender blue I've ever seen. It's very cold and the world slumbers beneath its blankets and cocoons of snow. Melanie walks outside and stands beside me. We breathe in the clean, cold air. It makes me cough, and the sound of my coughing falls flat against the hushed snowscape.

We turn our faces up to gaze into the heatless sky. I can see forever, or as much of forever as we're allowed to see, and I feel as if I've been freed from a cage. I give a silent prayer of thanks, then spit my remaining bile into the snow. A breeze chills my ears and sighs away through flocked trees. Branches sway and creak and then fall silent. We plow into the fresh powder snow. Sometimes it reaches our knees and sometimes it supports our weight only after we've fallen waist deep. We fumble and flutter until we break a trail to the creek. We dig to its frozen surface, and I fall to my knees and put my ear close to it, and I'm overjoyed to hear the trickle of water moving freely beneath the ice.

Melanie stands beside me. She's smiling. I'm smiling, too. It's mid-spring now, and the plants aren't blossoming. Maybe they won't blossom this year, and maybe we'll have another huge thing to worry about, but we're not worrying about it now. There isn't a cloud in the sky, but the high haze remains. Only a small fist of sun shines down on us.

We return to the cabin. I light a fire and then we set about cleaning up after ourselves. Melanie pitches in and we have the place squared away in no time at all.

We're getting very low on food. We have a well-stocked bar, but we're down to our last dusty cans of Dinty Moore—the ones that we set aside because they're dented. I think it's about time for me to try my hand at shopping for protein at Mother Nature's stores. I could catch some trout or shoot another deer, if any of the local game is still alive and uncontaminated. At the very worst, I could hack some meat from animals that certainly froze to death in the storms.

But then the government finally puts in an appearance. A C-130 flies over. It flies low over the smoke from our fire, its four big turboprops clawing the air. We run outside. Melanie's cheeks are flushed and mine probably are, too. I want to cry, but I don't. We wave and jump and shout, and the next day, the sky is thumping and clattering with helicopters. They're flying nap-of-the-earth, and they turn toward the smoke from our chimney. A National Guard Huey buzzes the house and gives us its loud-slapping rotor sounds. The Huey is big and real, and it's the prettiest bird I've ever seen.

The crew drops us a military survival walkie-talkie. We don't have much of a conversation on the radio. The crew chief takes down our information, how many living and missing and dead, the possible locations of other survivors, then he tells us to draw a big "X" in the snow if we need supplies. We stamp one out, and the C-130 makes a run on us. The heavens open, and our lean times are over. Parachuted supplies float down on target, three big boxes, and we have to get under cover to avoid being hit. The last of the packages thump into the snow and we run out like kids and tear into them. We have MREs and bottled water and blankets and first aid kits. We have pamphlets about how to survive in extreme weather and how to decontaminate ourselves and how to make traps to catch small game and how to do all the other things we've already been doing to make it this far into the longest winter on record.

There are also a few copies of some kind of newspaper. It reads like propaganda, and it's written at about a fifth-grade level, but we finally get some news. The lead story is an address from the new president of the United States. I don't recognize his name. His pamphlet urges us to come together in this trying time. Apparently, we've wiped North Korea and the tribal areas of Pakistan from the map. The Russians and Chinese and Europeans are assisting with the global mop-up of Al Qaeda. There are a half dozen fluff pieces about people who displayed the right stuff and towns that overcame the odds. There's also a piece written in an official tone about how "it was decided that displaced peoples should remain in their places of domicile for the immediate future, unless those places of domicile are officially declared hazardous for human occupation. More information will be forthcoming."

Melanie and I read the official notice together. We guffaw from opposites sides of the political spectrum, but then we get back into character. We open the packages, and it just about blows my mind when I find a patching kit for bicycle tires, and a compact sewing kit and fishing line and hooks and tiny space blankets and shampoo with conditioner and potassium iodide tablets and a bottle of prenatal vitamin tablets. I laugh and I leak a few tears when I start to believe again that we're still citizens of the richest and silliest nation that God has ever tolerated on His earth.

Susan

We aren't attacked. We don't have to defend the town from barbarians, praise God, because the government is here now, pulling off what appears to be the biggest disaster response in its history. I'm as happy as I can be about it, but Scott frowns when the helicopters fly over. The lines of scar tissue that fragment his brows and cheeks and jaw pull tight, and he turns away from me.

"We'll get your sister and father back now," I say.

"One way or the other."

"I know they're alive. How could they *not* be?"

Scott snuffles and then makes a big show of blowing his nose.

"Either way, the monsters have to pay."

"Shouldn't we leave that to God?"

"I *am* leaving it to God. It's what He told me to do."

I don't know what to say. He walks outside to watch the helicopters land. From his turned back I hear:

"He told me. I heard it."

Melanie

We'll be leaving soon. We're gentle with each other while we divide the MREs. We trade for our favorite entrees. I get the veggie entrees. Dad takes the meat dishes—Pork Rib and Beef Enchilada and Pot Roast w/Vegetables and Meatloaf w/Gravy and Chicken Fajita. I get a pile of meals, too—Veggie Burger w/ BBQ Sauce, Cheese Tortellini, Vegetable Manicotti, Cheese & Vegetable Omelet, and Vegetable Lasagna.

We eat our first meals fast and cold. I don't know how many we eat, but it's a lot. The place is littered with foil packets and slimed with food. We have food on our faces and our hands are greasy with super-preserved sauces. We burp and smile, then we see what pigs we've made of ourselves and we get kind of shy.

By evening, we're getting back some of our almost-forgotten etiquette. I light lanterns and pump some water and clean my hands and face. Dad cleans himself, too. While he's cleaning up, I clear the dining room table. I scrub the table as clean as I can, then I cover it with a linen tablecloth and set it with place settings I find in the hutch. White china plates with real silverware. I wonder when they were last used—a holiday meal, the celebration of a new birth, a wake. I light candles and heat our MREs in unfamiliar pots and pans. I find spices in the kitchen cupboards, and I add them to our meal, just because I can. Garlic and pepper and Tabasco and oregano and ginger powder. I add tiny amounts that I can barely taste, but it makes me feel rich to know that all those spices are in my food.

Dad stokes a long-burning fire in the fireplace, and we sit down at the table. We're lit by soft flames. Dad bows his head and gives thanks, his lips moving, but no sound coming out. It's the way he prays in public. It's not like he's shy about his religion or anything, and it occurs to me that he's praying quietly like he does when he doesn't want to embarrass me.

But I'm not embarrassed. He lifts his head and sees me looking at him. He smiles a huge smile. He hardly ever smiles like that when he's sober, but he's doing it now.

"What?" I say.

"Nothing," he says. "It's just that I think we might be on the other side of this thing."

"I think you might be right."

He nods and makes his "I'm pretending to be serious" face. I nod back at him. He hasn't changed a bit since this whole thing began. He's still worried about me, and he'll still kill in my name, if it comes to that.

I must've let something show on my face, because he asks me if I'm okay. I tell him everything's fine, then I squish everything back down inside me. That's what cowards do, right?

But then almost nothing else matters as we dig into our last high-calorie meal of the day. I feel the proteins and carbs going to work inside me, and for the first time in weeks, I start to worry about getting fat. I tell Dad about it, and he laughs a real laugh. We eat in the flickering light, and our stomachs accept the nourishment, and it's almost as good as all the dreams I've had lately of unlimited room service in a nice hotel.

*   *   *

After the first day of feasting we cut back to two meals a day. After we eat, we go outside and stare into the blue sky, but no more airplanes or helicopters fly over. After two days, Dad goes out scouting to see what's around us. I go for a walk, too. I have nowhere else to go, so I follow Dad's tracks, trying to be as quiet as I can.

I like the hard work of being quiet. I walk slowly because speed makes me noisy. I try to walk on the hard parts of the world, rocks and logs like slippery balance beams. I'm a gymnast, and I've trained for years to be very careful about where I put my feet, and I can walk with almost no sound at all.

Dad's tracks go on and on, and sometimes they have deer tracks around them, but he's still walking straight away from the cabin. I'm not a mountain girl or anything, but I think the deer tracks are fresh. And then I see a deer. It's a doe, and she's pawing at the ground and eating snow-dried grass. I stop walking and she looks at me, but I don't think she can really see me. She tunes her ears at me like antennae while she lifts her tail and lets fly with her pellets, fertilizing whatever might still dare to grow in this world, then she slides into deeper woods.

It's a soft day. The creek gurgles under its layer of ice, and in some places the water splashes onto snow. The ice is clear and grainy like an unflavored snow cone. It looks crunchy and good, and I eat some, and it is. Robins and jays make a racket in the trees. Squirrels and jackrabbits stand and chew on their meals of stored acorns. I space out for a while in that mild place, and I try to forget everything, but I can't.

I start walking faster. The creek is about a quarter mile behind me when I know I'm not alone. I get the feeling that something dangerous is nearby. I slow down. I see Dad standing at the edge of a clearing. It's a snowy meadow with a big McMansion in the middle of it. There's smoke coming from the chimney. Someone is outside chopping firewood. It's only about thirty-five degrees out, but the wood-chopping guy has his shirt off. His skin is the color of unsweetened chocolate and his muscles are big. His hair has grown out since I saw him last. He has a big 'fro now, like athletes had in the seventies, but there's no doubt that it's Luscious.

My breathing speeds up and my vision gets super-clear. Luscious doesn't see us, so that means he's vulnerable. I like seeing him vulnerable. Dad has an arrow strung in his bow. His head is down, but his eyes are locked onto his target. For a few heartbeats, I want to watch Dad shoot Luscious. For a few heartbeats I wish I had a gun, so I could do it myself.

But no. Hell no. I get more pissed off than I've ever been in my life. I'm pissed at Luscious and Dad and most of all I'm pissed at my own cowardly ass.

I move closer. I'm all done with trying to be quiet. This is the last straw. It's the boys and Dad again, with only their violence in common, but it's me, too, and I'm running past the edge of the woods and straight out into the clearing between them. The snow is the same pale color as the sky. The air is cold but softening, and I can feel mud beneath the snow.

Dad runs after me, but Luscious sees us then. He drops his axe and reaches for something. I see the whites of his eyes as his big hands close over a rifle. It's like my worst nightmare, but somehow I'm not afraid.

Dad takes a shot with his bow. His arrow arcs over my head and misses Luscious by an inch and goes cracking into the far trees. He shoots another arrow, but Luscious dives behind his stack of firewood. Dad drops the bow and takes out his little revolver and pop, pop, pops away, but no one is killing anyone yet.

There's still time, so I get exactly between them and I hold up my hands. A voice comes out of me that I've never heard before. I tell them to stop, for once in their lives to stop and *think*! It feels damned good to say it. Maybe I'm crazy because I'm not afraid anymore. And now that the fear is gone, I'm lifted up into the buzz of what I'm doing.

I stand between them, waving my hands over my head like a crazy woman. And they *do* stop. Dad stops shooting. He reloads the revolver, but when it's loaded he keeps it pointed at the ground. Luscious points his rifle at us, but he doesn't fire.

They look at me. They look at each other. Dad tries to move sideways so I'm not in his line of fire, but I sidestep to keep myself between them. He says, Please, baby, but I'm not a baby anymore. I'm doing the first logical fucking thing I've seen anyone do since this shit began.

I hear Dad start to move behind me. He walks straight toward me, and I immediately walk straight toward Luscious. Dad stops. I stop. Luscious smiles and shakes his head.

"Y'all are crazy," he says. "All y'all."

"Well then, let's be crazy together," I say.

"Let her go. She hasn't done anything to you," Dad says.

"Well, maybe you missed the part when she did a whole lot of things to a whole lot of people. Maybe we want our little whore back."

Dad raises the revolver and Luscious raises his rifle.

"Stop," I say. "Let's talk. We have food. We could sit down and eat and talk."

It's like they don't hear me. They're looking right through me. The anger flares up so high that I can barely see.

259

"Dammit! Damn you all! Can't you pull your heads out of your asses?"

I hold my arms out and take a few steps closer to Luscious.

"It's over," I say. "The National Guard is on the way. FEMA and cops and insurance adjusters and bail bondsmen and all that crap. The world is putting itself back together. It's time to get back to being normal."

Then Bill Junior walks out of the back door of the house. He's carrying a black rifle, but he's not pointing it at anyone.

"We've got the most normal thing in the world going on right here, girl," he says. "Come over here, why don't you, and give us some sugar."

His voice is soft, but it makes me want to puke. With Bill Junior and Luscious and Dad out in the open, the geometry is impossible, and I can't stand between them all. Donnie Darko comes out of the house, too. He's holding a pistol down behind his skinny butt. I don't think he'll shoot us, but he's another life to worry about. I back up until Dad is close behind me. He grabs my shoulders. I let him. He whispers to me.

"You've had your say. Let's just back away now."

He points his revolver with his right hand and wraps his left arm around me. He pulls me backward, but I don't move my feet. How could I? I'm doing something worthwhile and I can't stop now.

I try to peel his arm from around me, but he tightens his grip. He pulls me backward. I'm back to screaming again, because I scream at him to stop. My boot heels leave twin lines in the snow. He says something about running, and then he twists me around very fast. He's shielding me from the boys, but he doesn't know that my power can't save us when it's not in plain sight.

I hear the popping of gunshots. Dad lifts me off my feet

and I have no traction to fight him. He fires his revolver over his shoulder, then he drops it and holds me leg-straddled in front of him and he starts to run. I hear more shots and something hits me and I can't catch my breath. I don't want to, but I rest my chin on Dad's shoulder and he hikes me up higher to get a better grip. I look down and see the backs of his boots, running. The snow is granulated here, too, and there's blood in it, and I can't help but think it's a properly flavored snow cone now.

Scott

The helicopters land. Six Black Hawks and two Apache gunships. Their green paint is so dark that I can't read the black letters and symbols that identify them. They put down in a field of snow not far from the skeleton of Old Bill's Cessna.

"Here's our ride," Mom says.

She's wearing a daypack. She found a new shotgun in town, and she's carrying it in her good hand. She looks down at it, then props it against the wall of the saloon. She motions to the helicopters.

"Shall we?" she says.

I roll my eyes.

"Our heroes," I say.

The townspeople throw their doors open and run long lines across the buried roads and fields to meet the helicopters. Their packs are light, but their feet are clumsy in the snow.

They smile at each other as they run. It might be one of those good times that people keep in their memories and tell their kids about, years later. It might be a rescue and the beginning of a return to a normal way of life, but I'm not ready for normal.

I slip into my pack and walk the other way. Of all the guns in town, I chose a scoped Kimber 30.06. I'll be walking in open country, and it feels good to have a rifle that can reach out across it. I have a .40 caliber Glock at the small of my back, for close-in fighting, and plenty of ammo for both guns.

Mom was heading toward the helicopters, but she stops right away when I don't pull up beside her. She turns and runs after me. She has a spastic running form, with her arm in the sling, but she's still pretty fast. She picks up her shotgun and follows me. Part of me is happy to have her with me, but I don't want her to be around when I catch up to the ambushers.

We get some buildings between ourselves and the rescuers. Mom pulls up beside me and I stop. I lift my head in the direction of the helicopters.

"You should go," I say.

"We both should go," she says.

"I'm not going."

"Okay. But I'm coming with you."

She looks right into my eyes, and her lips are welded together.

"I won't take any orders from you. If you see something you don't like, I'll appreciate it if you keep quiet about it."

"I'm not here to be your conscience."

"Good."

"But I do have one request. Let's find your father and sister first."

"That's the plan, but it might not work out that way. What if we find Bill Junior's crew first?"

"If we do, I'll help you. God help me, but I want to hurt them, too."

"I'm not talking about only hurting them."

"I know."

She's looking straight at my face. My freak-show face. I turn it away from her and we head to the center of town.

I put on my best pace. The snow in town is packed hard, and I'm really moving. Mom has trouble keeping up. I slow down. I can't wait to see Dad and Melanie. I can't wait to see the little assholes who brought us so much hell, and return the favor. I believe some of them are alive, and I want to see them through my rifle scope.

But Mom is still skinny from the radiation, and I'm not exactly in the best shape of my life, either. We lean against a building to catch our breath. We turn to watch the rescue. The helicopters are still on the ground, and their rotors are still turning. The pilot of the first helicopter motions for people to hurry. The dark visor of his helmet is down, so we can't see his face. I try to imagine what it would be like to be him, but I can't.

When the people from town get right into the whipping rotor wash, soldiers jump out of the second helicopter and point their rifles. They shout something and the people drop what they're carrying and lie down with their hands straight out from their sides. My tongue gets really cold because my mouth is open. Sam tries to run back to town, but the soldiers shoot into the snow around him. The snow flies up and sticks to his clothes and clouds of it swirl around him. Mom makes a little strangled sound. Sam stops. He drops the Mini-14 he had slung over his shoulder. He looks right at us and gives us a nod, and we crouch down behind the building. The building has old gray wood siding. It's the café that Sam's mother used to run. It has a wooden boardwalk in front of it, all snowdrifted, and I go prone in the snow and watch the rescue turn into a mass abduction.

The soldiers put plastic zip ties on people's wrists. They drag them to the helicopters and lift them inside. Engines wind up and rotors beat harder and they make a big mushroom cloud of snow. When the helicopters lift out of the top of their cloud, they're dark and loud and they fly with their doors open. The faces of the good townspeople are down against nonskid floors as they're taken away to God knows where.

We walk south. I borrowed something from a tourist shop in Virginia City. I'm wearing a pair of badass Oakley sunglasses. They feel like armor for my eyes, but Mom is squinting in the snow-glare, so I offer her the sunglasses. She refuses, but I say, "We'll trade off wearing them," and she takes them. They look good on her.

The cold numbs my patchwork face, and almost makes it feel bulletproof. I break a trail in the snow that leads straight down the middle of the road. I know what I need to do, and I'm not worried about anyone stopping me. I'm not afraid of ambushers or soldiers because I'm following the still, clear voice of God. The ambushers will be like fruit on the vine when I find them, and so shall I reap them.

I have no fear of man or beast. The soldiers might be running wild, but I don't think so. I think they're just being careful. They probably got shot at in some of the other towns, so they're just taking precautions. The people of Virginia City are good people, and the soldiers shouldn't have treated them like assholes, but like Jesus said, "Forgive them, for they know not what they do."

No. The soldiers aren't the enemy. At least not yet.

Donnie

I'm the only one left. I shot those other two. They were shooting at Melanie and I had to stop 'em, didn't I? Captain Bill was pretty surprised when I popped him with his own fucking Beretta. Blood came out of his neck. It squirted like a hose. He put his hand over it, but he couldn't stop it. He smiled at me, and his teeth were bloody like a vampire that just bit someone. He tried to say something, but I don't know what. Probably one of his little speeches about pirates. Then he fell and didn't move anymore.

I don't remember shooting Luscious, but he's dead as shit, too. It's no use trying to bring them back to life, so I pick up their guns and go back inside the house. It's quiet and maybe it's safe, but I don't like being alone. Maybe it's stupid, because people always do bad things to me, but I like to have some people around. Especially Melanie. But I think she got hit. I know she did, and her old man took her away and I'll probably never see her smile again.

Life is a trip. There's nobody to boss me around now. No skanky mom to bring her johns home and no drunk assholes putting their cigarettes out on me and no lying social workers making up stories about me then sending me to get ass-fucked in juvie. My ass is mine for the first time in my whole life. I'm not sorry I shot those other two, but I wish I had someone to talk to.

It's cold in the house because we burned up all our firewood in the night. I bring in the firewood that Luscious chopped up before he got killed. I build a hot fire in the woodstove, then I go upstairs and tear apart the room Captain Bill stayed in. He had some cans of food stashed under his bed. I open a can of pork and beans and eat it cold. My belly gets full and tight, and I like the way the sauce coats my mouth with a brown sugar taste. I sit and listen to the wind in the trees. Branches creak and snow falls from them in big clods, but it doesn't scare me. It makes me kind of sad, because no one else can hear what I'm hearing.

I sleep until first light. When I wake up, I know exactly what I need to do. I need to go find Melanie and her old man. I'm still Melanie's doctor, and I need to check on her. I don't think her old man would shoot me just for trying. It didn't seem like he hated me enough to kill me. I *had* to shoot him with my slingshot that time, or Bill Junior would've killed me. I hope he knows that.

Anyhow, they're the only people in the world I give two shits about, and I want to see them again.

Jerry

Only three rules are left: Start the breathing, stop the bleeding, and treat for shock. But she's lung-shot and I have to seal the hole first. Her skin is slick with blood. I'm wired on adrenaline and I'm sick to my stomach, so it takes me a while to get her sealed up, but I finally get the entry and exit holes covered with duct tape. I have to breathe for her at first, but then her left lung inflates and she's breathing on her own, thank God. But her breathing is labored, and then blood comes from her mouth. It's choking her. I roll her onto her side and I put my knee into her back and pull her into it, trying to put pressure on the bleeder. I pray *please, please, please*, praying that pressure will stop the bleeding, but she's coughing blood everywhere and I know I'll have to unplug the patches and find the leak. Find a way to pinch it closed.

Her coughs grow weaker and my arms are about to fall off from the effort of holding pressure against her chest. I'm as cold as I've ever been in my life, but I can see dust in the air. We're in a pool of blood and the fibers of the floorboards expand like tiny ropes as they drink it in. It's no use. I'm losing her. I need to try something else.

I roll her onto her stomach so she won't choke on her blood. I run to the kitchen. I searched it when we first arrived, and I remember finding a drawer filled with miscellaneous possibles. I open it, and yes, yes, yes, it's just what I need to tie off bleeders. A small pair of yellow-handled needle-nose pliers and a roll of six-pound-test fishing line.

"I found it, Mel," I say. "We'll be okay now."

But when I get back to her, she's gone quiet. I give her CPR again, my breath wheezing into her lungs and my numb arms pushing contractions against her ribcage. The universe is black and there's only this, the grunting of one alive and the quiet fighting of one on the brink.

I try to bring her back until I'm neither here nor myself. I stop only when my arms refuse to move. I'm angry at my arms. I shake some blood into them and try to resume the compressions, but I almost pass out. It's very quiet. The front door is open, and a gust of wind gives the trees a good shake.

I look at her face. Something pops inside me, and I fall to the floor. I don't understand how I failed her. I had her in my arms and my body was shielding hers, so how did she get shot? And that's when I look down and see the blood pulsing from my side. The blood is dark, almost black. It's a high liver hit, probably, and it doesn't hurt until I see it, then the pain powers against the horror, and I'm almost glad for it.

I'm saying no, no, no, and then I'm floating somewhere in rusty water, and then I come back to living hell. I look at her face again. I ask her how she's doing. She's being very quiet, but I think I see her eyes sparkle, so maybe she's up to something. I slide across the bloody floor and stretch out beside her. I listen for the slightest sound, but there's nothing. She's very good at this game, so I join her. I don't move a muscle, holding as still as possible, seeing how long I can last before the game comes to its natural conclusion.

Susan

We walk through time and space and random humanity. We crest Donner Pass and continue southwest on Highway 80 in order to move north on I-5. Pine woods. Cabins on the hills, some of them puffing woodsmoke into the weak sky. Gun muzzles track us from time to time, but we're serving God's purpose and we pay them no heed. We pass plywood-patched convenience stores. Some of them are open for business, with few saleable goods and astronomical prices and nodding clerks and alert armed guards.

I use one of the gold coins to buy six cans of ready-to-eat chicken noodle soup. A thin man sees the coin. He follows us out of the store and we unsling our guns and he goes back inside. I stand watch with my shotgun while Scotty lights a fire and heats two cans of soup. The glorious smell of hot food rises into the air and my stomach clenches. We sit back to back with our weapons at the ready as we slurp it down. We burn our mouths tasteless, and the feast is over too quickly, the warmth fading from our bellies as we walk, but hope no longer seems like a fool's errand.

Every turn of the road is a mystery. The radiation was concentrated in certain places, and we cover our faces and pass pools in the river fouled with rotting trout and corpses of deer and bobcat and skunks and porcupines and opossums. Human corpses are rare but not absent, the expressions of their final pain preserved by the cold.

We walk until I no longer need the sling for my arm, and I toss the filthy thing away in the snow. The exit wound is a puckered anus, but it seems to be sealed against the world's infections. The muscles are wasted thin and the skin of my forearm is itchy from its confinement, but it feels fine to swing both arms as I walk. It makes me feel wider, somehow, and more substantial as I march with restored symmetry

We walk down the middle of unplowed mountain roads, the lichen hanging thick on mason-built retaining walls, the rust growing Rorschachs on green bridges. The sun sends its rays through flocked trees, but the sun has no heat and we walk in strobes of glare and shadow, paying no mind to people sitting on porches, calling out to us for food or news but offering us nothing in return. We're armed, but our weapons remain on our shoulders until we stop in the nights, shivering together in abandoned houses, not standing watch. The soup lasts a week, then we eat whatever scraps we find in strange cupboards, but most often we eat nothing at all.

We pass through abandoned mountain places. We grow very weak, but then Scotty manages to shoot a deer. We roast the meat in fireplaces and atop woodstoves and over open fires, and then we're down in lower country, winter-fallow fields, and there aren't any deer, so we fall to scavenging from the frozen carcasses of cattle and sheep and llama, hoping they died of thirst or starvation and not radiation or disease.

Walking downhill out of the Sierra and onto the floor of the long Central Valley, the road hidden beneath its blanket of snow, but with power lines and fences and abandoned vehicles to define its path. The big sky of the valley is high and inscrutable because of the fallout that hasn't yet fallen. The valley is warmer than the mountains, but not by much.

We merge onto I-5 North at our top speed of three miles

per hour. We trudge through the snow, and the only sound is of our trudging, and then vehicles approach us from the rear. We move away from the road, plunging through the snow-filled ditch and up onto its western bank. A fleet of all-terrain tow trucks is powering through the snow. They clatter up from the south with the industrial smell of diesel exhaust, their tire chains ringing like steel crickets. They feed on the cars abandoned on the highway, all the tow trucks left in the state, maybe. Men joke in the cold air and attach heavy chains to the cars and hoist them onto flatbeds and lift them by their tow hooks. One of the men stands at the ready with a rifle as we pass, but all of us are here with a purpose other than killing, and our weapons remain unfired. We trudge ahead. The men get into their trucks and clatter back to the south. I can see their flashing red lights for many miles behind us.

More vehicles rise up out of the snow. We stop to watch a big orange snowplow approach and, behind it, a truck belonging to the United States Postal Service. The drivers of the trucks blow their horns at us as they pass, but they don't wave, and we don't, either.

After days of walking, the air seems to be warming. Maybe it is. Sometimes the snow feels like wet concrete beneath my boots. Sometimes I think I see gleams of liquid water in the highway ditches, and the climate of people seems to be warming as well.

We begin to see other people on the road. A woman standing alone on the road's shoulder who shows us wallet-size pictures of her family, and then turns and walks southbound over her northbound footprints. A boy with no hair or teeth walks out of the ruins of an old roadside fruit stand and joins us, begging with plaintive gestures of hand to mouth at first, but then just walking. He seems fascinated by Scott's torn face. Scott gives him a good look at it, then pulls the hood of his coat over his head. The bald, toothless boy at least pretends to fall beneath the trance of our mission, though we tell him nothing about it. I become accustomed to his presence, wondering what he might talk about, and then one day he turns west on a coast-bound road and leaves us without a word.

Military convoys pass, trucks and humvees loaded with soldiers who look as if they should still be in high school. Scott watches them, and maybe he already thinks he's one of them. Other cars and trucks pass, one or two groups per day, their occupants holding their gazes fixed on whatever lies ahead but watching us from the corners of their eyes.

We haven't heard gunshots for many days, but we stay on the freeway through Red Bluff and Redding, staying well clear of the manned barricades that block their freeway entrances and exits. We walk past the highway signs for their amenities, their closed restaurants and burned hotels and looted supermarkets, and we don't look back.

I once had pleasant memories of Redding, summer road trip memories from when the kids were young and Jerry drove with his hand on my leg, in times when we were free to stop anywhere we chose. Music and air-conditioning and frivolous snack foods and the life-affirming backbeat of quickly resolved bickering. Above it and through it and all around us was the unwinding thrall of the road.

I try to remember what a pleasant journey feels like, but I can't conjure up those silly old emotions. I'd always been grateful to leave the rote of homebound responsibility behind me, and so all the world seemed new and lovely. I once had an almost absurd fondness for the places we're passing, the Redding boat dealerships and retail outlets stretching to the foothills, but now I walk armed on the ribbon of interstate that once symbolized freedom, and I can't look back.

We cross the bridge over Lake Shasta, the lake frozen below us, and we climb into the Siskiyou Mountains. The airspace over Dunsmuir is filled with carrion birds. We pass through the steep, valley-shaped town, the smell of bodies making our eyes water. Some of the vultures are too fat to fly, and some of them take runs at us. Scott shoots one of them and it explodes meat and black feathers across the filthy snowscape and we walk up a steep grade to put Dunsmuir behind us.

Donnie

It's time for me to go. I should bring some presents with me. Maybe Melanie's old man won't shoot me if I bring presents. I grab a suitcase from a closet upstairs and I fill it with the food stashes that the others were hiding in their bedrooms—sliced peaches and pork and beans and chili and beef enchiladas. I don't bring any cans of green beans or peas or creamed corn because I don't see how anyone can eat that shit.

I'll bring the first aid kit, for sure. The rich people that owned this house had a *huge* first aid kit, and a big jar of penicillin in the fridge, and even a few vials of morphine. I found the drugs before those others could, and I took them out of the cold refrigerator and hid them in the snow. I was saving them in case it got too dangerous here and I had to shoot up those other two with morphine and make a run for it. So yeah, I have enough shit to doctor up just about anyone.

I bungee cord the first aid kit to the suitcase, then I see the guns. Should I bring a gun? I won't shoot at Melanie or her old man, even if they shoot at me, but what if I run into a bear or wolves or some human assholes? So yeah, I'll bring a gun, but only the pistol, and I'll keep it jammed down next to my dick and covered by my coat.

I open the door and pull the suitcase into the snow. It's colder than a witch's tit outside. The suitcase has a handle, and I pull it out and get a good hold on it. The suitcase has little wheels on it, but they don't do shit in the snow, so I pull it behind me like a sled.

I walk to where Melanie's tracks got closest to the house. I follow them to where they meet her old man's tracks. A few feet past that, there's blood in the snow. I follow the blood and tracks into the woods. I hope they aren't too far away, because this fucking suitcase is heavy. I walk and drag my shit behind me, and the suitcase gouges our tracks and mostly wipes them away.

It takes less than half an hour to find out where they went. It's a log cabin, like the log cabin on maple syrup bottles. Their tracks lead into the cabin and don't come out again. The front door is open. I drop the suitcase and say, "Hey, it's Donnie. I brought you some presents."

They don't answer. I look around. Nothing is moving but me. I'm alone and I don't think anyone is watching me, but all that quiet creeps me out. I want to pull the pistol out of my pants, but I don't. I walk onto the porch. The snow is kind of slushy and I move my feet forward like I'm ice-skating, even though I haven't ever really ice-skated before, except with shoes on frozen mud puddles.

I knock on the open door, but there's a whole lot of nothing talking back to me. I walk into the cabin and see them lying on the floor. There's blood everywhere and they're not moving. I want to run away, but my legs won't move. I want to run away, because I don't want to get blamed for this shit. But then my legs take me over to them. The blood is slick, and I have to ice-skate again.

I've seen dead people before, and this is what they look like. I wasn't ever sad when I saw dead people before, but I think I'm sad now. Melanie's eyes are open and I reach down and close them. Her face is still pretty and I wish she'd say something to me, something nice or just something kind of ordinary, but I know she won't.

Her old man's eyes are open, too. He isn't pretty at all. He's got cuts all over him, for one thing, and for another thing, he's making a face like he died needing to take a massive shit. I reach down to close his eyes, too, but they turn and look at me. I just about piss my pants. I back away and he lifts his head. He says, "Shhhhh. Can't you see we're playing a game here?"

He's got no blood inside him and he's crazy as a shithouse fly, but that doesn't stop me from getting into my doctor way of thinking. I run outside and grab the first aid kid from the suitcase. I'll patch up his holes, neat as anything, and if I can't save him, it won't be because I didn't try.

Scott

We pass the sign that welcomes us to Norris, California, but nobody is home. It kind of freaks me out to see the blown-up food market. The sight of it makes my head hurt, and it pisses me off. We check it out, but there's nothing we can use in there. Nothing but blasted lumber and broken glass and maybe some DNA evidence of our family blood, all mixed together.

We walk in wider and wider circles around the store, looking for anything that might help us find them. I'm not afraid of running into an ambush, because God would tell me if I was about to. I'm not afraid. Mom doesn't seem be afraid, either. She's wearing the Oakley sunglasses and carrying her twelve-gauge shotgun at the ready. She looks like a female Terminator. I probably look like shit, with my cut-up face and skinny body, but I'll look like a nightmare to anyone who tries to fuck with us.

We search the empty houses along the main road. We knock at the first few places, but then we don't say anything before I kick in the doors. No one is home.

The Golden Eagle Motel is trashed, and it's no mystery who trashed it. All the rooms are filled with random, rotting things, food and stinky clothes and stains of all kinds on the sheets and walls and carpets. But the motel is empty.

We search both lumber mills. One of them has a line of rail cars beside it, and it used to make real lumber. The other mill made these little wooden fenceposts that people use for landscaping projects. We walk like hunting animals inside the buildings and all around them, the Chamber of Commerce building and the Mexican restaurant and the junkyard and the Moody Brews coffee shop, but there's nothing. We find a workshop in one of the buildings that's full of leather and leatherworking tools and custom-made horse saddles. The saddles look awesome, and I wouldn't mind meeting the person who made them, but there's nobody home.

We walk around and around, our orbits getting bigger, taking nearly the whole day to search a town with a population of a thousand. The sky is starting to go pale when we find ourselves climbing up into the hills on the north side of town. The town is below us on the edge of a big bowl that looks like it used to be full of water. The light is going away, but my rifle scope is very good, and I use it to look for anything we might've missed. I see a house out past the eastern edge of where we searched. I turn up the scope's magnification. It's a Leupold variable 3- to 12-power scope and it takes me a while to get the house back into my field of view. The place is white with green trim. At least I think it used to be those colors. The walls are blown out, and I can see inside the living room.

I tell Mom I found a house where a fight happened. She sees where I'm looking. She stands up and we walk through the last sunrays of the day. We walk the main drag and take the alley we took before, back when we were all together. The junkyard is covered with snow, but it doesn't look any prettier. There's evidence of the little assholes everywhere, graffiti and garbage and broken things. It's like walking through a place where zombies roamed, but none of these assholes had the decency to stick around long enough for me to put my scope's crosshairs on them.

*   *   *

We spend the night in the blown-up house. The main floor is covered with spent brass, a layer of 7.62 NATO empties and little steel pieces that look like the links that hold machine-gun ammunition together. I look for a machine gun, but can't find one. Sandbags are set in the windows. The walls are full of random and not-so-random holes. It must've been a hell of a fight, but I can't tell how it turned out. There isn't any blood or blood trails, but the absence of blood doesn't prove anything.

We set up camp in the basement. There's a little woodstove down there, and enough firewood to get our faces red and itchy. I put some strips of frozen beef on the stove and we eat it without talking. I leave the last of our scavenged meat outside in the snow. The whole world is a deep freeze now, and we wouldn't have any protein if it wasn't.

In the morning I force myself out of my sleeping bag. I go outside to take a piss and get the last of our meat, but we're not alone anymore. There's a National Guard convoy rolling up from the south. Mom is outside watching it come up. Maybe the soldiers are looking for something in particular, because they have a Black Hawk helicopter spotting for them. It's armed with door guns and it circles like it's hungry. The damned noisy, beautiful thing circles the town for half an hour before it lands next to the convoy trucks.

Then we're off again, walking a trail that leads north from the house. It's as good a direction to go as any. If Dad and Melanie were here, they probably took this trail. We walk until the trail leads to an unplowed road. We follow the road, using our senses and instincts to look for the parts of God's plan we want to come true.

*   *   *

It takes us two weeks to find them. We're out of food and burning through our supplies of faith when we smell woodsmoke. We follow the smell to a log cabin. It's not the first house we've come up to. We take cover and I shout out that we're here, and that we mean no harm; it's just that we're looking for the rest of our family. Mom covers the door with her shotgun. I scope the windows for movement. The front door opens a crack. A kid's voice asks us to show ourselves. I say, No way in hell. A black-haired kid peeks out to take a look. I get his face in the scope, but he ducks back inside before I can decide whether or not to cancel him.

He says we can come inside if we put down our guns. There's zero chance of us doing that. I sling the rifle and pull out the Glock. I walk across open ground and move to the door. The adrenaline lifts me far above hunger and doubt, but I know it won't last long. Mom moves to my side. I push the door open and step through it. The kid is inside with a pistol. He's a skinny little dude, and he's holding a Beretta down alongside his leg. I put the Glock's sights on the base of his throat and take the slack out of the trigger. He's all tensed up, but he doesn't raise the pistol. When he sees Mom, he opens his mouth. No words come out. After a few seconds he starts to calm down. Mom takes off her sunglasses. The kid gives her a long look.

"I won't shoot you," he says. He puts his pistol down on the floor and backs away from it.

"Have you seen them, a man and his daughter?" I say.

"She looked a lot like you," he says to Mom. "Come in. I'll tell you what happened."

He sits down on a couch and we stand across from him. He tells us a story. He's nervous, but he says it's everything he knows about Melanie. It's not a happy story. I can't tell the lying parts from the true ones. Mom is crying hard. I'm pretty sure the kid is telling the truth, but I keep the Glock pointed at his guts.

"I wouldn't blame you for popping me," he says. "If I had a sister and she got done like that, I might want some payback."

Mom says, "No." She gives me her no-bullshit look and I put the Glock away.

The kid is a nervous little shit. His eyes are brown and shifty, but then he gets them to lock onto mine.

"It's true that I never did anything bad to her," he says. "I helped her every chance I could get, but I couldn't help her in the end." Then his little chest puffs out and he gets a look on his face that makes him look like a juvenile delinquent Napoleon.

"It was too late for her, but listen," he says. "I saved the old man. Come on. I'll show you."

Jerry

I stretch out to die, then I wake up with that little black-haired kid checking my pulse. He's looking at the ceiling and counting out loud. He's breathing through his mouth. His breath is rank.

I have no idea what day it is. I'm in a warm bed, covered with blankets. The thin light from the bedroom window is either gaining strength or dying away. There's a tube running from my belly. I look for Melanie, but she isn't here. The black-haired kid says, "Hey, he's awake." I tell him I already know it. Someone else comes into the room. It's Susan and Scotty.

The reunion goes as well as it possibly can.

Susan

The snow starts to soften in mid-July. Our tracks grow as big as dinner plates during the day and then freeze hard at night. Jerry sits up in bed, then he can walk far enough to do his business, then he can walk downstairs for meals. His goal is to walk outside to visit Melanie. He'll be able to do it, soon.

I've been visiting Melanie every day. The ground was frozen when she died, and God's temple spoils when it's empty, so Donnie burned it. He picked a good spot, a hillside under a spreading oak, with a view of Mount Shasta and Broken Top and the dry lakebed.

He didn't tell me the details, so I make them up myself. He wrapped her in white bedsheets taken from a rich man's summer house. He sewed her into a shroud, then he built a tall, foursquare woodpile and soaked it with gasoline siphoned from one of the useless cars on the road. He put her on top, the only girl in the world who treated him like a human being. He lit the match and the fire put its arms around her and it wasn't only the smoke that made him cry.

It's only ashes and black bits of charcoal in the snow now. The fire was hot enough to scorch the oak. When it cooled,

Donnie carved her name into it. He didn't know the exact date, but he carved her name on the blackened bark. He carved a heart beneath her name. It's the most pathetic heart I've ever seen.

In August, the thaw achieves a more complete victory. The icy stream moans and leaks at the edges of its banks and then its water breaks. The icicles fall from the eaves of the cabin and shatter when they hit the porch. The world is dripping and soggy. The underbrush here is thin, but it's made up of the same kinds of plants as the underbrush in Oregon. I watch it try to reassert itself—vine maple and nettles and wild black-berries—and I hate it. Tender buds unfurl and push blossoms into the sky and I want to pinch them tight and shove them back into their rough branches. But the new climate does it for me. Random freezes take place all summer, and the trees are dying. Even the hardy grasses lose their grip, and the slightest breezes blow dust into the house and into our lungs and eyes and dreams.

More days pass. We've almost exhausted our supplies. God no longer allows grasses to grow and leaves to open, so I don't talk to Him anymore. I'm helping Donnie change Jerry's dressing when another kind of change comes into our lives. I hear a familiar sound. A small airplane is approaching. I walk outside and a lit-tle plane comes into view above us, circling the flattened mush-room of our chimney smoke. Scott is standing in the yard. His scarred face is twisted into a scowl. He's aiming his scoped rifle at the pilot and his finger is on the trigger.

A hand emerges from the airplane's open window and makes a peace sign. Scott lowers his rifle, but doesn't put it on safe. The pilot waggles his wings, and then throws something out. Sheets of paper flutter in the sky and float down to litter the forest. I walk into a swirl and pluck a flyer from the air. The front side announces the locations of regional federal aid centers. On the back is a census form, with a notice that martial law is in effect, as if that makes us safer.

I'm not exactly overburdened by my trust of strangers, but we're hungry, so I set out to walk fifteen miles to the nearest aid center. It's an overnight trip, at best. Donnie stays home to watch over Jerry and Melanie. Scotty follows me, and I let him.

We're wearing empty packs in hopes of filling them. We're dragging sleds we made from the metal of an old garbage can. There's no snow and the sleds rattle over rocks and keep getting caught on shrubs and low branches.

I'm carrying Donnie's pistol at the small of my back, and I'm sure that Scott is carrying a concealed weapon, too. I'm walking armed again in open country, and I can't quite believe there was a time when we rode fast and warm and whole in a big American SUV.

We walk the fifteen miles. We're not spoiled people anymore, so we don't complain. There aren't any clouds, but the sky is gray. I try to enjoy the fact that I'm walking with my son. I'm sure he'll be leaving us soon. He's been talking about joining the army or the air force. He's a pilot, after all, and a young man, and I can't expect him to stay in the middle of nowhere with us.

Jerry and I expected him to go to college, but I can't imagine it now. There's much work to do in America and in the world, and now isn't the time for passive learning and beer parties and flirting. I watch him pull his sled through clumps of dying grass, and I hardly recognize the boy he once was, last year.

When we near the town, groups of people are converging on the aid center. It makes me nervous to be near them, and they don't look happy to see us, either. On the main street of the town there's a sign welcoming us to the Shasta County Federal Aid Center. There's a sandbagged position manned by National Guard troops. A machine-gun barrel tracks our progress.

We stand in a line. I have no idea what it's for. The other people in line crowd us, and we glare at them and they glare back. A thin guy with tattoos cruises to the front of the line and takes cuts in a place that opens up in front of a woman in her fifties. The guy says something to the woman and her face goes dark. Scotty pulls his pistol and points it at the tattooed man. I draw my pistol and back him up. The guardsmen at the checkpoint aim their machine gun, and the line-cutter smiles as if someone has made a mistake. We keep our guns on him. He tries to say something, but his voice is small and raspy and I can't hear his words. When he goes to the end of the line, Scotty puts away his pistol and gives him a small round of applause, and the tension seems to recede below the temperature required for killing.

But then something else happens. The woman in her fifties is shouting at her linemates, asking them how they could be so selfish, so cowardly. She's thin in her ragged jeans and middle age. Her coat is much too big for her. She pushes up her sleeves and waves her pale hands and shouts at her immediate neighbors, then she turns and shouts at Scott.

"What the hell do *you* know?" she says. "What gives you the right?" Then she starts in on me, saying, "What kind of monster did you raise?"

It's too much and I take a grip on my pistol and pull it into plain view. The woman doesn't appear to be armed, but her face is twisted with rage.

"Oh sure," she says. "Shoot me, why don't you. But that man you kicked out of line? He wasn't trying to take cuts. He was here a long time before you even showed up. He went to check on his sick little boy. The boy didn't make it. I was saving his place, lady, if you must know."

The others in line are looking at me. All of them. I safe the pistol and put it back into the small of my back.

"You're no different than the ambushers, lady," she says. "Can you tell me what makes you different?"

I try to apologize but she turns her back and doesn't say another word.

The first line allows us to register for aid. There's a second line to determine how much aid we need, and another line to receive it. We finally enter a small warehouse. Its shelves are stocked with MREs and a few cans of chili and stew. A girl wearing camouflage gives us a single shopping cart. The girl is Melanie's age. I have the cart half filled with vegetarian items before I remember that Melanie is gone.

We make the trek back to the others. Our little sleds are heavy with canned food, and they raise dust and wipe away our tracks behind us. We're in the middle of nowhere, and that suits me fine. In the past, driving cross-country, I'd see the damnedest places. Not cities or towns, but places where people isolated themselves, living in hollows and stands of timber and in the middle of deserts. Standoffish people, and I never understood why they chose to live in such places. "Must be hiding something," I'd think. Drug dealers or perverts or crazy people with bad secrets. But now we're living in this isolated place, and I know one of the stories that cause people to live alone. We have nothing to hide. We just don't trust anyone. We'll live here with the ashes of our daughter, and the boy who cremated her.

Jerry has no intention of leaving, and neither do I.

*   *   *

When Jerry gains enough strength to walk cross-country, he walks directly to Melanie's final resting place. He needs to be close to her because the Ignoring Game doesn't work if its players are too far apart to acknowledge each other's existence. Melanie's ashes are melting into a hillside beneath a spreading oak, but she's still with us. She's taken control of her father's actions. She lives through him, his every move weighed against what she might say about it. He talks to her sometimes, but mostly they play the game. Sometimes he winks at me, as if to say that our girl is getting really good at it.

And who's to say that she isn't actually communicating with him from the great by-and-by? Maybe later I'll try to help him stomach the truth, but for now I let him believe that our daughter's silence is only a perfected form of the Ignoring Game, and that humor and love and forgiveness and redemption still exist in the world.

I tally up the government food in our cupboards, then I sit in a rocking chair on the cabin's porch. I watch the world dry into a weak parody of summer. I'm knitting a pair of socks for Scotty. He'll be leaving soon to join the military, what Jerry calls "signing his life away."

I'm mostly trying to concentrate on the knitting, trying to let the work crowd against the black weight in my heart. My shotgun is propped against the wall beside me. Every day I place it a quarter inch farther away from my chair. Someday I might leave it inside, but not today. We have to be smart and hardworking and careful, so we won't be caught flat-footed when winter returns.

I'll stay here with Jerry, and maybe I'll even love him. I know he won't drink anymore. Never, never, never, he says, and I believe him. And he's trying to be a good father to our daughter, even as my own grief threatens to take away all hope for the future. If it weren't for Jerry and Scott and Donnie, our needy new addition, I might commit a great sin against myself. But I'll stay alive for them. I'll try to join them in the Ignoring Game, looking for rays of love at the crazy edges of it. Maybe Jerry will expand the game to include me, and maybe someday when we're riding together on the porch through a long sunset, he'll turn to me and smile, and I'll remember how to find enough trust to smile back.

acknowledgments

I wish to thank Dr. Alan Robock (Rutgers University) for information provided in his "Climatic Consequences of Regional Nuclear Conflicts" (*Atmos. Chem. Phys.*, 7, 2003–2012, 2007, http://www.atmos-chem-phys.org/7/2003/2007/acp-7-2003-2007.pdf) and the fine volunteers who run the Calflora Database. This book could not have been written without the love and forbearance of my wife, Sabra, and our daughters, Terra, Brenna, and Riley. I owe an impossible debt of gratitude to the Loney family, who put up with the lot of us, and to Jack and Jan DeHart and my brother, Tom, and sister, Tammy, for never doubting. This book was brought into the wider world by the ceaseless efforts of Jill Marsal, my agent, and my editor, Dong-Won Song. Thank you. Thanks also to my inimitable Oregon friends and to Francis Ford Coppola's *Zoetrope* online writing community for the encouragement and support that allowed me to suspend my own disbelief.

extras

orbit

meet the author

Credit: Sabra Loney-DeHart

TERRY DEHART is a former U.S. Marine and NASA security analyst. Three of his stories have been nominated for the Pushcart Prize. His short stories have appeared in *The Barcelona Review*, *Zoetrope All-Story Extra*, *Night Train Magazine*, *In Posse Review/Web del Sol*, *Paumanok Review*, *Smokelong Quarterly*, *Vestal Review*, and *Opium*, among others. Terry lives with his wife and daughters in the San Francisco Bay Area.

interview

Have you always known that you wanted to be a writer?

When I was a boy, I didn't think such a thing was possible. I've always liked to watch people and relish the deep feelings that certain places can bring and wonder about methods and motivations and ways of being. I've always thought it a waste that we can't preserve more of our most moving experiences. Even though we can never answer the big questions about why we're here, or what exactly we're supposed to be doing, I wanted to try to somehow pull my weight. A writer can entertain, pull readers away from their daily troubles into worlds of speculation and, hopefully, small truths. It seems like a useful vocation, even if nothing real is produced, and I'm grateful to be working at it. Looking back now, it's always been my dream job.

How has your past experience as a Marine and as a security consultant informed your writing?

I guess it's given me an affinity for ordinary people who stand in the breach. The soldiers, sailors, airmen, Marines, and coasties who give years of their lives to stand up against those with malicious intent aren't any better, as a group, than anyone else. They have the same weaknesses and flaws we all have but, for whatever reason, they've decided to put their posteriors on the line. Their jobs are often boring and lonely, and sometimes dangerous and frightening, so it's sort of a concentrated version of life, the slow parts and the fast parts compartmentalized in the months and years of active duty—kind of like the chapters of a book.

Working in IT security has allowed me to meet some truly paranoid folks, and shown me some good reasons to worry. Virtual battles are being fought around us, every minute of every day. It's not a bad field for writers interested in apocalyptic themes.

Who or what inspires you in your writing?

My family gives me all the reason for *being* I'll ever need. If I want to interact with my wife and children, I only need to put out a bit of effort and time to reap the greater rewards of love. Writing is like icing on the cake. Being alive inspires me to write.

How did you develop the idea for The Unit?

I've always enjoyed post-apocalyptic books and movies. It's one of the classic story premises, and I wanted to write something that would frighten me as I wrote it. I suppose I was trying to break out of complacency.

It's any parent's nightmare to see their family in danger. When that happens, all bets are off, and characters reveal things about themselves that would remain invisible in calmer days. As I came to know the members of this family, they came up with ideas of their own, and my primary job was to remain true to them.

Did you have to do any research to write this novel?

Yes. I had to look up recent military MRE (Meal, Ready-to-Eat) entrees. Some of them made me hungry. Some of them made me wonder if it might be better to get my jaw wired shut. I used satellite imagery to map the route the Sharpe family takes after the bombs go off, so I could picture them casting shadows against real landscapes. I'm not a botanist, but the Calflora website is a salve for my ignorance.

But most of my research involved the effects of nuclear weapons. I found a recent study on the likely effects of a limited, regional nuclear exchange, the blast and fires and radiation and EMP effects, but also the way that tons of ejecta from the blasts would hit the stratosphere and bring about a sudden reduction of temperature. The part about ozone depletion really got to me. I'd never thought very carefully about all those effects occurring at the same time. I tried to imagine a world of freezing storms, the snow laced with radiation, and in the times of icy calm, the sun's unfiltered UV burning the skin and blinding the eyes of the surviving animals and people.

Even a limited nuke war, say an exchange between India and Pakistan, could turn our friendly planet into a cold hell. I was an aviation ordnance technician in the Marine Corps, but I don't understand how anyone sane can truly love the Bomb. (Maybe there's a book idea in that.)

Was it challenging to write from each character's perspective?

Yes, the multiple first-person structure didn't come easily, but it allowed me to climb into the skins of the characters. It was fun to get into their hidden thoughts and emotions, all the cross-purpose stuff that people do inside their heads. After I learned the rhythm, I came to enjoy the challenge of keeping the plot moving from character to character. Also, I've always admired the way Faulkner used multiple first-person present tense in *As I Lay Dying*, and this story seemed to lend itself to that setup.

Do you have a favorite character? If so, why?

At first it was all about the father, Jerry Sharpe, mortally afraid for the safety of his family. That's how it began. But then the other characters asserted themselves, and none of them would allow me to write them as "lesser" characters. The lives of Susan (the mother) and the children were in the balance and they insisted upon being heard, so I was forced to give them equal billing.

The Unit *depicts what might happen in a post-apocalyptic United States. Literature, movies, and television shows that explore this territory have become increasingly popular. What do you think this says about society's current mind-set?*

Well, we have good reasons to be gloomy these days, but the post-apocalyptic genre can also be uplifting in a dark way, because it reminds us that things could be much worse. When I was writing about people without shelter, exposed to radiation and barbarism and starvation, I began to pay closer attention to the things I'd taken for granted, soft puffs of warmth from heater vents on cool days, the textures and flavors of a nice meal, walking in public with my family and feeling a sense of community rather than threat.

The post-apocalyptic world is a portrayal of ultimate poverty. The survivors lose all of their "stuff" and their sense of safety and all the systems and structures they'd come to rely upon, including some of the beliefs that previously sustained them. In that light, we're doing pretty well for ourselves these days.

How realistic do you think the novel is? Is it speculation or should we be taking notes from the Sharpe family's struggle?

We have determined foes who have demonstrated their desire to use weapons of mass destruction against us. *The Unit* is set in the aftermath of simultaneous nuclear detonations in seven of our major cities, but smaller attacks are probably more likely, in the real world. It's probably a sensible idea for people to keep a few days' of necessary supplies on hand, as we do here in earthquake country.

Disasters and attacks can certainly bring people together. We were gentle with each other after 9/11, united by horror. Disaster response efforts call forth the resourcefulness, hard work, and generosity of countless people. But when all infrastructure is destroyed, and there's no expectation of a quick recovery, more primitive power relationships are likely to come into play. The very definition of what it means to be *strong* or *good* could be up for grabs.

Can you tell us anything about your next novel?

It's a sequel to *The Unit*, following the story of the newly adult son, Scott Sharpe, as he ventures into a world of increasing government repression, with militias growing in the hinterlands and rumors of starvation in the surviving cities.

You know, *cheery* stuff.

Finally, as a first-time author, what have you found to be the most exciting part of the publishing process?

I've really enjoyed working with my editor, DongWon Song. He's as determined as I am to make this book as clear and gripping as it can possibly be.

introducing

The Sharpes' story continues
in the exciting sequel.
Coming 2011

by Terry DeHart

After the bombed cities burned themselves out and the first hard spikes of radiation began to fade, the survivors in the surrounding suburbs and country rose from their improvised shelters, hungry and helpful and determined not to botch their new chance at life. The body count was unknowable, but as the embers cooled, much work lay ahead.

While their leaders unfurled their steely fingers to push the buttons that ground their enemies to dust, and the skies continued to grow darker day by day, the people donned gloves and masks and layers of clothing to protect them from the sun's unfiltered UV rays. They turned to rebuilding, as best they could, what was left. They hung radiation signs around their ground-zero nightmares and posted yellow flags far downwind, mapped in the shape of giant teardrops. They looked for new places to grow crops and build communities. The best and

301

worst of America were on display, still and again, standing with equal parts brutality and kindness before what remained of the world.

And it was into this world that young Scott Sharpe set off from his mother and father to seek a path of his own making. He was determined to answer the call of duty, or at least that was the story he told himself. It was five in the morning when he said his goodbyes. He stood beneath the fantastic nuclear sunrise and hugged his mother and shook his father's hand. There weren't many tears left in the world, but his parents shed what they could spare as he climbed aboard the bus that would carry him to the rest of his life.

He knew he would always remember his last glimpse of his parents standing on the cold shoulder of the road in the Sierra Nevada, their thick hats and sunglasses making them look like eccentric tourists as they waved at the black-tinted windows of the recruiting bus and then through the departing swirl of its frozen exhaust until a curve of the road took their waving away. When they were gone behind him he felt very light and very free, even though he was on his way to the Klamath Falls military induction center to "sign his life away," as his father put it.

It was a hard-frosted Northern California September morning, nine months after the last of the bombs fell. The previous winter had been a nuclear winter, with icy storms raging from the Pacific and even colder ones flowing down from Canada. Scott wasn't happy to see the shortening of the days, and the pines were casting shadows that looked to him like thin, blackened bones, but still he couldn't shake the light mood that had taken him when he left home.

The recruiting bus moved at top speed in the government lane, a commandeered tour bus, spray-painted olive drab. Scott hadn't been aboard an operational motor vehicle since before the bombs. The driver, if there was a driver, was invisible in his hijack-resistant compartment as the bus thrummed past dead crops and the half-cremated remains of what had been blinded and sunburned livestock.

The bus floated on its soft suspension, giving almost the feeling of flight. It steadily put miles between Scott and the dregs of his childhood. After a half hour of listening to the diesel growl and the hiss of filtered air flowing from the heating vents, the glow of the sun rising through its nuclear layer caused the bus to cast a long shadow to the west, its elongated box morphing and flowing like a runaway flag over the imperfect canvas of rocky meadows and patches of contaminated snow.

Scott sat with twenty-four other passengers, young men and women in their late teens or early twenties. They were accompanied by two acne-faced Army MPs who sat so close behind the driver's armored box that it could've been a bonfire built to warm them. One of the MPs leaned into the aisle and peered at the road ahead. The other one sat facing the recruits. Both of them kept their locked-and-loaded M-4 carbines close at hand.

Most of the recruits were sprawled in their seats, alternately scowling at nothing in particular and pretending to sleep. They held their heads loosely, so the bumps and dips of the road caused them to nod. Scott imagined they were trying to look bored, like battle-hardened soldiers riding a helicopter into combat, but their quick glances betrayed their excitement. It was pathetic, but Scott himself was nineteen that year, and he had to force himself not to join their show of pretend nonchalance and make-believe courage.

The bus left the alpine plain and began to shoulder its way into the Sierra. As the miles rolled beneath heavy wheels, the young passengers became bored at their game of pretending to be bored. A long-haired kid said something about how good it would feel to get some payback, and his rowmates nodded. A boy with a shaved head let loose an almost impossibly profane string of insults about North Koreans and Al Qaeda, and then the recruits were laughing and punching each other on the arms and aiming imaginary rifles and becoming brothers and sisters already, in their shared mission.

Even the MPs smiled, and Scott smiled, too, the muscles of his face moving beneath the ropy whorls of scar tissue that surrounded his eyes and lined his forehead and cheeks. He hadn't smiled in a very long time, and he wanted the feeling to last. One of his new comrades slid into the seat beside him and offered his hand. Scott shook it. The kid was thin, but his grip was sharp and crushing, the grip of a farm boy or a high school wrestler, probably both. He examined the pocks and scars on Scott's face. Scott could tell he was dying to ask about them, but he didn't.

"Can't wait to stick it to the bastards, huh," he said. "How 'bout you?"

"They asked for it."

"Damn right they did. Every last one of them."

"Let's hope there's some targets left for us."

"Oh yeah? Hey, what if our nukes took 'em all out?" The kid was crestfallen, the hair on his upper lip quivering like a caterpillar in a wind. "Damn, I hope there's some assholes left to shoot."

The kid moved away without introducing himself and accosted someone else. Another inductee slid into the seat next to Scott. Her black hair hung over her face, and she reached up and pushed it away. She was dressed in shapeless khakis and a billowy black shirt and Scott wondered what she was concealing, weapons or rations or maybe just the curves of her body.

Her dark eyes held the spark of intelligence. She made a not unkind twist of her lips that could've been shared camaraderie or joking mockery.

"What's your story, scarface?"

Scott felt his eyes go hard. Serious. And the girl smiled again, a disarming smile that spread warmth to her eyes, and said, "Sorry. I didn't have what you'd call a refined upbringing. But we're on this bus together, so we might as well talk."

"Someone tried to kill me. With dynamite. It didn't work." It was the response Scott had worked out in front of the mirror at his parents' cabin, but he said it too quickly, forgetting to pause in the right places.

"And where is this mad bomber now?"

"Dead."

"You kill him?"

"He's dead. I killed plenty of others like him."

"Was he militia?"

"No. He was with a group of assholes."

"Plenty of that going around."

The girl looked straight at him, measuring him and having some sort of conversation with herself, then she held out her hand.

"Name's Chrissy. It's my middle name. My real first name is Melanie, but I won't answer to it."

"My sister's name was Melanie."

"Was?"

"Yeah."

Scott told her his name and they shook on it. Her fingers were warm and strong.

"What are we getting ourselves into?" she said.

"Someone has to clean up the mess."

"We have to do *something*, right?"

"The job market's not so hot in the civilian sector."

"What are you going for? What job, I mean?"

"Pilot," he said.

"Can't wait to look down on the common people, can you?"

"I already have a pilot's license, so I might as well go for it. What about you?"

"I come from a long line of grunts. They were always telling me about their good old days in Iraq and Afghanistan. Seems as if they had more fun in their sandbox than they could ever have here, living in God's country."

"Yeah?"

"Anyhow, it's not like we'll be able to choose. The government will put us wherever they get it into their pointy little heads to put us."

The way she said "government" held a practiced disgust that caused Scott to sit up straighter. She said it in the same way that the militia members he'd met had said it.

"We're probably asking for trouble," he said.

"Probably."

"We could end up cooks, or something boring like that."

Chrissy pulled a can of Spam from a pocket of her fatigues. She leaned close enough to whisper.

"Could be worse things than being a cook when there's a famine on. Want to eat?"

Scott nodded, his suspicions about her receding behind the more immediate matter of protein.

Chrissy held the can in her lap and worked the key to open it, and Scott wondered what drove women to do nice things for men. He felt his heart rate increase and then a blush rose to his face. She shook the meat from the can, broke it into two exact halves, and pushed one of them into Scott's hand. They ate quickly, furtively, managing to finish the food without losing any of it to the recruits around them. By the time the smell of the salty meat reached a larger audience, the Spam was gone. Scott hadn't eaten meat for weeks, and he sat back and relished the feeling. Chrissy handed him the empty can, and he licked the oils away until not even the smell remained.

They leaned back in their seats on a tour bus that had once carried old people out for larks. Now there weren't many old people left. They looked through tinted windows at a land both burned and frozen. Smoke rose at random intervals. The bus passed a collection of battered cars driving slowly in the civilian lane, Chevelles and Galaxies and Jeepsters, primitive machines that hadn't been disabled by the electromagnetic pulse of the bombs. The cars were driven by suspicious-looking men, all of them armed and equipped with hungry-looking families. Scott noticed that every vehicle they encountered was headed in the opposite direction, away from town.

VISIT THE ORBIT BLOG AT

www.orbitbooks.net

FEATURING

BREAKING NEWS
FORTHCOMING RELEASES
LINKS TO AUTHOR SITES
EXCLUSIVE INTERVIEWS
EARLY EXTRACTS

AND COMMENTARY FROM OUR EDITORS

WITH REGULAR UPDATES FROM OUR TEAM,
ORBITBOOKS.NET IS YOUR SOURCE FOR
ALL THINGS ORBITAL.

WHILE YOU'RE THERE, JOIN OUR E-MAIL LIST
TO RECEIVE INFORMATION ON SPECIAL OFFERS,
GIVEAWAYS, AND MORE.

imagine. explore. engage.